"O'Hehir sketches o [...] the old people in this b [...] oth quirky and dignifie [...] ic, funny, insightful voi [...] ust another cozy unforge [...] *lobe*

"A story that will move and captivate all who read it."
—*Booklist* (starred review)

"When memory and fantasy collide, truth is up for grabs . . . O'Hehir scores big with her wry heroine . . . and intriguing snippets of Egyptian poetry."   —*Kirkus Reviews*

"The narrating voice is a pleasure from beginning to end."
—Vivian Gornick, author of *Fierce Attachments*

"A quirky outlook . . . delightful prose will draw readers right in."   —*Library Journal*

"Combines an intriguing amateur sleuth tale with some Egyptologist elements inside a deep family drama . . . a fine contemporary thriller."   —*Midwest Book Review*

"Sparkling prose enlivens every scene and gives the story the heft and luminescence of narrative art at its most energized level. Ms. O'Hehir's mastery of her subject is effortless and engaging . . . A fun and funny book, but one with heart and unfailing insight into matters achingly human."
—James W. Hall, author of *Forests of the Night*

"O'Hehir spices up her elegantly plotted novel of . . . skullduggery with keen, sympathetic, and often amusing insights . . . with a gift for spot-on metaphors . . . and with laugh-out-loud wit."   —Aaron Elkins, author of *Unnatural Selection*

"Introduces us to a delightfully unconventional pair of sleuths . . . O'Hehir is at the top of her form here . . . I couldn't put it down!"
—Sandra M. Gilbert, author of *Belongings*

Berkley Prime Crime titles by Diana O'Hehir

MURDER NEVER FORGETS
ERASED FROM MEMORY

Murder
Never
Forgets

Diana O'Hehir

BERKLEY PRIME CRIME, NEW YORK

THE BERKLEY PUBLISHING GROUP
Published by the Penguin Group
Penguin Group (USA) Inc.
375 Hudson Street, New York, New York 10014, USA

Penguin Group (Canada), 90 Eglinton Avenue East, Suite 700, Toronto, Ontario M4P 2Y3, Canada
(a division of Pearson Penguin Canada Inc.)
Penguin Books Ltd., 80 Strand, London WC2R 0RL, England
Penguin Group Ireland, 25 St. Stephen's Green, Dublin 2, Ireland (a division of Penguin Books Ltd.)
Penguin Group (Australia), 250 Camberwell Road, Camberwell, Victoria 3124, Australia
(a division of Pearson Australia Group Pty. Ltd.)
Penguin Books India Pvt. Ltd., 11 Community Centre, Panchsheel Park, New Delhi—110 017, India
Penguin Group (NZ), Cnr. Airborne and Rosedale Roads, Albany, Auckland 1310, New Zealand
(a division of Pearson New Zealand Ltd.)
Penguin Books (South Africa) (Pty.) Ltd., 24 Sturdee Avenue, Rosebank, Johannesburg 2196,
South Africa

Penguin Books Ltd., Registered Offices: 80 Strand, London WC2R 0RL, England

MURDER NEVER FORGETS

A Berkley Prime Crime Book / published by arrangement with the author

PRINTING HISTORY
Berkley Prime Crime hardcover edition / September 2005
Berkley Prime Crime mass-market edition / December 2006

ISBN: 0-425-20903-2

BERKLEY® PRIME CRIME
Berkley Prime Crime Books are published by The Berkley Publishing Group,
a division of Penguin Group (USA) Inc.,
375 Hudson Street, New York, New York 10014.
The name BERKLEY PRIME CRIME and the BERKLEY PRIME CRIME design
are trademarks belonging to Penguin Group (USA) Inc.

PRINTED IN THE UNITED STATES OF AMERICA

10 9 8 7 6 5 4 3 2 1

Thanks

To my friend and agent, Ellen Levine, who got me to write and rewrite.

To Carol, Cyra, B. K., and Allison, who read the manuscript, some of you more than once.

To the rest of you who listened and responded, month after month: Whitney, Carol, Mary, Annegret, Diana.

Special love to Mel for help on this project and many others.

Disclaimer

Many books about Egypt and Egyptology and several translations of Egyptian poetry and of *The Book of the Dead* have supplied background knowledge for this tale.

Among these are translations by E. A. Wallis Budge, Miriam Lichtheim, and R. O. Faulkner, and accounts of ancient Egyptian life, language, and culture by Miriam Stead, Maria Carmelo Betro, Bridget McDermott, and George Hart.

These very interesting sources do not always agree. Nevertheless, mistakes in this book should be ascribed to my own inadequate transcription and not to any fault of these helpful scholars.

1 Prologue

It was difficult from the cliff above to tell what the people on the beach were doing, although they were very clearly presented, as if on a stage lit by the last rays of a low-lying sun that shone flat out across the water. Orange sun-glare highlighted their figures and threw exaggerated shadows across the sand, until finally, just before sunset, just before the people finished whatever they were doing and the tableau below ended, the shadows grew and stretched, active finally, merging with each other, to spread halfway up the cliff.

At first there was just the woman and her companion; then those two were joined by two others.

They talked, but what they said wasn't audible to the person who watched from the cliff. At one point the woman gestured and looked up. The other person, a man probably, it was hard to be sure from this distance, also gestured and looked up. Perhaps they were worrying about whether someone was up there.

The person who waited above and watched didn't care. These days the things he cared about came and went quite fast. And fur-

thermore he knew, with an inner physical knowledge he'd picked up in some other existence, that he was safe. There was no path here from his place, only a route down a drainage pipe which he had squeezed through with pleasure because it seemed like an adventure from his earlier life. The cliff was like that, too. He knew that the beach cliff projected out far enough to hide the outline of a head.

The people moved back and forth; they leaned forward and back; they gestured. The woman gestured more than the others; her arms came up, her head went back; he could see that she had short white hair; she looked in some way familiar. Finally someone took her elbow and they started walking.

It was a tiny beach, bounded north and south by rock outcroppings and by three conical rocks, east and west by ocean and cliff. The pair below proceeded arm in arm, slowly, steps coordinated; it seemed almost as if she were being marched by him, left, right, left, right.

The watcher was interested. Also troubled. But the troubled feeling, the sense that something wasn't quite right, this meant nothing new to him; he had that feeling often lately.

When the walkers reached the south cliff they turned abruptly and began retracing their steps. The two extra people were there by now and fell into step behind; it made a curious four-person parade.

Their observer was an old gentleman in a tweed suit who lay on his stomach on the cliff-grass above. During the quieter portions of the beach tableau he hummed softly to himself. Apparently he liked country and western tunes.

The woman now, he said to himself, perhaps she looks familiar. But then, many things, many people these days look familiar. This beach below reminded him of another beach, the one at Sharm el Naga in Egypt. He had been younger at Sharm el Naga and the climb had been easier, but the people were surely the same people. That was it, he understood it perfectly now; they were the ones from

The Book of the Dead; *the woman was on trial; the others were judges; she was being tried for her sins in this life.*

All of us have committed sins in this life.

I will say a prayer for her: Oh, you judges who gather around me, I will become perfect, perfect . . .

He felt sorry for her with her familiar straight carriage: the soul and her three judges. This must be one of the Trials further along in the Journey, perhaps a trial of the soul's ability to cross water.

He tried again for the right spell: Oh, you who bring the ferry boat of the Abyss to this difficult bank . . .

Sometimes he knew he was forgetting and didn't care because it was all part of the Process. And other times, like now, when he couldn't remember a spell, those times a heavy, gray helplessness welled up in him. He put his face down on the grass, which prickled, wiry and damp.

When he looked up again, the scene below had changed. The people were moving in what seemed ritualized measures back and forth. And circling around. Strange. They made shapes he seemed to recognize; perhaps they were playing a game—a children's game— Blind man's bluff? Musical chairs? One of those exercises where one person is in the middle and the others move up to that person cautiously and dodge and then move in again. The person in the middle has to outwit the others by moving, by running.

The woman wasn't very agile; it was hard to watch her.

He tried to send her another spell: I am one who passes by, pure and . . . *Pure and what? Once again, he couldn't remember. There must be a spell against forgetting.*

When he looked again at the beach, the woman had started trying to climb the rocks. She wasn't very good at it; the rock crumbled, someone started pulling. It took only one of her pursuers to drag her down. But then maybe the gods helped her; she seemed to get stronger, knocked on her back and flailing. Two of them now had to fight hard to hold her down. Down on the sand, on her back.

The third person had been behind the rocks, now this person came out holding something that unfolded and unkinked, cumbersomely. The watcher recognized the object finally as it undid itself across the sand: it was a net. A net shining golden in the final sunrays. Together they flung it over the recumbent figure, now all of them together, everyone helping, they climbed on her and around her like ants on a captured caterpillar. She was bound and netted; they rolled her over and over.

The man on the cliff couldn't watch any more. He put his head down. The grass came up and wet his cheek. Briefly, he fell asleep. When he got up finally to go back to his place, it was quite dark.

He still had good eyesight, fortunately.

"My goodness, that was a long walk," they said to him back at his place. "Should you go for such long walks? Watch out you don't fall. Did you have a lovely walk?"

🐦 Chapter 1

I am working in Susie's health food store when the call comes from Green Beach Manor.

Susie's Health Food Store is on the first floor of a small teetering Berkeley building, one of those wooden Victorians that survived the 1923 fire; the inside of the store is either calcined green splintery pine or beat-up oak cabinets with brass pulls. Berkeley health stores aren't supposed to look glossy or enameled because health, Berkeley-style, is organic; it has crumbs. Susie is the nicest person in the world.

I am standing there holding the phone receiver away from me; it's one of those movie-era phones with a dial, and I'm going, "Yes, yes, I see," while at the other end an officious voice recites the ways my father is causing trouble. "He creates diversions. He calls out in the hall. He wanders out into the woods. He is disturbed, Miss Day; I'm sorry to say it, disturbed. He has inappropriate responses. We are

considering the quieter auxiliary facility." And so on for a
while, during which I nod, as if the person on the other end
can see me, and sigh and make faces at Susie and fiddle with
a protein-booster candy wrapper.

Finally I hang up and ask Susie, "What are inappropriate
responses? This woman told me, 'Green Beach Manor is a
colony for independently functioning adults.'"

Susie flips a page. She's a beautiful old hippie with scraggly hair and peasant skirts; she looks up now from scowling
nearsightedly into an advertising brochure, *Mother Nature's
Baked Organic Lovies*. "People that say that stuff want to put
your ass in a vise."

"*Auxiliary facility* is not good," I suggest.

Actually I know about *auxiliary facility*. At Green Beach
Manor it means Hope House, which the aides call No Hope
House. "For when you forget," Daddy's aide told me, tapping the side of her tight gray wiry hairdo. Daddy was
afraid of that auxiliary facility. "They make your heart
heavy. I think I won't go there."

Susie stares at me. "Carla, I'm really, really sorry about Ed."

Sue knows my dad well; she's what you might call a
good, a very good friend.

All that morning I think, all the time I'm dishing up
Rice Dreams and unsticking the chai machine and rearrang-
ing the milk cartons to get the oldest ones in the front, and
by lunchtime I've made up my mind. "I have to go down
there. Maybe I can calm him down. Maybe get them to keep
him." Susie, who is packing ice cream using the back of a
pancake turner, says, "I was thinking that, too."

Neither of us talks about how it will be for her if I quit in
the middle of the week, because we both know it will be
good. Susie doesn't really need me working mornings in her

store. She offered me the job out of purest chivalry and because she thought I needed something to do in a time of crisis, but she can't really afford to pay me. The store is a hobby, an organic pure-foods missionary enterprise. She's proud of it, and she loses money on it.

I go home to my basement apartment, which is just down at the shopping center, and when I come back, Susie loads me up with nutritional-advantage health bars and walks me out to the street where I can catch a bus to the Greyhound station.

"Listen," she says, and then goes, "Oh, hell, Carla," and kisses me pretty hard and shoves some twenties into my pocket for my this-week's wages.

We have a little tussle with me saying it's too much and her saying not enough.

I've known Susie all my life; she's been a neighbor and a kind of aunt, and for a really long time I was in love with her son. That makes a bond, unless it does just the opposite. "Do you know what kind of stuff Ed was doing?" she asks now, "I mean, he *said* something?"

"Something about Egypt." I'm not going to repeat the exact quote to her; these old hippies tend to be mystical about body parts. What he said, and the Green Beach Manor woman told me unwillingly, "He yelled it out in the hall, Miss Day. Very loud. He said, 'You whose eye is eaten, you with your heads on backwards, you will not entrap me in your net.'"

Those heads on backwards and eaten eyes really bothered the Green Beach Manor administration.

"Don't worry about us, Susie; I'll do something." I feel pretty sure of myself. I like helping people, and this is a specific job: help your father get calmer, help Green Beach

Manor feel less jumpy. Clearly defined tasks, not like the nebulous ones Fate has been throwing at me lately.

Susie and I kiss again and she accepts the key to my apartment. She looks at me doubtfully for a moment, and I'm afraid she's going to say something about her son Robbie, but she doesn't. She grins, "Hey, let the goddess shine down on you, darling, okay?" And she adds that she'll water my two geranium plants.

I like riding on Greyhound buses; it reminds me of our life before everything got so very complicated, of coming up to Berkeley from Santa Cruz and wondering what my father had been doing while we were playing house. The *we* in this case was me and Susie's son Robbie; he and I shared a redwood-lined attic and a tin shower above Mrs. Stein's garage on Ocean Avenue. I was twenty-one years old, Robbie was twenty-four. This happened four years ago, but it seems like more, with everything that has gone on since.

My parents were old when I was born; my father was sixty and my mother, Constancia, pushing forty. (I don't usually think of her as *my mother*. Constancia was her name, and it suited her, a cold name, esthetic and people-unfriendly.) Constancia was a world-class expert on Phrygian bronze bowls, handsome symmetrical artifacts from the mythical country of Phrygia, someplace in what is now Turkey. When I was ten years old, Constancia went off with a Turkish archaeologist named Dr. Hakim Kasapligl. As far as we know she is still in Turkey with him, tending to an archaeological dig east of Istanbul, dusting off her Phrygian bronzes.

So my father, who is eighty-five by now, has inappropriate responses. And I have gotten to be twenty-five years old. That's an age at which a lot of people have already started doing *it*, whatever their particular brand of karma is, climbing mountains or selling real estate or writing books on South American Surrealism. I remind myself that I have taken care of my father and gotten A's in disparate subjects like English Literature and Urban Reorganization and worked for the college animal lab and, most recently, worked for Habitat for Humanity in Baker's Landing, Tennessee. For now, I should settle back on this bus and think about what to say to the people at Green Beach Manor.

The bus rolls down Highway One, through Pacifica, a damp suburb hanging on to the side of a hill, then along a cliff above the ocean. Electric-red ice plant shines on one side of the road; on the other side surges the slate-blue ocean, as alien and removed as anything can be. I think, there it is; knockout beautiful and it doesn't know anything about me nor care anything, and that's a good thing, too. I like that indifference of Nature's; it makes you feel stronger.

Daddy is asleep when I arrive in his rooms. He lies on his back in bed with his hands crossed over his chest and his nose pointed at the ceiling. He looks like a crusader on a tomb, perfectly calm, the way the crusader always looks, but with those lines down beside his mouth and horizontally above his nose that might become worry marks when he wakes up. He's fully dressed in a sweater and vest, with a green chintz quilt tucked in around his legs. I sit on the bed beside him and slip my hand between his two clasped ones. "Hello, darling," I say, not expecting any answer.

I'm very fond of my father. He did a terrible job of raising me, but he tried. He was vague and affectionate and every so often he would come to and look at me and realize he ought to do something fatherly, and then he would take me along to Egypt for a while.

Right now he opens his eyes. "Why, there you are." He sounds absolutely all right. But then he sits up and isn't all right.

"Oh," he says, bent over, still holding my hand. "You came. I thought, I *hoped*, you'd come."

"Of course, Daddy. Listen, you look fine." He doesn't, but it helps, with him, to pretend.

"We have to go," he says, "you'll come with me; of course you will. We need to look for . . ." He lets go of my hand. "We need to find . . . There was a fishing net. And I didn't help. I didn't help at all. I did nothing."

The Alzheimer's books give you conflicting instructions. "Go with his fantasy." "Ignore his imaginings; change the subject." "Get him to *elaborate* on the fantasy." The books may tell you different things to do, but they're unanimous in calling the patient *him*, even though most old people are women. Sometimes I do it one way, sometimes another.

"Let's go for a walk," I suggest now.

And I put my arms around him, trying to straighten him up. He feels funny, like my father but different, skinny and wiry, a pipe-cleaner man with little ribs poking out from beneath his vest.

"So," I ask again, "a walk?" He says yes and feels along the edge of the bed for his shoes.

Green Beach Manor sits on the grounds of a former lumber baron's estate. After the lumber baron died, his children sold the property to be a model retirement colony, all beams and Norman roofs and views. It's kept beautifully washed and mowed and trimmed; even the fog shines controlled and glistening. "I will live here myself someday," my aunt Crystal announced, in the triumphant voice that meant she knew she wouldn't, and she took Daddy's money, only a medium amount, and gave it to Green Beach Manor to buy a set of rooms for him. The money was not refundable, and the Manor pledged to take care of him for the rest of his life. But they did not pledge, if he started to go peculiar, to keep him in the elegant part of their establishment.

Of course, Aunt Crystal consulted me about Daddy's money, but I was busy at Habitat for Humanity doing good for people who weren't related to me, and I just told her, "Go ahead, spend it, put him in that place. Who cares about money?"

I used to imagine Daddy would come live with me some day, but I didn't think he'd crumble so suddenly, and I wasn't counting on my own life getting that confused.

My father and I pass through a set of double oak doors into a bright blue afternoon where the Manor garden is showing itself off. This garden is lush, green, wet, and both tropical and seacoast. It has palm trees and ice plant, ferns, seacoast rocket and moss. Yes, believe it or not, moss on the ocean side of the palm trees. Someone, a long time ago, worked very hard at the overblown surreal effect; God and the Pacific climate have done the rest. The garden has flourished, flowing down the hill in profusion, up the hill in triumph, as far as the base of the Manor where an assortment of spires and stained glass windows and awkward Manor towers finishes the effect. It looks like Harry Potter's school, which my father wouldn't know anything about. Or like Jack-and-the-Beanstalk's castle.

I stop and put my arms around a fat palm tree. "So where is my harp of gold," I ask the air, "if this is my beanstalk." Meanwhile telling myself, you total lunatic; you're crazy, too, it runs in the family. How could your poor parent not be confused? The palm tree has crystal fog droplets trembling at the ends of its fronds.

In a minute a lady joins us at the tree, a small question-mark lady, bent sideways over her walker. I know this person, whose name is Mrs. Dexter; she's one of Daddy's three-person fan club. That is, three ladies, all old and in different ways attractive and interesting, who like to eat with him when he goes to the dining room. I think that they eat with him because they see that he is also still attractive and interesting, although somewhat damaged in transit.

Mrs. Dexter bump-clunks down the path toward us and stops to stare up at the palm tree. "There are monarch butterflies living in that tree," she says. "Hello, Carla, hello, Ed, how are you?" And she reaches out and grabs a butterfly and holds it, upright wings together, under my father's nose.

Her white hair is smashed into even, accented waves, and her pink face stares sideways at the sun. She tucks the butterfly back in its palm tree cleft.

"They sleep all winter, a butterfly doesn't dream." She adds, "It doesn't have the nerves."

"They stand for the soul, of course," Daddy says. "Like . . ." He had straightened up cheerfully when Mrs. Dexter first arrived, but now his body contracts. "There was a woman on the beach. They *seized* her *soul*. Three people. With a fishing net."

Mrs. Dexter looks over at him, her flat, heavy face creased. "Perhaps it just looked that way, Ed."

"No. No, Miss . . ." Names are hard for him.

"Dexter." She touches his arm briefly. "It's easy to misinterpret." She's firm in proposing this. "Things change in a certain light. Or if events happen quickly it can be confusing."

"I did *nothing*," my father says. "I simply was there. I didn't *act*. That's a sin. The Negative Confession pledges: *I did not cause to weep. I was not deaf to the words of truth.*" He touches his hand to his cheek as if he's feeling a sore place.

"Daddy," I put an arm around him, "let's go look at the mermaid."

This mermaid statue glimmers down at the end of the path, a bronze copy of the one the travel brochures show in the Copenhagen harbor. She has a plaque on her pedestal that says she's a memorial to somebody's parents. Unlike the original mermaid in Copenhagen, this one has blonde hair. Or reddish-blonde. The sculptor did something to the bronze to make it that color. My father is fond of her.

The mermaid statue area is also a local hangout for the long-legged hares who frequent this garden, inquiring noses quivering, ears aloft. My father likes them, too. "They look like former President Coolidge," he says.

"I'll examine the mermaid alone." He rejects me with a shoulder movement and plods away down the path.

Mrs. Dexter leans on her walker to watch. He's still agile and moves all right, but his back looks stiff and unhappy. "What a pity," she says.

"He's worse," I suggest.

She inclines her head.

"How long?" I ask.

She shrugs, which is difficult for her, bent over the walker and not in a good position for shrugging. "One week? Two?"

I say, "The books all talk about plateaus. The person goes along fine for a while and then crashes for a while."

She makes an explosive noise, "Poo," or some similar sound; I had never heard anyone actually say, *poo*. "Books. You don't need books, Carla. It's this *place*."

I had been thinking something like this, but now I argue. "Hey. It's a silly place. Pretentious. Overstuffed and phony. But not *that* bad."

"The place is *weird*." Mrs. Dexter relishes this word as if she's just thought it up. "There's a tense atmosphere. People go around looking pursued."

"Pursued?"

"Afraid to look behind them."

I resist asking her if she'd been watching *X Files*.

"Someone fell out of a window," she says.

That's a stopper. I gawk. "You're kidding."

"I am not, as you put it, kidding. She is all right, but she might not have been. She might have died. It was a floor-to-ceiling window, one with a door; those doors are supposed to be nailed shut, but someone got the door open and left it that way."

I think of practical questions that I'll pose later: Was the maintenance crew painting? Repairing something? Putting in a new TV line? "And she just fell out?" I ask.

"We don't know exactly. She has a bad sense of balance. The new chef caught her."

Down the path my father is bent over, reading the sign on the mermaid's pedestal. I start walking toward him.

"Daddy has a very good sense of balance," I say.

Mrs. Dexter clunks along behind me. "There have been other things. Also fairly serious. A fire in the beauty parlor. And a gas fireplace unit that leaked. Management says these are accidents, but we residents know they aren't."

"Of course they're investigating," I say.

"*I* am investigating," Mrs. Dexter's voice, normally a nice contralto, grows sharper. "I have been listening. If you're old, they don't pay attention to you, and you can listen. You'd be surprised. You can come up behind, and no one notices you. You're a cipher, a nonentity. You can learn things."

We've almost reached Daddy now. I have a silly impulse to hold on to him when Mrs. Dexter talks like this. What a shame, I think, Mrs. D. is starting to go, too, and I was counting on her to be sensible. If she and the other residents are sensible and the Manor itself stays stable in spite of being pretentious and overdone, then maybe my father can quiet down. For a while, anyway.

That's what you ask for with Alzheimer's. A while.

"Do you know," he says, "the modeling on the scales of this tail is quite good." He seems perfectly okay for the moment. Early-stage Alzheimer's is like that, one minute you're vague about your own last name and an hour later you're delivering lectures on the Chaos Theory.

"Perhaps we should start off toward dinner," Mrs. Dexter gets cheerful at this thought. "Dinner is one of the better things here. Did you know that we will have oysters tonight? Many older people do not like oysters. I, personally, love them."

* * *

The dining hall has an arched oak entryway and a circular front lawn where the management is always running the sprinkler. You can hear the sea; it seems to be inside your skull. Sometimes, with an extra-long breaker, you can feel it there, too. The ocean surges back and forth just beyond our reach, a quarter mile away.

We go through the beveled doors and stand in the lobby, which is high-ceilinged and has a dark red carpet. The wall is also dark red with a pattern of braided gold rope criss-crossing against the scarlet background. There are lots of heavy gold-framed pictures stationed in relays up to the ceiling. Some of these contain Renoir-type women in blue tunics, and some show sad Victorian dogs beseeching up at an invisible master. The double doors to the inner eating area are closed.

Mrs. Dexter wants to talk some more about Green Beach Manor. "The atmosphere in this place—" she stops her sentence to gesture menacingly at the art gallery with her square baby's chin. "Carla, no wonder he's reacting. They, here, are so cheerful and glossy, and underneath that the atmosphere is tense—know what I mean?"

Sure, you already told me about it, on *X Files* where the woman agent whispers, "Watch it," to the man agent, and the computerized music synthesizes away in the background, and the TV screen glows darkly film-noir. Poor Mrs. Dexter. I smile down at her.

"And I've *listened*," she goes on, "and I've learned."

"All of us can learn," my father says reasonably. "Did you say oysters, Miss . . ."

Mrs. Dexter tells him *Dexter*, and he says, "Oysters," and I excuse myself and go off toward the restroom.

Mrs. Dexter's paranoia bothers me. I stand in the rococo

marble and gilt bathroom with my hands on the edge of the washbasin and scowl at the mirror.

My ex-boyfriend, the one that ran Habitat for Humanity in Baker's Landing, told me an only child always thinks well of herself. He didn't mean it as a compliment, but I decided to remember it that way. I am tall and have reddish hair that gets brighter when the sun hits it, and I look younger than my age. The Habitat boyfriend used to say I looked radiant and lusty; Susie's son Robbie just said I was pretty. Today I'm wearing blue jeans and a black T-shirt and a black jacket on top of that for respectability. I stick my tongue out at my reflection. That seems a corrective gesture and I'm imitating the faucet handles, which are shaped like those medieval decorations high up on the cathedral, the ones with griffin heads or lion heads and long, lolling tongues.

When I get back to the dining room, Daddy and Mrs. Dexter are sitting at a table in the corner. The walker rests beside the table; Mrs. Dexter has hung her pocketbook on it. She and my father are talking about the food.

"Oysters are interesting to eat," she is saying. "My uncle, long ago, taught me." She demonstrates with an imaginary shellfish, holding it by its edge and slurping. "It seemed barbaric at first, and then it seemed the height of sophistication. Did they have oysters in ancient Egypt, Ed?"

I think, oh, Jesus, now he'll start again about fishing nets; that's his phobia for today, but he doesn't. He answers perfectly rationally, describing a search he once made among Egyptian banquet paintings for "not oysters exactly," he says, "but shellfish. And I didn't find any! Perhaps the shells were too small to look good in a tomb painting." He sounds exactly like his old self, Edward Day, Professor of

Egyptology, Head, Department of Near Eastern Studies. Thank you, Mrs. Dexter, for treating him like a real person.

"But I won't have oysters today," Daddy says. "They're special, aren't they? I'll sit here and admire yours."

I also don't want oysters. They were a favorite with my mother, Constancia, and I don't want to think about Constancia just now.

So Daddy and I are involved in spearing bits of salad lettuce and aren't watching when Mrs. Dexter begins making the noises.

She holds an oyster out in the air and coughs out the half-choked, half-explosive sounds that go with having something stuck in your throat. Then she drops the oyster and puts a hand to her collarbone and leans forward. Her face screws up, her eyes bulge.

And liquid begins to run down her chin. A juice that looks red, almost like blood, at first runs in a narrow glaze below her lip, then in two angry rivulets, one from each corner of her mouth. And yes, it is blood. Definitely.

She puts a hand to her collarbone and leans forward, eyes bulging.

A red puddle drips from her chin onto the oysters that still sit in front of her.

I stand up and run around the table, knocking my chair over. I'm trying to remember the details of the Heimlich maneuver. And saying to myself, *No, not Heimlich, she's bleeding*. And then telling myself, *Yes, but something's stuck there*. So what I finally do is part Heimlich and part invention.

I pick her up and shift her around. It's almost like handling a child, a child with scrawny shoulders and a projecting ribcage. I think, *Oh, my God, I hope I don't break anything; her bones are bird bones only; here is a tiny frail rib, like a chicken rib; here is a knobbed curve of backbone. And the blood; blood coming down her face and into the creases in my wrists.*

I turn her partly upside-down, concentrating hard, staring at the jug of flowers in the middle of the table. "Don't swallow now," I say, and move my hands into position on her diaphragm and lift her into the air, half upside-down, squeezing.

Behind me the dining room gets silent. Maybe my ears have clogged up, but the room seems to get totally still, and then there is the explosion of a lot of chair-scraping and feet coming our way. But I can't pay attention to that. Mrs. Dexter pats the air; her little rump presses into my chest; the rest of her body hangs rigid and tensed, black-shod feet pointing outward, everything hanging from my squeezing hands. But finally she coughs, an awful, painful noise, wrenching, as if some part of her throat is coming up. It sounds final, as if she can never do that again. I turn her around and lay her on her back.

A couple of waitresses have materialized nervously behind me. I feel them but don't even look up at them; I'm busy.

"Now don't bite me, for God's sake," I say, kneeling over her. And winch and wangle her mouth open. She is good about the way I maul her; it's hard not to gag when someone does this to you.

A lot of blood has puddled under her soft palate. I feel something—a sudden triangular wedge of sharpness. I get a finger underneath and catch the sharp thing; she gags, but I've pulled this little sharp bit forward. Then I turn her over onto her face, and she spits the sharp object out, along with a gush of blood and oyster and moaning.

A lot of people are standing around us now, including a

waitress who says, "Oh, my God, oh, my God," over and over.

I reach for Mrs. Dexter's napkin and wipe her face. "Oh," she's saying, "oh, oh," drawing in a harsh, bubbling breath each time.

"You were wonderful, wonderful," I tell her, "Jesus X that must have hurt. Oh, poor Mrs. D." I bend over and kiss her on her poor quivering blood-smeared cheek.

I'm not sure what makes me pick that fragment of sharpness out of the blood and oyster mess on the floor and put it in my pocket. I tell myself something like, *If the infirmary wants to see it, I'll show them, but meanwhile I'm taking charge*. I thought at first it must be a piece of oyster shell, but now, as I feel in my pocket, it seems more like a piece of glass.

People are around us in a circle. Someone is saying, "Call the infirmary," and someone else, "Doctor, get the doctor." Poor Mrs. Dexter will hate this, being on display.

I get up to go to my father, whose voice I hear threaded through the other babble; he's saying, "If she lies there, they will come for her. When you lie down like that is when they grab you."

ヿ Chapter 2

I spend a bedraggled night churning across a Manor guest-room bed and staring up into a fluted ceiling. What's going to happen to my poor confused father? And to gallant, paranoid Mrs. Dexter? And what's with that piece of glass? Because it *is* glass; it sits now, wrapped in toilet paper, in the front pocket of my backpack, looking like a sliver of that microwave-safe milky stuff they use to make baking dishes.

I don't want to believe that Mrs. Dexter's dramatic warnings are fact-based. Four A.M. flickers across the motel-type clock before I turn out the light.

But the next morning I get up feeling okay and go off to find Daddy, who seems moderately glued to reality, although he wants to talk too much about Horus's Eye, which is a hieroglyph of an eye with stylized markings below it. We have breakfast sent to the room, and he cracks the top of his egg and worries about the eye: "It represents eternal renewal, did you remember? An image of hope, of course."

Snap, off comes the top of the egg. "You know, I think I am in danger."

"Surely not, Daddy." This has to be more of Mrs. Dexter's paranoia. "The Manor," I enthuse, "such a safe place." I gesture at his small-paned, mullioned window, elegantly old-fashioned.

"Hmmm," says my father. "They may send me somewhere to keep me safe."

I don't like this talk one bit, but I decide the way to handle it is to ignore it. I kiss him and position him in his easy chair in front of the TV, and by the time I leave for my appointment with Manor administration he seems perfectly all right, clucking over the timber construction of the prairie mansion in *This Old House*.

The appointment with Manor administration is the one where I'm supposed to discuss what to do with my father.

They want to send him off to Hope House, and I want them not to. It seems to me that he has paid for the luxury of residence in the good parts of the Manor, and he should have that for a long while more.

Manor administration is a lady named Mrs. Sisal, who has an asymmetrical haircut and is wearing a long-waisted black suit. She focuses on me in her lozenge-shaped glasses and lets me know that I am famous. "Excellent thinking last night," she says. "Admirable." She sounds as if it hurts to say these things. "We are going to have to give Mrs. Dexter medication lessons," she adds right away, being the kind of administrator who needs to balance any nice thing she accidentally does with a mean one.

I ask, "Medication lessons?" and she agrees, "Yes, of

course," and goes on to explain: "We have had many clients—the people we work with here are not *patients*, Miss Day, but *clients*—we've had many clients who did that. Forgot. Tried to swallow a pill inside its aluminum casing."

I'm lost here. "A pill in an aluminum casing?"

Mrs. Sisal moves her head irritatedly. "Some of the medications are arranged on an aluminum-covered card. You have to separate the sections, which are sharp. And after that, you must pry the pill out."

"And you think she tried to swallow it, piece of card and all?"

"Certainly she did. There's no other explanation for those throat abrasions. And this client has had medication problems before; when she had pneumonia, she could not keep straight the rules about when to take calcium and when to take Cipro."

So Mrs. Dexter is being blamed for cutting her own throat with a pill casing; that certainly will take care of any ideas she might get about lawsuits. I feel a flood of anger that I can't let show because Mrs. Sisal is moving on to the business of the day, hassling me about my father.

"Embarrassing for him, too," she says, and "He wanders, he calls out, he is distressed, he is upset, Miss Day, more upset than we find useful. Perhaps he would be happier in Hope House? Hope House," she gets a fashionable pointy-toed foot over the edge of her file drawer, "is our comfortable, controlled facility."

I work hard at looking unfazed; I smile gently. It doesn't do to go weak with these bullying types. The question of who moves to Hope House and who gets to stay here in overstuffed luxury will probably be settled by Mrs. Sisal. "My father has been a very famous man," I remind her.

Both she and I know that *famous* once-upon-a-time has nothing to do with Alzheimer's now but the reminder works just the same. She relaxes a bit, the glasses turn to their *admit light* mode; she likes the idea of fame and agrees, "We have many famous people at the Manor."

It's at this point that it happens. The Devil makes me do it. I open my mouth and out it comes. I accomplish something that is totally outrageous and apparently unplanned, although later when I stop and review, I realize that I have indeed been planning toward it.

I ask Mrs. Sisal for a job. For a job for me at Green Beach Manor. A position as an aide, one of those helpers who assists the old people in taking their pills and finding the bathroom.

It is ridiculous, and at the same time it's not.

I want to be near my father and keep him from talking about his woman on the beach and his eye being eaten. I am feeling guilty about having left him to go off to Baker's Landing and Habitat for Humanity. My father needs me nearby, a buffer against Hope House.

He has a lifetime sentence in the Manor, thanks to Aunt Crystal.

I have no job and no ties except for him; I've just had a final and irrevocable falling out with the Habitat boyfriend.

I thought of maybe working here while I was riding down on the Greyhound bus, and I thought of it again this morning as I crossed the garden toward Administration with the sea air all fresh and vigorous, and one of Mrs. Dexter's butterflies coming to life among the ridiculous palm trees, and the coastal moss spangling itself with dew. I looked around and thought, *It's a weird atmosphere but maybe a pretty place to be for a while.*

And just now with Mrs. Sisal being so meanly stupid about Daddy and also about Mrs. Dexter, I think of these possibilities again. Perhaps it's the case of Mrs. Dexter even more than of my father that kicks me forward; *You're an uncomfortable person*, I decide, analyzing the glasses, *somebody better watch you.*

"This may seem like a complete change of subject," I tell her, "but actually it's not . . ." I pause and warm up into my spiel. "A job as an aide. I am very well qualified." I list my charms, not bothering to be modest: good grades, college animal lab (those lab cats with glasses should be worth something), Habitat for Humanity. Service with others, experience helping people. Et cetera, et cetera.

Sisal is a very cool, not to say chilly human being and can't let herself be amazed that I might change the subject so suddenly, nor that I might want to work at her establishment.

I don't add, *I know I'm overqualified*, which is true, but I do imply that although highly trained, I'm willing to come down in the world and that I'll stay for a while (". . . stable, I have a really great work record"), and generally I'm a terrific bargain. I murmur about a devotion to Sociology, a possible personal future in Aging, "This will be work experience; such a useful field," I say, all the while chin up confidently, smiling into the glasses.

Mrs. Sisal mutters about my father, and I reassure her, "Yes, I want to be near him, of course, but, no, that won't affect my work."

"Well," she murmurs, looking favorable.

I'm remembering Mrs. Dexter's stories about someone

falling out of a window and somebody else with a gas leak and now her own oyster-glass sandwich, and I think, but don't say, *Hey, if you're having all these weird accidents, you certainly can use more staff.*

"We cannot pay a great deal." She takes her foot out of the file drawer; business is beginning.

Some sheets are summoned into her computer, and she begins asking job-application questions, pecking the answers in rapidly on her keyboard: *education, previous employers,* (Susie becomes a Marketing dot com). Suddenly, Sisal stops and looks up, inquiring, "There are almost no young people here; will you be lonely? Do you have friends nearby?"

I hadn't suspected her of understanding the word *lonely,* but maybe the question was in her *Executives Procedures Manual.*

"I have friends from college in the town of Green Beach."

"Oh, good, good." She returns to the rest of my vital statistics.

Actually, the friend in Green Beach is Susie's son Robbie, who is a doctor at North Shore Hospital and thus an adjunct doctor at this establishment, one of the extra ones whom the Manor calls in when they can't reach the usual guy.

It may seem the height of coincidence for Robbie to be here and also for me to be here. But it isn't coincidence at all; it's cause and effect: Robbie was the one who told Aunt Crystal about Green Beach Manor in the first place, when she was shopping for a residence for Daddy. I've stayed away from Green Beach more than I should because Robbie might be around.

Susie, in the parking lot, when she was saying goodbye to me, almost talked about Robbie; I could feel her take in a deep breath for: "Hey, Carly, say, 'Hi,' to Robbie for me," and "Don't be mean to my boy when you see him, huh, girl?" But then she didn't say any of these things. All she did was look doubtful and kiss me. Susie is too nice to torment ex-lovers, even when they're related to her.

Mrs. Sisal rips a long page out of her computer and hands it over to sign. "Now you understand . . ." and she enunciates a list of days on and days off and a salary figure (yes, low) and a fraternization rule which means *do not have sex with the old men.*

I leave Mrs. Sisal's office loaded down with directions, schedules, a chit for the laundry room where I'll get an aide's smock, a room key, and an armful of gold-embossed literature about *The Manor System, Your Way to New Life*. "Seize the Day," the brochure says. "Live the way you've always wanted to live." And it supplies a long list of classes you (that is, Daddy and the other clients like him) can take to do this. Besides an online stock-trading class, so useful to those of us with early-stage Alzheimer's, there are sessions in Watercolor, Found Sculpture, Tai Chi, Macrame, and Contract Bridge.

Mrs. S. had smirked at me, "That is our message; you need to *project* it."

She was busy gloating over her new cheap aide and appeared to have forgotten about sending my poor confused father to Hope House.

After I get my uniform and move my backpack into my new, minimal, utilitarian little room, I stop by Daddy's apartment to give him the news. "Guess what? I'll be living here now."

He sits in his easy chair looking pink and hopeful, his tweed jacket neatly buttoned, his face a childish round. He's balancing, slightly too close to his face, a *New York Times* folded into that standard *Times* quarter-fold. Although at this moment the paper is upside down. Maybe it hasn't been that way all these hours since breakfast.

"Live here, darling?" He lowers the paper and turns to assess his apartment with its oriental rug and redwood window seat and bay window. "How nice, how fine. Of course you live here. I will sleep *there*," a gesture at the window seat; "You will have the alcove."

"I like a hard bed," he persists while I start explaining, and then he continues with, "Do you remember, camping at Sharm el Naga, oh, I was such a good camper, Carla, although that woman in the net . . ." Here he seems to lose track of his thought, and I jump in with words like *job* and *experience* and *temporary*. Which results in a big pileup of misunderstanding. "Oh, no, no, not *temporary*; Daughter, of *course* you live in my hotel." And he settles back determined to beam at me.

"Come see my room, Daddy." I take his hand and lead him, *New York Times* and all, down the hall to show him the eight-by-ten space Mrs. Sisal has allotted to me.

Our way through the hall is wide and plush and overstuffed; someone has been hanging another van-load of those gold-framed pink-and-blue pictures. What is it about Renoir that makes it so easy to do a fake one, all misty and plump?

He wants to talk about other hotels. "There was one, I wonder where, they had a replica of a pyramid?"

The hotel he's talking about is the El Nil in Cairo, but I don't tell him that; offering facts sometimes results in extra confusion, as if he doesn't want to know the real names of things, just the possibilities that shimmer in the back of his head. I'd love to know how memory works for him. I think of it as a random pile of high-voltage electric wires, some of them with the rubber casings peeling off.

We have arrived at my new room, which is entirely different from the surrounding hall; maybe it was reinvented out of a utility cupboard or guest closet; it's lined mostly in white fiberboard and contains a sturdy little IKEA bed and cardboard dresser and one of those steel pipe arrangements with colored metal hangers dangling from it. A high window, half-open, lets in ocean noise.

Daddy looks troubled; he enters my new room; he bounces on the bed. "They can do better than this," he announces.

And for a moment, he's his old academic department-head self.

"You should speak to them, Carla, dear. I think it quite possible that . . ."

Here he stops, distressed. "This is quite a good hotel, isn't it? Did you get the reservation? I think you did; you usually do, don't you? And a good hotel. You always get good ones?"

He's quiet for a minute, long enough for me to decide I don't like his bent-over posture; then he says, "Daughter, I am worried about memory."

Oh, Jesus, here it comes, I think. The Alzheimer's books all prepare you for the moment when he says, "I'm afraid I'm beginning to forget." Then, and not before then, you say, *I'm terribly sorry, but we think you have a disease; the doctors are*

*working on a cure and the outlook is hopeful and so on and et
cetera.* Don't say this before he mentions something specific,
some worry about his control of things. Only when he raises
the subject himself. How would you like it if you were old
and dependent and your young relative suddenly started
lecturing you about how incurably forgetful you were going
to be?

But the general subject of forgetting is not the one he
wants to raise. I start out with "You know, memory is really
complicated," and he intervenes, "It was down there below.
It was a gold net." His Woman in the Net, that's what he
wants to talk about. "For a while I thought I knew her."

"Something Egyptian," I suggest. "You have so many
Egyptian memories." Maybe the way to reassure him about
this net fantasy is to put it in a pleasant context. "Someone
from Egyptian poetry," I blather on. "Or connected with
your Coffin Lid Text."

The Coffin Lid Text was one of Daddy's great moments.
He found this coffin lid in the anteroom of a "dry" (already
explored) tomb in the Valley of the Kings, and while Egyptian coffin lids aren't usually important, this one was because
written on it was a version of the account on the tomb wall,
and by comparing the two texts he could deduce the meaning of a whole row of hieroglyphs that had baffled scholars
before him.

The coffin lid is in a nearby museum now. It really belongs to the Luxor Museum, but the owner of Egypt Regained, a weird private California museum, wangled or
charmed the Luxor Museum into an indefinite loan. Egypt
Regained is run by an eccentric millionaire named Egon
Rothskellar, and I'm afraid Egon is interested in the life-

extension aspects of Egyptian artifacts. But, hey, my father's eccentric, too.

"Coffin lid? Text?" he asks now. "No, dear, I don't think so. She wiggled. She wiggled around in the net. And then dead. Dead, and I didn't . . ." He looks up at me, and there seem to be tears on his cheeks. "And someone fell out of a window here," he adds.

I don't like it that his fantasy, his strange, persistent woman-in-the-net obsession has been added onto the lady-out-the-window. That's just too eerie, I won't explore it. I grab him by the arm and say, "Listen, let's go back to your room. You can watch M*A*S*H; I'll turn it on for you."

Returned to his armchair with his quilt and his bay window and a snack package of his favorite peppermint Jelly Bellies, he's feeling well enough to lecture me again about how my new room isn't good enough; he will speak to Management. "They're quite nice at this hotel."

I kiss him and go back to my room and survey it some more. It seems all right to me. Sure, it's a really tiny crabbed space, scraped and minimal, like Orphan Annie living in a piano box over a Manhattan subway grating. So it makes me feel like somebody out of a story.

I do some unpacking, four garments, two get hung on the pipe-hanger arrangement and two go into the cardboard dresser. I unpack Mrs. Dexter's piece of glass and put it on the dresser in a plastic yogurt top I've had in my backpack. I stand back and look at this arrangement and think that the yogurt installation is an art object and the foundation of my new homestead. In my Santa Cruz esthetics course the teacher said the beginning of an individuated life was a personal esthetic; he meant you should do something artistic that was new and different and yours. Well, you can't get much more personal than a maybe-murderous piece of oyster glass in a yogurt top, can you?

🐦 Chapter 3

I'm headed to the hospital to visit Mrs. Dexter.

Most of Green Beach Manor is Victorian and overdone. But the hospital was added later and simply looks like a standard hospital. I am familiar with the breed because of the one we built in Baker's Landing; it was white and pink and chrome and looked a lot like this one.

The Manor Hospital also smells like our Baker's Landing structure, a combination of lemon disinfectant and instant noodles-in-a-cup. There is an entrance desk and a lot of fluorescent lights, and then down a hall you can see three rooms with two beds apiece. Mrs. Sisal and Co. aren't set up for a really big epidemic.

A short, skinny peroxide-haired person in blue whose name tag identifies her as "Hospital-Aide Mona" gushes up to me with the kind of gush you don't expect in a hospital. "You're Carla; you were so wonderful," she emotes. "You were the one who saved her. So great. So quick-thinking. We're just so, so proud." She extends a scrawny birdlike be-ringed hand, which she latches on to my wrist to pull me down a pink hall. "So wonderful," she says, presumably meaning me, not the hall.

Down at the end is a white room where Mrs. Dexter sits propped against pillows, her face scrunched into a vinegary, rubber grinch-mask, her body surrounded by a mountain of magazines, newspapers, and dangerously tilting glasses holding bent straws.

Mrs. Dexter stares for a while, glumly, and finally raises a hand, palm out, Indian fashion, and says, "How." She winces, she's hoarse; you can tell that even this one syllable hurts her throat.

Mona continues to hover, "What a shame. I was so upset when I got back from Provo, Utah; I'd been visiting my sister, and when I got back from Provo and heard—such a dreadful accident. But you were so wonderful." Mrs. Dexter hides behind her sheet while Mona won't stop. "Oh, that was so terrible. I nearly died when I heard about it. And now there's this silly, silly rumor—something about glass? And your dear father, they say he's been complaining?" She turns to me, her eyebrows raised. She has the kind of eyebrows that you paint on afterward.

When I don't answer, she says, "Well, I'm really upset about this, but I'm really glad I was in Provo."

She's hitting that button about being in Provo pretty hard. She has her mouth open to babble some more, but I level a thousand-watt scowl and she backs away saying, "Oh, well. Oh, yes." That scowl is the one I think of as my Aunt Crystal look. Aunt C. was very good at squelching people.

"Pretty weird," I tell Mrs. Dexter, since that's what I think she wants someone to say, sort of like supplying subtitles for a foreign film. She doesn't react much. This experience has damped her down.

I sit on the bed and remark, "Well." We stare at each other. "I guess you're better than you were last night," I venture.

She contorts her face. Of course it's a dumb remark, but how do you make small talk with someone who can't even say "uh-huh" without hurting? That, however, isn't what she's contorting about. She lifts her hand again in the Indian or traffic-stopping gesture, swallows, moves her head, and whispers, "Thank you. For saving. My life."

I lean over and hug her, which I guess she hates; she makes her body uncooperatively stiff. But, I'm sorry, Mrs. Dexter, a person has to do something and "No problem," or "You're welcome," is not a good response.

I like older people, I might interject here, especially older women. That was part of my success at Habitat—I got along with the seniors. Probably it's because I'm looking for a mother. What a bore. I hate dragging all that ancient history around all the time.

When I emerge from the hug, I say, chaotically and too fast because I'm embarrassed, "I thought about you last night. About you and those questions you had. How you had suspicions and talked about them and were trying to listen in and maybe investigate. And then this awful thing happened to you." I stop and take a good look at Mrs. Dexter.

She's making pained, everything-hurts faces and giving me the palm-out gesture. She mouths, carefully, lips very controlled, "Accident."

"Accident?" I repeat, not sure I've read the lips right. "Oh, but, hey. I mean . . ."

I'm about to go into an explanation of *That was a real piece of glass: I've got the little bit in my room now . . .* But she preempts me again, shakes her head vigorously, shapes the lips. "Accident. I was. Wrong."

It's a funny thing. Up until now I've felt tentative; yes, it is strange, suspicious even, that Mrs. Dexter should have noticed the accidents in the Manor and talked about how she was listening and spying and then should have had an accident herself. I wasn't ready to say that all this necessarily added up, just that it gave me an *aware* feeling. Until now, when Mrs. Dexter protests, "Accident. Accident," and I don't believe her. Something clicks; I tell myself that there's too much accident and denial around here, it adds up, damn right it does. That piece of glass is a real piece of glass. Mrs. Dexter has to have known that it was alien and sharp and didn't belong in her oyster. And now she's acting scared and paranoid. I don't like this set of facts.

She and I regard each other. I debate arguing and decide against it. In the first place, she has an abraded throat and can't argue back, and, second and more important, she's feeling rebellious and frightened. She doesn't want to be hassled.

I'm debating the various harmless nonthreatening subjects I can raise now: the weather (stable and occasionally sunny), the news of the world (stable, with war, disease, poverty, corruption), local news (my new job at the Manor could figure here—but I have a feeling Mrs. Dexter would be horrified). Then the day is saved by Mona, who bursts in announcing, joyfully and with hand-twitches, that "The doctor is here; so concerned, so interested. Such a caring doctor."

I'm pleased. I really want to meet this Dr. Kittredge, who appears in the literature as ". . . our eminent resident physician, one of the three Resident Directors of the Manor." As a resident director and as the Manor doctor, Dr. Kittredge will certainly have a say on whether my father continues living in Victorian luxury or gets exiled to Hope House, which I imagine as more pink formica. And my opinion on the rights and wrongs of this has gotten inexorable. The man has paid high for Victorian kitsch; he should have it. I turn to meet the doctor.

It's funny how some names make you decide in advance what a person will be like. Dr. Kittredge, I knew this when I saw his name in the Manor literature, would be older, trim, neat, a version of my father except for a spade-shaped beard.

But the doctor who blusters through the door is handsome, bulky, and tousled-looking. Somewhere in his forties and with no beard of any kind. "Well, now," he pushes past me without acknowledgment and heads for Mrs. Dexter, "So here you are. Louise, my old darlin', what a scare you've been givin' us. You're better this morning, Mona says? Thanks be to God. Now, let's see, can you open wide for me? There we go, old sweet."

This doctor takes up a lot of room. And he has an Irish accent. I'm not sure how I feel about that combination. I want to lecture him about his treatment of Mrs. Dexter, "For God's sake, quit calling her by her first name; give her some respect; she's old enough to be your grandmother."

"Hello," I announce loudly to his back, "I am Carla Day."

"I know all about you." He's still bent over Mrs. Dexter's open mouth. "You're the girl who does the Heimlich maneuver."

Well, great, I decide. Now I'm *the girl who*. Here's a man with no manners and no p.c. on top of that. Living in Berkeley gives you extra radar for negative p.c.

But the next minute he turns around and announces in a carrying baritone, "This is a tremendously brave lady," and holds Mrs. Dexter's hand up in that successful boxer's gesture. He cocks his head and looks so silly and hopeful that I get a different set of messages, straight out of an old Bing Crosby movie. While the voice keeps on announcing he's Irish. Or at least part Irish. Enough to lengthen the vowels and put a *J* in *tremenJously*. Irish voices do something basic to my sentiment glands; my Habitat boyfriend once put it that the Irish can make you nostalgic for something you never had. That boyfriend was perceptive and bright; his personality problem lay in his being also a neurotic mess.

Dr. Kittredge grins, one of those lopsided Irish things with an eyebrow going up toward the hairline. "You did great the other night."

"Yeah, okay," I continue being ungracious.

"And, *Jaysus*." That Irish accent now. It comes and goes, waxes and wanes. He puts Mrs. Dexter's hand back on the bedspread. "What an awful thing. The palate abraded. Some of the other clients are saying it was glass; can you imagine that, glass in an oyster?"

I say, "Oh?" And no response. I wonder how that glass rumor got out. Not from me. I haven't talked to anybody.

"Ah," says Dr. Kittredge, "such a dreadful idea, really dreadful." He sits down heavily on Mrs. Dexter's bed, slumping his shoulders as if I've agreed, but then he gets right up again; probably he's remembered the doctor isn't supposed to sit on the patient's bed.

Mrs. Dexter is making convulsive Greek-tragedy faces.

"An accident in the kitchen, I guess?" the doctor says, still as if I've confirmed the glass theory. "God almighty, we'll have to investigate." He thinks about this for a minute, massaging his chin. And scowls and appears to change his mind. "Probably just oyster shell, don't you think? That's bad enough. Careless, terribly careless." Suddenly he gets very sincere. "There is entirely too much peculiar stuff going on around here these days."

I don't get it, I tell myself; *what's he up to?*

He bends toward Mrs. Dexter. "Sweetheart, we'll send you home tomorrow, but stay on the clindamycin four more days and don't forget to swish out with the chlorexadine. Feelin' a little better now, are we darlin'?"

Mrs. Dexter says, "Mmmf." She rolls her eyes at me. She wishes I would go away and shut up.

"Oyster shell. Glass," the doctor says, half to himself. "Holy Jay. Out of our own kitchen! Or maybe someone put something there, in her oyster. Somebody consciously set out to slit this little lady's throat." He holds Mrs. Dexter's hand; he flexes it up and down; he looks as if he's posing for a TV commercial: *The Caring Doctor*.

"Carla," he calls over at me, "wait a minute till I sign these forms, and I'll walk back to the main building with you."

I don't much like getting to be *Carla* so fast for this doctor, but yes, fine, I'll walk over to the main building with him; I want to hear what else he's going to say. He's certainly going for the opposite of Mrs. Sisal's aluminum pill-card theory.

"Tomorrow," I tell Mrs. Dexter, who receives the suggestion stonily, and then Dr. Kittredge and I start out into the sunshine. I'll let him do the talking. He's a word-spinner; I'll just mutter *uh-huh* and *oh*.

He's also one of those bulky men who wants to lean at you when he talks. "Dreadful business," he says lugubriously, and cants a shoulder into my personal space.

"Uh-huh."

"Poor woman. Painful, of course. But, thanks be to God, the palate heals fast. That was one of the wonders in med school. How fast the mouth and throat area heal. Lots of blood vessels.

"Yep." He's certainly spending a lot of broadcast time on this. "But scary," he goes on. "Tremenjously scary. Far too much of this sort of thing here lately."

"Ah," he goes, looking at my face, "you've not heard? Maybe partly rumor. But also, maybe not. Other accidents. Bad for the Manor." He waves an arm here. "No good at all."

I say encouragingly, "Oh?" and he grins and puts his head back; he likes it that I want to hear him. "Accidents. You know, and we can't pretend; that gets you even worse lawsuits. I'm a director of the Manor, you know."

"I heard."

He hasn't forgotten his duty as an alpha male, and we're jittering a little dance along the path with him moving toward me and me pulling away, but curiously I don't feel much of the focused irritation I'd usually get, maybe because Dr. Kittredge so successfully projects the image of *puppy dog*, bouncing and panting along like a large, friendly hound that doesn't know it shouldn't slobber.

"Ah, I'm worried about the Manor, Carla. Am I gettin' too personal too fast? It's been that kind of a day, pileup of troubles; it's a help to walk in the sunshine with a pretty girl. Too personal, is it? I guess so." He pronounces *personal* as *pairsonal*.

"Um," I say.

"Did I hear right?" he asks, "You're goin' to be workin' here?"

"Just an aide." I look sideways at him. News certainly travels fast in the Manor.

And he goes, "Ah, girl, you're daft."

At least half of that Irish accent must be fake. And anyhow, how, with a name like Kittredge does he get to sound Irish at all?

"But, ah," he says, "I feel strongly about the Manor. We do good; we get a lot accomplished. I work here because I think it's a force for good. Ah, it's a cause close to my heart. . . . Now, some of the directors, they think we should try to . . . how is it? Obfuscate? Fib a little bit? About all these accidents we been havin'. But I, now, ah, well. I don't think you ever get away with that stuff. A fact is a fact. And the fact is, some pretty peculiar things been happenin' around here. Before this. You heard about it?"

A leading question. I say, "Some."

"Well, sweetheart, believe it, you will." He manages to sag his shoulders while keeping on walking and to send along a new and different story about puppy dog with mas-

ter gone. "Carla, I just can't tellya . . ." A pause here. During which I think, *Okay, organ music, please.* "It makes me
sad, dear girl, to see people tryin' to hide the truth . . . however bad, it's the *truth*."

I guess I have to say something now. "Ummm," I try.

We've arrived at one of the Manor buildings now, all
brick and wainscoting and ivy; Dr. Kittredge leans against a
corner, dislodging some ivy leaves. "Plenty to think about,
huh? Listen, dear girl, I'll call you, and we'll go for a walk
some evenin'. Am I right?"

I say, "Yeah, okay," and watch him dodge into a handsome side door of the Administration building, one with a
cutout of a seabird nailed on it. He still hasn't buttoned his
lab coat, which flaps out behind him.

♟ Chapter 4

A woman named Belle is going to teach me my Manor job.

I already know Belle. She's Daddy's own aide, and I saw a lot of her the times before this when I came down here to visit him. She's the one who hands him his morning pills, checks he doesn't have his shirt on wrong side out, gets him out into the hall and pointed in the general direction of the breakfast lounge. Belle is a tall angular woman with faded hair who looks like that painting of the lady poised in front of the New England–type church-cum-barn and peering through the rake—the one that gets onto all the T-shirts these days. But she's not like that, really. I like her okay. She's nice to my father, straightforward and respectful, not unctuous the way the Manor literature is, and she has a wry, direct way of talking right at you that's reassuring.

I meet her in the hall underneath a fake Renoir of a woman with one pink breast hanging out.

Belle has a cartful of bottles that she's rocking squeakily back and forth. She stares at me in an irked manner. "Well, hi, I guess."

"Hi, yourself, Belle." I'd expected more of a big hello than this.

"So yer working here?"

I tell her yes, and she asks me *why* as if she's caught me out in a minor crime, and when I say, "Well, I needed a job," she snorts. *Hmmff.* A juicy throat-clear. "You don't need a job, sweet pea. You're rich."

I'm amazed. I take a minute to digest this. "Rich? Why'm I rich? What gave you that idea?"

Belle turns and tries to stare a hole through me. She has the kind of watery see-right-through-you blue eyes that go with that T-shirt image. "Lissen. Yer dad lives here. If you got a dad that lives *here*, yer rich. You don't got *any* need to work here."

I say, "Oh." Then I try to explain. Yes, there used to be some money, but no, not any more, it all went to buy him in here. I'm poor. Poorer than anybody. Not that it's any of Belle's business, but I hate to have people misjudging me. As a matter of fact, I need Belle to like me, if I'm going to be around here. "I'm poor," I reiterate. "I *need* this job."

She stares at me some more. "So. You got no other job?"

"Other job? No."

"Oh, yeah? Well. Okay, then. I guess." She snorts again and points at her cartful of bottles. "See all that stuff there? Now every morning you knock on all these doors—you got fifteen, not such a bad load—and you check up, do they look okay, an' does the room smell funny, an' does it look like they slept all right, are they able to stand up and not teeter, and you give 'em their pills—each set of pills is in a little plastic doohickey, see, all except the antibiotics; they're down on the lower shelf—gottit?"

I'm bent over, looking at the antibiotic shelf. "The antibiotics have red lids."

"Yeah, right, right." Belle still hasn't moved the cart, she's kept on rocking it back and forth; it squeaks, one of those *help, help* sounds. "*Why*, exactly, you want this job?"

"I told you. I need to work. I'm broke."

"Yeah? What about your *other* job?"

I put my hand on the cart to stop the squeaking. "What other job?"

She stares me up and down. This part of the hall has flocked wallpaper—that stuff where one busy design has been pasted on top of another busy design—and the whole tangled mess seems to be leaning at me. Which Belle is doing, too. I think her stare is supposed to be scary. "You're here *observing*. I knew it the minute I heard. About you bein' here. A spy, I said. Watchin' us."

"What in *hell* are you talking about?"

I'm sufficiently amazed that I apparently connect; she examines me some more, and then scratches up under her blue-striped smock. She says, "No?" and I say, "*No*," with force, and after another minute she agrees, "Yer not," more to herself that to me.

"What would *I* be spying for?" I ask.

"You kiddin', baby? There's plenty stuff around here to spy about." She gestures in the direction of the half-exposed Renoir matron. Her voice gets ruminative. "Well, maybe not. Okay, kid, I apologize; yer just a innocent wage slave like the rest of us. You want to be near yer dad, too, I guess?"

"I do."

"That's a dumb idea, too. Don't be near him here; get a

good job with money, call him up, come in an' see him a lot, send him stuff; he likes those chocolates with a cherry in the middle, you noticed? Be his rich daughter that comes to see him. This is stupid."

"They want to send him to Hope House," I say.

"Oh, uh." Belle frowns a little extra. "Well . . . takes time that. Gettin' somebody into Hope House. Doesn't happen right away. Don't worry about it."

"I thought maybe I could help. Calm him down."

She's too old to say, "Duh," the way somebody my age would, but she stares and makes a noise that means the same thing and then goes on, "Lissen. This place is peculiar. I mean, nothin' adds up lately, gettit? Could take 'em a long time to get anything organized. Gettit?"

All I'm getting is an uncomfortable feeling. "Uh-uh."

"So you *don't* gettit. You sure yer not investigating?"

We're far enough into this peculiar conversation that I decide this is a flattering thing for Belle to think. Investigator/observer/spy equals professional. It's a new way of looking at me. But I turn down the honor. "No, Belle. Absolutely not."

She takes another minute to analyze me and then switches focus at last. "Okay, then. We gotta get these pills out. Come on along with it, now."

The cart is activated; we squeak down the hall past Renoirs, Chagalls, dog pictures, and swirling red-and-gold flocked wallpaper; finally she knocks on a door that has an elf in a yellow jumpsuit hanging from the nameplate. "Good morning, little lady, you won a sweepstake, four kinds of pills. My God, are you lucky. Howya feelin' this morning?"

The woman at the door wears a flowered housecoat and

peers at us through powder-spattered glasses. "Belle," she says, "I'm so glad to see you, I always feel better after I have my morning dose of Belle. Belle is my morning fun package." She turns to me, and when we're introduced, says, "Why, you're Edward's daughter. A *young* aide; how good, so nice to have a young face, helps us, know what I mean?" Mrs. Cohen is another person here whom I've met before; she's one of Daddy's special group of three old-lady admirers.

Belle watches the door close on this lady and tells me, "Now that is Mrs. Cohen. Like you can see, she is nice an' won't give you any trouble, which is not what I'd say for all of them."

And she goes through my client list: another of my father's special trio: this one is named Mrs. La Salle, a Mr. Rice, a Mr. Taylor ("an they're a coupla hellers"). A bunch of others. Mrs. Dexter is on my list. "It's not exactly hard work, but it's hard on *you*, if you gettit. You gotta watch, and sometimes they're scared, and then they take it out on you. There's Mrs. Cartwright has Parkinson's, shakes so bad I have to hold the pill cup for her, and Mrs. Krech with arthritis, some days so bad she's in a wheelchair and has to have a bag for going to the bathroom. You really wanna know, it's a lousy job an' I think yer crazy, and that's my candid opinion."

We trundle farther on down the hall. Halfway through our pill delivery, I have my mouth open to ask Belle about the Manor accidents—"Hey, what do you think about the woman who fell out the window? What about Mrs. Dexter and the oyster?" And then I decide not to ask these questions. Those are just the sort of questions an observer (or a company spy, or whatever else it is Belle thinks I might be) would be asking. I'm flattered by Belle thinking that of me, but I don't want her to fix on that opinion and never have any other.

Instead, I ask her about my father. "Mrs. Sisal says he yells around in the hall."

Belle shrugs. "So. A little *vocal*ization don't hurt anybody."

I smile, acknowledging the big word, but keep right on. "And that he wanders up into the forest. What's that about?"

"Dunno. Don't hassle it." She looks at my face and says, "Some kinda favorite place he's got up there. I think it's a well or something. He calls it 'Dark Lake.'"

"Dark Lake," I repeat. I don't much like the sound.

I start to ask her about my father's visits to the beach and then decide not to. I don't want to investigate that beach too much with Belle. Instead, I try some ordinary character-assassination gossip. "What do you think of the doctor?"

"Kittredge? Old mega-testosterone?"

"That's the one."

"Big blowhard," she adds.

I think, *Yeah, that, too.* "He took me for a walk," I volunteer.

"Excitement." Belle looks cynical.

I stress, "Not *especially*."

"How about him and Mrs. Sisal?" I ask. "Do they get along?"

"Maybe just great when they're in bed together." She stalls and examines me. "Hey, you *are* an Observer."

"No, I'm not. Just ordinary curiosity."

She makes a face and reminds me what happened to the cat. "Pussycat hamburger. Don't get too damn curious."

* * *

"Okay," she tells me at the end of the corridor. "You gottit, I guess, the routine. You pick up quick. The rest is just common sense, and don't scream if you find somebody passed out on the floor. They're old, and they do that. There's a string with a red button . . ."

"Yes, I know about the red button."

"Okay, then. That's what you do *in extremis*. You push that red button." She looks pretty pleased with herself for that Latin phrase, *in extremis*. "Now when you get finished, you check everything off on this clip sheet an' take it down to the desk. Gottit?"

I tell her, yes, I've got it. I say, "Thank you, Belle," and she says, "No charge, babe."

I've taken the cart handle and am trundling down the hall when she calls after me, "Hey, come see me when you feel like talking."

Which I take it is her way of saying she's keeping her lines open. She thinks I'm an Observer. She just hopes that I'm a friendly Observer, or maybe a stupid one.

The whole thing adds to the general tenseness here. Any situation that needs an observer is not a great situation.

⅃ Chapter 5

Finally, I telephone Susie at the grocery store to tell her I've taken a job here. "They call it joining the Manor family," I say. She's at first amazed and then supportive. "Working in that place," she says, "what a blast, where do you get these ideas? Listen, it might be *okay*."

She agrees to close up my apartment and adopt my two geranium plants. That apartment is just a one-room deal with a couch and microwave.

"So how is it? Working there?" she asks, and I tell her, "Okay. Not bad, actually."

"It's *okay*," I repeat, "the old ladies are nice to me."

"Tell me, tell me," she infuses enthusiasm into the telephone.

I try to remember if I've ever had one of those "Carla, now seriously, you can do better; you're not living up to your full potential" lectures from her in all our life together, and I decide I haven't. She's always total support and interest and enthusiasm. She sends these over the airwaves now. "What do you *do*? What happens, like, first off in the morning?"

I describe wheeling the cart down the hall, half-admiring and half-hating the misty, moist pictures—"Listen, Sue, they put their gold frames *inside* of gold frames"—and knocking on each old lady's door and saying, "Here's your morning stuff, one calcium, one Tylenol, and we got a prescription for Cipro today, and how are you feeling?"

I don't say anything about Belle thinking I'm an "observer," whatever that is.

"And the ladies—or, there are two old guys, too—always announce how they're feeling, in a lot of detail, and then they have to talk about the accidents. There was one where somebody fell out of a window, and one where the beauty parlor burned down, and then something else about a gas heater—really a lot of weird things, Sue, and now this latest one, with Mrs. Dexter and the oyster."

Susie is all ears about the accidents, which I describe pretty thoroughly, including the glass in the oyster. I don't tell her about Daddy's woman in the net. I pretend to myself I omit this because Sue is so fond of my father, and why worry her unduly? But maybe I just don't want to think about it.

When we're back to discussing the clients, she asks, "How old is *old*, Carly? And who's your favorite?"

It's like her to want to know which one I like best instead of who makes the most trouble. I tell her *old* is like Daddy, and my favorites are the ones that love Daddy: that's Mrs. Cohen and Mrs. La Salle and Mrs. Dexter. They call themselves the trio because they're his fan club; Mrs. Dexter is bent and smart and cross at me right now, and Mrs. Cohen is small and chirpy. And Mrs. La Salle looks like the news-reels of royalty, maybe Monacan royalty; there's a duchess or princess or something who looks just like Mrs. La Salle, with a straight back and modernist jewelry and a bright blue superior gaze.

"And, Sue, there are the two old men; they hide behind their doors and say, 'Who is it? Who is it?'; they're the only ones that give me grief . . ."

She cuts in here with, "Listen, Carly, when you see my boy, be nice to him, will you?" and I decide it's time to end the conversation, because when she talks about me and Rob-bie, it is the only time Sue almost criticizes me. "I love you, Sue; lots of kisses." She always tells me to be good to Rob-bie, when the actual truth was that nobody was good to anybody between me and Rob; we were too much alike. He's a can-do type from having taken care of Susie, who is loving but scattered, and I'm the same way from tending to Daddy, so that between Rob and me, we could never figure out who should do what to whom.

But it still hurts—the fact that he and I aren't together anymore. When you've spent your whole life with some-one—living next door to them, and then sharing parents. Susie was for a long time the only mother I had. And my fa-ther, who mostly couldn't remember that he was a father, would sometimes pull himself together and decide he should take me with him to Egypt. And then he would take Rob, too, who didn't have a father. Daddy really liked Rob, and Rob truly admired my dad. And Rob got into Egyptian archaeology. He and I wanted to go back to Egypt and do good for the populace; Rob would be a doctor, and I would be a social worker or maybe Peace Corps. We were very heavy about those plans. I like remembering them.

I go back to my corridor. I still haven't dispensed vitamins and Tylenol and antacids to Mr. Rice and Mr. Taylor, the two who hide behind their barricades. "Hi," I call out cheerily, "it's just me." Mr. Rice begins making echoing noises, as if he's dropping a box full of nails into a tin wastebasket, but I'm not worried, I know what's happening; he's undoing the four bolts on the inside of his door.

I finish off my morning duties by writing a postcard to Aunt Crystal. I'm careful not to be too specific about Daddy's condition because I don't want her up here on the next plane; she'll be irritated enough learning that I've taken a job at the Manor. I can hear her voice now: "Carla, that is ridiculous, when I was your age . . ." When Aunt Crystal was my age she was halfway through her graduate librarian's degree, but I guess even she would admit that's not the right career for me.

Aunt Crystal lives in Venice, California. That seems a peculiar place for Aunt Crystal to live, but that's where the old family cottage is, the one she and Daddy knew as kids. Back in Daddy's and Crystal's childhood, Venice was a sleepy resort town, and my grandparents had their summer cottage there and their "big house" in Berkeley. Crystal and Daddy were co-owners of both houses until she sold the Berkeley place to get Daddy into the Manor.

I emerge from my room with the postcard in my hand; I'm on my way to the brass-enclosed mailbox in the main sitting room when I run head-on into Mona from the hospital. She's draped against the wall outside my door, and I get the impression she's been waiting there for a while. *Lurking* would be the word I'd use, I guess. She looks at me with big, mascara-ringed, watery blue eyes. Her face is thin, and her hair scraggly bleached-blonde. She looks, in spite of being quite young, like a seasoned barfly. Like the woman in the movie who sits down at the end of the bar and hopefully greets every guy that comes in.

"Hi," she says to me now, not sounding very hopeful.

I say, "Hello." I add, "It's Mona, right?" to let her know I hardly remember her, which isn't really true. I noticed her especially in the hospital because she was so effusively jittery.

"Can I come in?"

If Mona comes in, we'll have to sit side by side on the bed, since there isn't any chair. I suggest the downstairs living room, and she says, "No. Ohmigaw, no," as if doing that would be life-threatening, so I give in and throw wide the door of my broom closet, motioning at the bed. I sit on the floor, cross-legged.

There's a silence while she pulls at her skirt, a flowered something, quite short. Then finally she bursts out, "Oh, gaw, I've done so many things wrong."

I resist saying, "We all have." I wait. "I mean," she goes on, "I wanted to talk to you because you're younger, you know? I mean, nobody around here is younger."

Again, I don't answer. What am I supposed to say—"Mona, you sure got that right"?

"And then, you look like you know so much. And you understood about what to do when Mrs. Dexter had that thing in the dining room. That was so great! How'd you learn to do that stuff?"

There are a lot of women that got told when they were little that they are absolutely adorable when they're enthusiastic. "Oh, she's Daddy's little darling. I just love little Tootsie when she gets all thrilled." I'm willing to bet Mona heard that from some Daddy-type back in prehistory.

"And," she's continuing, not waiting to see if I'll answer, "you're so smart. I could tell from the way you were talking to Mrs. Dexter how smart you were."

"Mona," I intrude, "what *exactly* are we talking about?"

This pulls her up short. "Talking? About? Ohmigaw, well, I guess *you* know. I mean, I made so many mistakes. Around here. Got in trouble all down the line. Did it all wrong. Everybody hates me."

I stare up at her. She might have been a pretty little girl once, when that relative was telling her how darling she was. "I haven't the foggiest notion what you're saying."

"You haven't?"

It dawns on me that Mona, too, thinks I'm the Observer. Somebody from the outside world sent to take notes. To figure it all out. Learn about secrets, love affairs, stealing from the clients, pilfering from the Manor, whatever they've been up to. And about the accidents. And any other dirt.

"The dumbest things I ever did," Mona is saying, "the real bottom-line dumbest—but you know about that, I guess, don't you? And now I can't do anything about it. It's just there and—oh, gaw, I get so worried. Tell them, will you, I wasn't thinking, and I didn't at all mean it. And I was just trying to help. People get in a lot of trouble, don't you think, over trying to help? I figure helping is one of the things you can do. But this time, ohmigaw, was it dumb."

I probably look pretty blank about this, so she stumbles

on. "But that's not the only dumb thing. I did another dumb thing, and I don't guess you know about that. I mean, it's a secret, but I thought you might have found out."

I stare at her. This situation is weird.

Mona certainly has me cast in this observer role.

Is it better to convince her that, no, I don't know a damn thing? Dr. Kittredge knows more than me. Mrs. Sisal knows more. Belle, too. I don't know enough to know what it is I don't know. If you follow me. Or is it better to pretend and get some power out of that?

"Like with this other dumb thing," Mona is stumbling on, "it was really dumb, jeez I can't believe that was me; I wasn't exactly thinking straight, know what I mean? You do know what I mean, don't you?"

I avoid this slippery slope.

Something tells me that knowledge is dangerous around here.

"Listen, Mona, I *don't* understand you. I don't get it. I don't even know what you're talking about."

It's obvious she doesn't believe me. She stares in disappointment. She says, "Boy, I thought you'd be more upfront than this." She broods for a while. "Listen," she says finally, "when you hear . . . 'cause I know you're gonna hear . . . bound to . . . well . . . tell them I didn't mean it. You know how that is. Didn't mean it at all."

"Mona," I say; I'm going to grab her with a question while she's here and obviously upset—strike while the iron is hot, so to speak—"Mona, do you know something about Mrs. Dexter and that oyster? And what about—" she's halfway out the door now, so I have to raise my voice, "what about my dad? Someone's been getting him upset; who's been doing that?"

Mona leans against the door and says, "Oh, my gaw, my gaw." She adds, "Things are kinda different from what they look. I guess you know all that, though. Oh, geez, is this gonna be a *mess*!" Then she exits, head turned, arm flapping vaguely. Out in the hall, she stares back at me with mascara-smeared eyes, making me want to reach out firmly and shake her. But also partly making me wish there were something reassuring I could say.

🦅 Chapter 6

I've decided I'll take advantage of some of the stuff described in the Manor's enthusiastic brochure *Your Way to a New Life* and go with Daddy to a watercolor class. Maybe I'll learn something. And maybe keep my father from any more descriptions of the eye of Horus. I have a suspicion that aides aren't encouraged to take landscape painting classes, but until someone specifically tells me I can't, I'm going to try.

"Landscape painting," Belle says, "yeah, sure, why not? Sisal more or less lets you do anything you want, right?"

Belle still thinks I'm an Observer.

The painting class gets assembled on a bright, green breezy field, seven of us lined up on folding metal chairs among the scatters of poppy and dandelion and wild blue iris. Everybody receives some watercolor cubes and an easel plus a handful of pastel chalk crayons. Paint jars are strategically positioned.

"They come off on your hands," Daddy says of the pastels; he looks at his blue-streaked palm, then presses it against his blank paper to make a handprint. "Arabic," he announces pleasedly, "for good luck."

"Our job," the painting teacher is saying, "is to capture into ourselves the essence of this beautiful scene, the spirit of sea. And sun. And coast." The teacher is Ms. Deirdre Chaundy who, along with Mrs. Sisal and Dr. Kittredge, makes up the Resident Manor Directors. Ms. Chaundy is a pop-eyed Norse-goddess type with an admirable bust and a sheaf of blonde hair; she looks as if she came off the prow of a ship.

She half-turns her metal chair in order to lecture us. "Please," she advises, "sit back. Do not stress, don't strain. Surrender yourselves to the scene." Everyone does this, *plop*, *plop* of shoulders against chair backs. People that tell you what to do with your body often get obeyed. "You have the powers," she broadcasts. "You can do it. Get in touch. And do not, *do not* attempt to paint yet." She scowls at Daddy's handprint.

There are a lot of ladies like Ms. Chaundy in Berkeley. They are always coming around to your house or your school and wanting to teach you something you can do with string or clay or autumn leaves. Susie knows all of them and is tolerant: "They provide good energy," is how she puts it.

Ms. Chaundy wears a chiffon scarf around her neck and projects her words distinctly: "Lean *for*ward. Lean *back*. Life force. Coursing. Joining with the roots of trees, the pathways of rivers."

She asks us to close our eyes and reach down into those tree roots toward our hidden inner powers.

It's difficult to do this leaning back in a metal chair balanced on meadow grass. The chair legs are uncertain; your balance gets loused up. Also, I have a perverse need to look at the other people from under my half-closed eyes and figure out how they're doing.

Daddy sits beside me, his head on his chest; he looks as if he's fallen asleep. Next to him is Mrs. Dexter, released from the hospital, healthy and irritated, with her walker balanced against the side of her chair. She, like me, is being bad; her eyes are open, and she's watching some black-and-white ducklike birds on the tufted meadow edge.

The meadow edge is fenced and (I ascertain all this by continuing to peek) directly overhangs a big slice of ocean.

"Now," Ms. Chaundy says. "Open your eyes. Slowly. Return to this beautiful world. You have your powers; you are ready. Paint!" Her scarf flips back in the breeze; she spreads her arms wide. I'm waiting for her to tip her chair over, but she doesn't; she has a good sense of balance.

Daddy hasn't been asleep. He sits up and says, "Interesting. Did you think so?" and starts arranging his pastels on the easel tray. Pastels, in spite of their soft-sounding name, come in brilliant colors, and my father marches them along his tray in a brisk sequential rainbow.

Mrs. Dexter squints at the teacher. "Utterly ridiculous." She makes a ritual of wearily unwrapping her paintbrush. "Would you fill my paint jar, please," she asks generally of our circle; she's still mad at me and won't ask me to do this. And her stiffness prevents her getting down there with the water pitcher.

Daddy rips off his handprint page and draws a blue line across the middle of a fresh sheet.

On my left is Mrs. Cohen, the lady with the elf on her door, bubbly as always; she's having a good day with easier breathing; she has a red scarf tied around her black-and-gray hair.

"This teacher is enthusiastic," Mrs. Cohen tells me now. "Enthusiasm is half the battle, don't you think? And creation is a battle, don't you think?" She sloshes her paintbrush in her water jar.

The other person here from my corridor is Mrs. La Salle, the third of my father's fans, who looks especially elegant today with a gold Hermès scarf carelessly knotted at her throat. "I simply close my ears," she whispers. "Pretend it's bees or birds. I do that with half the things people say." She examines her page. "I would like a pencil so I could outline shapes, neatly, the way I like, and then color in the middle of them, also the way I like, but I know this teacher would disapprove; she'd give me an intolerable speech about how a pencil stifles your hidden powers."

"You bet," Mrs. Dexter agrees. She's using yellow paint to sketch in a recognizable bluff-edge with silhouetted tufts of yellow grass.

I have decided to go abstract. Abstract, if I do it right, with just a hint of shape behind the colors, might capture some of the strangeness of this bright scene and our peculiar little class.

There are several moments of silence while we all dip and dribble. Daddy is using both pastel and watercolor; he's the only one trying this, a tricky process, because pastels smear when they get wet. But my father is actually an accomplished artist; all archaeologists have to learn to record their finds by drawing them.

"I wonder," Mrs. La Salle says to Mrs. Dexter, "this moment seems so peaceful that it's hard to imagine bad things, but do you remember my theory? That our accidents are caused by a mad old lady?"

"No," Mrs. Dexter is applying paint in heavy blobs. "It was just accidents."

I've been wondering if Mrs. Dexter has talked frankly to her friends since she got out of the hospital, but I guess not.

"I don't understand you, Louise," Mrs. La Salle says. "I hope you're getting a lawyer." Mrs. Cohen joins the discussion with "Lawyers, my goodness. And lawsuits. The Manor is in for *trouble*. Everyone is talking lawyers. And leaving. Because of the accidents. You know, the Manor'd be better off offering cash settlements—some of those suits are going to be big-time. Did you hear about Mrs. Goliard? Carla, this Mrs. Goliard—you don't know her, she's the lady that went out the window—Mrs. Goliard has one of the lawyers from the O.J. case."

We're briefly silent in tribute to this.

"Lawsuits all over the place," Mrs. Cohen says, with her usual enthusiasm. "Big time. All the way back to the beauty parlor fire."

Everyone wants to tell me about the beauty parlor fire. "Seven months ago," Mrs. La Salle says, "and in retrospect, yes, it was the first of the series of unusual events. But when something's the first of a series, you don't know that then, do you? What about it, Louise?"

Mrs. Dexter just grunts.

The other ladies apparently haven't noticed that Mrs. Dexter falls silent during these accident discussions.

"I *do* think it was a mad old lady," Mrs. La Salle says. "So

easy to lose your bearings around here. *You've* noticed that,
Carla."

Our next moment of quiet is broken by Mrs. Cohen, who
suddenly points at my father's easel and cries out, "Why, my
goodness. Why, look. Edward, your painting, that is *amazing*, it's so real, so imaginative. Look, everybody, come see
what he's done!" She's half out of her chair, her gray-black
hair ruffled by the breeze, and pointing at Daddy's now-
filled page, a scramble of bright chalk colors, all the right
yellows and blues for this vivid day. It's a recognizable picture of our landscape; here's the meadow with its clumps of
wildflower and grass. But there's more than our landscape in
his picture; by a miracle of extended perspective he's made
his view stretch over the bluff edge, which is unfenced in his
picture, and down to a beach below, bounded by three conical rocks. Of course there isn't any beach below and also no
rocks like that, as I've just determined by squinting at the
view during our meditation session, but in Daddy's picture
there is a beach and conical rocks, and on it is laid, arms
wrapped against its sides, a mummylike figure, trussed and
crisscrossed with yellow stripes. My father has used a bright
yellow crayon for the stripes. I know right away who the
figure is; I recognize her. It's his woman in the net.

I think, *Oh, Jesus Christ*.

In the corner, where the artist's signature might be,
Daddy has drawn the Eye of Horus, wide-open, staring, and
with marks below that look like running feet.

I didn't, I tell myself, want him to do something like
that.

He sees it so clearly that he draws a picture of it. The
bluff, here in his picture, was another bluff, and a different

prospect below, but he still sees it bright and true; doesn't that mean it really happened? I don't think your imagination works like that, to supply all those physical details . . . Especially if you're an old gentleman with Alzheimer's . . .

The Manor ladies are standing up now, exclaiming. My father is a favorite; they want to give him praise. "My goodness." "So interesting." "So odd." "It suggests something. Edward, do you want to explain?"

Daddy says, "I've painted a lot, you know." He says, "I saw her." He seems a little troubled by the praise.

Ms. Chaundy is coming over to see; she picks her way regally between the grass clumps; she stops, she looks down at Daddy's picture, she says, "My word."

There's a pause while she pulls on the trailing end of her scarf, then she remarks, "*Quite* surprising."

"It's good, isn't it?" Mrs. Cohen asks. "I mean, really, really good."

"Yes," agrees Ms. Chaundy. And after a minute she elaborates, "Absolutely. A work of . . . of the imagination? Tell me, Dr. Day, of the inner spirit?"

"I've painted a good deal," my father says. "I like these crayons," he adds in a confidential tone. "They're good for difficult subjects."

Ms. Chaundy starts to say, "A welling up of the . . ." and then stops. She asks, "Your inner powers sent you this scene?"

Daddy shakes his head. "The yellow's not exactly right."

"Such an *original* scene," she says. She levels her shoulders and adjusts the scarf; she moves away to examine Mrs. Cohen's shakily indicated bluff and wildflowers; she says they show "the beginning of the life force."

"But not," Mrs. Cohen intervenes, "as good as Edward's. Nowhere near. That picture is *remarkable*."

*   *   *

I've been fighting a revelation in my chest that's like one of our upsurges of ocean waves. This idea lodges behind my lungs and is cramping my breathing; I'm thinking thoughts at Daddy that all have behind them the idea *danger*, and all start with the word *please*. Please be careful. Please forget about your net-woman. Please stop, stop. This is going to turn out dangerous. Please, darling, no more pictures, no more talk about a woman in a net; try to give it up now, oh, will you?

On the way back to the Manor, I fall into step beside Mrs. Cohen. Maybe what I need right now is frank publicity for some of what I know. I don't know anything as dangerous as my father maybe does, not as bad as what he has, if all those ramblings about the woman in the net are fact-based. But any secret information is dangerous. It can trip you up, or somebody can decide they've got to have it. I want to make my information about the piece of glass un-secret.

"Listen," I say to Mrs. Cohen, "There's something I need to talk about. I think it's important to share . . ."

Good California word: *share*. And I recount for her the story of Mrs. Dexter's piece of glass and how, yes, it *was* glass, and it was sharp, and I think it had to be in that oyster on purpose. Mrs. Cohen is enthusiastic; she loves to be in on new knowledge, she loves to talk. She has the kind of bubbly breathlessness in the face of gossip that makes it clear she'll go right home to her Manor apartment and call people on the telephone; it will seem almost a duty to get the word out. She'll be a fine resource. "Guess what? Do you know what I learned?" she'll ask, "Well, no, it's not a secret . . ." She'll have this story all over the Manor by dinnertime.

"Oh," she says now, and, "Oh, I thought so." She is so thrilled by my inside info that she stops short in the middle of the path. "But I couldn't get Louise to say a single solitary thing. Oh, just wait until I tell Daphne—Mrs. La Salle. Both of us thought, of course, but . . . Now why on earth would Louise want to keep quiet about it?" She waits, hunched over the drawing pad under her arm. "Well, maybe I have an idea. Things are endlessly complicated, Carla, don't you find?"

I tell Mrs. Cohen please don't let on how you know this; please just pretend the information dropped out of the sky. And she continues walking and burbling, and I follow, still subliminally projecting at Daddy, *Honey, have some sense, will you now.*

ᒣ Chapter 7

It's evening on my corridor, and I am doing my rounds.

"I'll get you a flashlight," I tell Mr. Rice. He has just stopped saying, "Who is it?" and has begun talking like a normal human being; he's worried. "The hall," he says, "has a dark corner. I am upset. I have been consulting my lawyer. I'm concerned." Mr. Rice is worried about the accidents. He explains: "I was concerned before . . . previously . . . when that woman went out the window. But now . . . an oyster with glass in it. Have you ever heard of such a thing?"

Mr. Taylor, his buddy next door, has also started talking to me; he is worried, he says, not just about the accidents, but also about locks. "Are there enough locks on the doors? Are they the right kind? I like the double-bolting one that makes a big click after you turn the key." Also, he would like some Ovaltine.

Mrs. La Salle, who lives down the hall, has been lying in

wait while the men harangue; now she pulls me into her apartment. Her problem is not so much that she's worried as that she wants company. "English Breakfast *with* or *without*?" she asks, meaning with or without caffeine. Then she gives a little lecture on her collection of block prints, which are very handsome and strange; they're modern Japanese and show architectural shapes, dark green and ink blue, cliffs and crags and monuments that assertively hold their own against the Manor's high-ceilinged rooms.

"Hiroyuki Tajima," she says, naming the artist, and I tell her that I like the prints.

Have I ever really described Mrs. La Salle? Maybe I've said she looks like a member of a European royal family, but that's misleading because she's not one of the fat dumpy royalty with a baffled expression and a square pocketbook suspended from her wrist, but the other kind—the skinny sophisticated duchess you imagined for your Cannes and Sundance movie; alert, tanned, handsome, and with earrings. Or today just one earring, a lumpy, uncut aquamarine. She wears a dark green dress and a twisted leather belt with a double silver arrow buckle. She has the look of not-caring that goes with the royal title.

"Carla," she says, tapping Hiroyuki Tajima's black enamel frame with a red fingernail, "I need to speak about your father; I am worried about him. You know, I have seen how upset he can get. And such a specific fantasy, that one about the beach. So clear. I've never known an Alzheimer's fantasy to be that definite. How long has he had it?"

We talk in a general way about Daddy, with me trying not to react too much. His pastel picture has really advertised his obsession; what did I expect? And Mrs. La Salle is a friend. "You are doing so well with him," she says. "I admire you so much."

I look around her apartment—extra subtle and expensive-looking in the right way, not just fake-opulent, like the Manor's Victorian halls and pink pictures. Mrs. La S. goes in for spare modern furniture and small African statues. And I can really appreciate all this—I've been missing Art (capital *A*). One good thing about having both parents in archaeology was the immersion in Art; all that stuff about proportion and scale and balance, they served it up with meals. Art was almost the only thing my mother and I ever connected on. "I suppose this is quite fine," Constancia would inform me, in a matter-of-fact voice, holding out a perfect ovoid bronze bowl. I told her it was *gorgeous*, and she half-closed her eyes and said, "I suppose so." She didn't go for superlatives.

Mrs. La Salle is talking. "My dear, there may be episodes for him later on. My brother had episodes."

We discuss Daddy's woman-in-the-net with me not saying much; I've decided to be—*circumspect* is the word—from now on.

"He has moments when he makes perfectly good sense," I say, and she agrees, "Certainly."

"And you're so professional," she adds.

I smile and shake my head and count out the pills for her evening Vicodin and calcium. Mrs. La Salle is the handsomest lady in the Manor and maybe the best conversationalist, but I'm not ready to make her into a confidante yet.

"I do hope you're coming tomorrow," she goes on, "to our party in the beauty parlor." She laughs dismissively. She's sophisticated enough to know that a beauty-parlor party is ridiculous and might happen more often in Welch, West Virginia, than here. But she still likes the idea; after all there's not much social life at the Manor. The party is to celebrate the beauty parlor being refurbished after the fire. "You know, I hate to brag," she says. "I've done a lot of things in my life: I was a manager at Gumps and on the board of the Ballet, and then I had a column for *City* magazine, the restaurant gossip one. And now I'm here. Well, times change. *Come* to this thing."

I tell her yes, we'll be there.

But first I have to talk with Mrs. Sisal.

I've been summoned to the Sisal office. "Hey," Belle says, delivering this message, wiggling her crunched forehead (maybe you remember the worried forehead of the woman with the rake and the church-barn behind her), "What *have* you done? The superpower is cross; trouble in River City."

Cross indeed. Mrs. Sisal is positioned with her back to me. Her secretary, Rebecca, hides in the peon computer alcove out of her way and shoots me a stricken look as I go by.

"Well," Sisal says, addressing a spot on the window.

Turns out, Belle and Mona aren't the only ones who think I'm an Observer. Mrs. Sisal thinks so, too. Or thinks I ought to be. "You didn't tell me," she accuses. "You knew, and you didn't say. And now it's all over the Manor." She's talking about the glass in the oyster, the fact that it really was glass. "You kept it a secret. Why didn't you say?"

She gives me a half a minute, which is enough. I'm pretty good with the impromptu lie.

I fix her window reflection in a stare of the utmost sincerity. "I was worried about the Manor."

She's stopped by that, as I guess she should be. "The *Manor*?"

"I was afraid Mrs. Dexter would want to sue."

Mrs. Sisal is not a dummy; in fact, she's quite smart. She's disbelieving. Her window reflection tucks in its mouth corners. "And you were *protecting* the Manor?"

"Mrs. Sisal," I shift my body forward, moving my voice into its extremely *real* mode, "my father is a lifetime resident here. He has invested all his assets in the Manor. It's the place where he lives. If the Manor goes down, he goes down. He would lose all his money. I was protecting my father."

People will believe what they want to in a crisis, maybe this is especially true of strong-minded people. Mrs. Sisal says, "Ohhh," a long, drawn-out, thoughtful exhalation. She takes off her glasses and examines them. Finally, she turns around to face me; she appears assuaged. "And you thought of all that in those few minutes?"

I tell her modestly, "Yes."

"And now you've learned that Mrs. Dexter does not plan to sue?"

I haven't learned anything of the sort. But I say, "Mrs. Dexter is a very private person." Which is true. And if, in the future, Mrs. Dexter decides that a suit will comfort her privacy, I can always exclaim about how fickle old ladies are.

"That is sensible," Mrs. Sisal says. "That will be better for . . . everyone."

She's probably residually cross at me for making her look foolish with her aluminum-card theory, but she's letting go of this for two reasons. First, she could never really believe she looked foolish. And second, she's feeling relieved. No suit from Mrs. Dexter. No Miss Day testifying.

Mrs. Sisal thinks Miss Day is being smart about this. Or at least very sensible. Miss Day is the kind of sensible person the Manor needs. "It was intelligent of you not to gossip about this. I gather that you didn't gossip?"

I sit back, pleased that the record of who said what to whom is apparently even more confused than I'd expected.

"Well," Mrs. Sisal says finally, resignedly, "I believe you behaved *sensibly.*" Her voice caresses this nice word *sensibly.* She positions both feet on the edge of her file drawer, apparently a sign of well-being for her. "We are pleased with your *adjustment.*" Briefly, she makes a sort of smile, which appears to hurt. "Now, let's have a look at your schedule, shall we?"

For a moment, I get the insane idea that Mrs. S. is about to reduce my hours or maybe raise my pay, but, of course, no such luck, we simply begin to go through a list of my clients.

When we reach the end of the client list, she clicks the computer good-bye and rearranges her swivel chair. "Miss Day, you are perceptive and intelligent; in working with these clients have you ever noticed anything untoward?"

"Untoward?" I ask, while thinking, *Oh, so that's how it's pronounced; I've always said un-two-ward.* "No," I remark firmly.

"Miss Day, I think some clients are worried about recent events—the kind of event you've witnessed—do you think that is possible?"

I resist saying, "Are you kidding," and agree, "Yes."

"How do you handle these client worries?"

I answer part truthfully, part untruthfully; I'm beginning to be good at this, "I don't encourage it. I listen. I let them get it off their chest."

"Ah." She runs a Gucci heel against the file drawer rim. "That is a constructive attitude. Just the right attitude. And of course you don't gossip afterward."

"No."

"Fine. Miss Day, we're pleased with your mature approach. But if a situation appears dangerous, I hope you will then come to me. I need to know if a situation is explosive."

I don't say, "I thought that was what you wanted." I just repeat, "If a situation is explosive." I don't actually tell her I'll come to her about the explosive problem.

But she's happy with my answer. "Not many of our aides," she tells me, "have your degree of education."

She half-rises, to signal that we've talked enough. "We are pleased with your work here, Miss Day. And it is agreeable with us that you continue some of the special things you've been doing. You may keep on going to your father's classes. Also, you may accompany him to the dining room."

She nods to let me know that *Yes, we knew all along you were overstepping the boundaries, but now we're saying it's okay because this is a bribe. Spy for me, girl, and your dad can stay and play.*

Mrs. Sisal looks good today in her long-waisted suit and short straight hair partly pasted to her cheek. I wish I could get my hair to do that.

"I will see you at the party tonight," she suggests, favoring me with a pinched Dragon Lady smile.

⏀ Chapter 8

Daddy has said, "A party, darling! How very, very nice!" He's not exactly sure what a beauty parlor is. "A place of beauty, dear? Many places are beautiful." When I say it's where you have your hair washed and set, he looks completely lost. I don't think Constancia ever did anything to her hair except to lather it up under the shower. After which it emerged looking great.

"My good suit," my father says, sliding his closet door open, "the one we got for me in—where was it?"

"Alexandria."

He agrees, "Yes, of course, just as I thought. And what will you wear?"

I get into the spirit of things. "My purple shirt."

The purple shirt is one Susie gave me for her Beltane festival. Susie thought Beltane was a rebirth celebration; she didn't listen to the rumors about blood and sacrifice. The shirt has sequins across the front in a moon-and-stars pattern.

Daddy is pleased by it. "Mythic," and holds my hand as we walk across the courtyard to a door with a banner proclaiming: CELEBRATE! DRAWING FOR A FREE SHAMPOO!

The beauty parlor, like the hospital, is mostly pink formica, but someone has been sufficiently knowing to add bits of Victorian nonsense; there is a fluted white molding and some scalloping, and every so often an occasional angel or winged being pasted in bas relief against the pink wall. Sandwiches, soft drinks, and white wine are lined up on a long sterilely wrapped table in front of the dryers.

Mrs. La Salle is present, sheathed in gray satin so crisp it could stand up by itself; she's stationed near a sandwich platter. "Olive and pimento," she says. "I truly hate those angels. Tell me honestly. Did you ever go to a party in a beauty parlor?"

"Beauty, did you say that, Carla? Yes, you did." Daddy looks pleased. "In Egypt, there were beauty procedures at parties. They put cones of fatty incense on their foreheads and allowed them to melt." He eyes one of Mrs. La Salle's sandwiches and moves his face close for a bite.

"You are an innocent man," she holds the sandwich steady. "I wonder, were you always so innocent?"

"My dear, ripeness is all. That's a line by Shakespeare . . ." He thinks about this for a minute. "Also, 'That time of year thou mays't in me . . .'" he winds down, looking pleased.

I don't like this quoting-and-smiling approach he's adopting here, it demeans him. Also, he's beginning to get it wrong. I change the subject: "How about a 7 Up?" He comes back firmly with, "White wine," so I try a counteroffer, "Diet Coke," and he goes, "White wine," again, at which we seem to be stalemated until Mrs. La Salle inter-

venes, "Carla, now, think. *One* wine won't make any difference." She's right, of course. Sometimes I can feel myself being bossy, as if Aunt Crystal has planted a Crystal-chip in
my brain.

I have a wine, too. *Relax*, I advise my inner me, and sip,
and remember how, in Santa Cruz, Robbie and I kept a
cardboard container of industrial-grade Beaujolais under the
kitchen table.

Those were good years, even if the drinks were terrible.

Daddy and I, he with his wineglass held high, start our
progress through the room. He smiles, he sips, he starts an
imitation of his old true-blue self, Dr. Day, archaeologist-
scholar. "How nice of you to come," this to a lady in pink,
apparently a perfect stranger.

Hospital Aide Mona is here, her peroxided hair up to one
side and fastened with a green parakeet clip; she's wearing a
purple cloak that must have been bought at the same moon-
and-stars bazaar as my T-shirt. I point at the two moon designs, and she bats her eyes confusedly. "Oh, you mean my
Astarte cape? Hey, sure. Isn't this a *great* event." She looks at
me big-eyed and beseeching, as if saying *Please forget our conversation*, and then gives herself a minute to flutter at Daddy.
"And the *dear* professor."

Mona is pretty creepy. She's like the little girl in your
kindergarten class that tagged around after you, acting as if
someone were going to hit her.

Daddy seems to kind of recognize her; he examines her
carefully and then looks beyond, over her shoulder, maybe
searching for something else. "My dear."

"That woman," he asks, as we are leaving her, "does she
have a belt with scissors on it?"

A belt with scissors sounds like something a hospital aide might have.

I agree, "Probably."

Mrs. Dexter is at the far end of the next room, propped beside the door and squinting up at Mrs. Sisal, who is skinny and New York–chic in a metallic sweater and orange scarf. Daddy and I start moving toward them, but there's a traffic jam; some clients want out, some want in, and some just stand around, looking helpless.

"What are they waiting for?" my father asks. "Is a train coming?"

"It's a party, Daddy. Remember?"

"A party in a train station. Did you get my ticket?"

He asks about the ticket twice as we maneuver and push and say, "Excuse me," but when we reach Mrs. Dexter, he's once again the cordial greeter. "My dear. So good. Thank you for the cookies."

Mrs. Sisal has disappeared.

"I remembered you liked chocolate chip." Mrs. Dexter has decided to be marginally polite to me again. "How are you, Carla?"

I say I'm fine. "Did you really bake cookies?"

She's defensive. "You can cook perfectly well with a walker, you just line the ingredients up on that little shelf in front . . . Hello, Sally," this is to Mrs. Cohen, who has come up behind me. "Isn't this *ridiculous*?"

Tonight Mrs. Cohen has a camellia in her hair. "Why, Louise, here we are, all my favorite people. Edward, how are you?"

"I forget. Carla, may I have my . . ." He pauses and clears his throat, "my *drink* back?"

He's lost it somewhere on our journey through the room.

I'd give him mine, except that I've just finished it. One look at his face tells me this will be an issue. Sometimes, especially when something's lost, he needs to talk about it for twenty minutes. "*I'll* get it," I say, and head back toward the drinks table. If I fetch the glass myself, I can control how much goes into it. Or even add some water.

I think, *Please don't start talking about fishing nets. Another wine could start you up.*

When I get back, the group has been joined by Dr. Kittredge, shoulders straight in a navy blue cashmere jacket with brass buttons.

My father is singing. " 'Oh, yes, I'm sick, I'm very sick. And I never will be better.' " He has found another wine glass, a mostly empty one, and is keeping time with it. He doesn't sing loudly; his voice is sweet and not obnoxious, and the whole display is only slightly disturbing and slightly embarrassing. He seems to be aiming his song at Dr. Kittredge.

"Ah, sure," Kittredge says. "I haven't heard that one for a while."

" 'Until I have . . .' " my father sings. His face crumples; he hands the empty glass to Mrs. Dexter and says, "I have forgotten the rest."

"You're tired," Dr. Kittredge says. "That's what it is. Tired. Totally expected."

"Poor man." The painting teacher, Ms. Deirdre Chaundy, has arrived beside the doctor, and she thrusts out her marvelous bosom under a festoon of amber beads. "Too much on your mind. Such a talented man," in an aside to everybody; "His history . . . so interesting."

Daddy looks at the doctor and smiles uncertainly. Maybe he's afraid of Dr. Kittredge, which makes sense. I'm afraid of him right now, since he's a doctor and probably can decide on whether my father goes to Hope House with the other loonies or remains here in coddled comfort. And now Daddy is acting irrational. "The rest of that song?" he asks. "Until I something . . . something?" His voice is getting louder. "*Carla?*"

Surprise, Dr. Kittredge is the one who supplies the missing line: " 'Until I have the love of one,' Dr. Day." He hums a bar or so. "Ah, the songs of our youth." Daddy's song is "Barbry Allen," a folk piece that got revived in the sixties; I guess the doctor's youth happened around that time, too. He beams at me, glass in his hand, stomach out, feet apart, handsome Irish head cocked. Maybe he's trying to figure out just how goofy Edward Day really is.

" 'Until I have the love of one,' " Daddy tries this in a sweet tenor. Then his face crumples, and his voice begins to rise, "How can that be? It doesn't seem possible."

"Oh." He stares at me. "There was a time when I knew everything, everything I needed to know. Carla, remember, in Egypt, in the City of the Dead, when we found the coffin lid. It was like a window into another world. I'd been up for three nights, waiting to get the container opened. And the desert around us, and the stars, and down at the silent dead city just a few flickers of torches from people camped, and the white fronts of the small buildings . . .

"Oh, I used to be able to understand, but now I do not . . . I do not . . ."

Of course, he's about to say *understand* again, but he doesn't get the chance. I move forward, a new drink extended like a lure, and put my arm around him and get him turned toward the door. "It's hot," I call back to our friends, "we need to get outside," and then we're through the passageway and into the evening garden and safe out of there at least for this minute.

🕴 Chapter 9

Once in the garden, silence and peace reign. There is a thousand-watt moon and several traveling rivers of fog. Palm trees dazzle in the mixture of fog and moonlight, showing off their feathery arched boughs. The path ahead glimmers between its rows of white rocks, showing the road like paint-by-numbers.

My father stands still for a couple of minutes to look at this heady mixture of nature and art. He takes several deep, ostentatious breaths. Then he heads off, lickety-split, across the savannah. Running full speed into the lunar-splashed fog.

Rob and I used to have a cat that did that on moonlit nights. Dashed madly away, in a declaration for feline freedom. But it's one thing when it's your cat and you can laugh and bless him with, "Run, Tiger, run," and another thing entirely if it's your aged, dotty father.

You wouldn't think an eighty-five-year-old gentleman

could outrun his twenty-five-year-old daughter, but he can if he gets a head start and she's asleep on her feet. Daddy and I cover a lot of fog-splashed garden territory, with me trailing along behind, calling, "Daddy! Watch out! Go slow!" And so on and so forth. I even have a moment to think that this would be funny if I had a sense of humor.

He has reached the far edge of the Manor property down by the highway before I catch up with him. He's sitting against a manzanita bush. He has lost his wineglass and one shoe. He stares up at me, moonglow highlighting his rebellious old face.

I ask, "Are you hurt?"

He's not even breathing hard. "Not at all. Are you?"

"You fell. Here, hold up your foot. Flex, flex."

He doesn't want to flex for me. "I'm fine. Aren't I a good runner?"

"I'm taking you by the hospital." Belle told me that last January he broke a finger, and no one knew about it for almost a week. "Doesn't complain," Belle said, admiringly. "Phenomenal."

I scramble around behind him, next to him, and find the shoe. "But I can tie my own shoes," he says, incensed.

"Come on. Up we get. Hup."

He doesn't want to hup. He wants to sit in his manzanita bush and look at the celestial orb, which is coming and going behind its fog cover.

"Up we get. What did you do with your wineglass?"

"I have had a very interesting e-mail."

You aren't supposed to attempt logical argument with an Alzheimer's patient; the person isn't logical and will just get confused. I immediately breach this sensible rule. "You don't *have* a computer."

"Of course not. This e-mail saluted me as 'O, Powerful King.' Don't you think that's nice?"

"You are limping," I accuse. "Where did you lose that wineglass?"

We are walking, moderately steadily, following the paint-by-numbers.

A field ahead is the place where, he says, the wineglass got dropped.

"Here? You remember?"

He gestures at an anonymous-looking plant. "I noticed. By the aloe bush."

So I start feeling around by the aloe bush. Maybe he noticed it especially because the Egyptians used aloe face creams. And me? Probably I'm being so compulsive because I want to teach him a lesson.

No question, I'm mad at him. Why does he have to pick tonight for a full demonstration of his Aged Adorable Delinquent Parent act? "Stand still," I command. "Don't get any more ideas. Stay exactly where you are."

"Carly," he says. He's standing on the path behind me a little to the left; there's a curious alert note in his voice.

"Yes?"

"Someone is *sleeping* here."

Sleeping? I get up. I start to put an arm around him, but he doesn't seem to need that. His voice is tight in what I think of as his "archaeology-discovery" tone, the one used for: "This is the entrance to a tomb." "Shoes," he says. "Nice ones."

The shoes are women's—small, flat, and thin-soled. The uppers are silver kidskin. There are small, bony feet and legs projecting out of the shoes, but not side by side and neatly arranged; no, one shoe has been almost kicked off, one white-stockinged leg is twisted on top of the other.

"Father, stand back."

My father doesn't want to stand back. He pushes up right behind me. I kneel down and fight off some of the long grass blades that are bent across the out-flung shape. It lies on its back, arms stretched. Its dress, a blue one with spangles along the shoulder straps, is disheveled. The person in the dress is someone I recognize perfectly well in her patch of bright moonlight. The last time I saw her she was wearing her moon-and-stars cape.

"Ah," says my father. I suppose he, like me, has recognized Hospital Aide Mona. Her peroxided hair is splashed around among the grass blades, but the parakeet clip still clings, a darker color in the bright hair. "She's not wearing her scissors belt," he says.

One of the things I didn't like about working in the Santa Cruz lab was dealing with the dead animals.

I've never seen a dead person before, but people are animals, too, and dead is dead.

And this person, not-sleeping on her back, really looks dead. Although . . . well, I saw her just recently, didn't I? Giggling and carrying on in her Mona way, part of a party, drinking a drink?

I touch the back of my hand to the pulse-place in her neck. Nothing. And then to her mouth. Again, nothing, no moisture.

But she feels perfectly warm. I bend closer and get my lips near hers. The eyes are half-open; there's moonlight reflected back in them.

And now I understand it—the twist of the head. The neck kinked back in that impossible angle.

Hospital Aide Mona is truly dead. With her head at that peculiar slant, I'd guess she died of a broken neck.

I notice that one of my hands is shaking. Not my right hand, the left one, the hand that an Egyptian fortune teller once told me had the fate line in it.

"Daddy," I say, "we should get back. Quickly."

My father is the world's biggest innocent, but he knows about death, not just because of dead pharaohs but also because of dead archaeology workers, people falling off ladders or getting rocks dropped on their heads or coming down with bilharzia. Sometimes, believe it or not, he had over a hundred workers asking him what to do. Right now, he looks down at Mona and seems to remember some earlier event. "The inspector will be here to investigate. Shouldn't we do artificial . . ." He can't think of the word. "This is alarming," he says.

"It wouldn't work. Let's just get back fast."

"I'm feeling dizzy." And I guess he is. I almost have to drag him.

We're approaching the Manor beauty parlor steps, Daddy being wobbly, and I inadequately attempting to support him, when a figure appears, fast, apparition-like, poised at the head of the stairs, and then swiftly down them to appraise the situation and reach out toward my stumbling father. It's Mrs. La Salle. She wheels forward, stiff silk snapping and shimmering. "Carla . . . Ed. Something . . . I can tell . . . something has happened. Come here. Ed, now then, I've got you, this'll be *all right*."

Mrs. La Salle had seen us coming. She must have been watching through the glass-paneled door. I take a minute, in the middle of everything else I'm feeling, to think about that.

She's using her grand-duchess voice and sounds very competent. I tell her there's been a serious accident in the meadow. "Serious?" she asks. "In what way serious? Oh, my God. Poor Ed," and at this point my father, whom she's been supporting by the elbows, starts to topple.

And Mrs. La Salle, gray electric silk sticking out stiff, sits down on the brick step and scoops him onto her lap. He disappears into an enclosing cowl of gray silk. Noises like *all right* and *there, there* emerge from inside it. Mrs. La Salle's narrow hand, embellished with an amethyst ring, rises to pat my father's shoulder.

The lady rocks, she even hums. "Now," she says. "It'll be *fine*." She cradles his head.

"Get somebody," I say, a little weakly.

After a minute more of ministration, Mrs. La Salle responds by lifting her head and commanding upward, "Somebody *come*," in a great volume of grand-duchess-yell.

Right away a little crowd arrives at the beauty parlor door, jostling down the steps to see what on earth can be happening.

"A very bad accident in the meadow," I repeat, projecting up and out, emulating Mrs. La Salle.

"Get Dr. Kittredge," I add.

There's a lot of commotion and questions as we are pulled and pushed up the steps and into, presumably, safety: Daddy and I each are supplied with a chair while a group goes to find the doctor; people saying to me and to him, "What happened?" and "How did you . . ." and "How terrible!" And I'm finally starting to react. What I'm reacting to mainly is this thought: *Accident?* That was no accident. You don't fall and break your neck in an accident, and then lie down on your back. You lie some other way, on your face, with your head pushed askew, or curled in a ball, head canted. Not stretched neatly, as if you'd been dragged there. Someone transported Mona to that spot, and then didn't have the *chance* to fix her up like an accident. They heard us coming. Maybe part of the time we were stumbling around, they were there, too. Watching. Maybe they were watching us and wondering what they should do about *us*.

I'm fighting with these thoughts all the time I'm arranging to get Daddy back to his room. Mrs. La Salle volunteers to be his guide, and he totters along with her quite willingly, leaning into her protective furl of gray silk.

I watch them go, and then I flash back to that scene on the steps and have a dumb, inappropriate association. They looked like Michelangelo's *Pieta*, the lady bent over a cradled prostrate man, like that statue of the crucified Jesus stretched out on Mary's lap. Latch on to something like that in a moment of crisis, and your brain will go totally numb.

But three minutes later, after I've been supplied with a glass of the beauty parlor's leftover wine and am waiting for the doctor and the sheriff, I'm back to wondering who was lurking in the underbrush and watching us fumble around.

Because now we really are Observers, major Observers. Also witnesses. Smack at the middle of a quivering spider web. I analyze each person in this room wanting to ask, "Were you out there while I was out there?"

The doctor arrives, breathless and for once, almost quiet. "Dead?" he asks me. "You could tell that? Do you know what *dead* looks like?"

Something in my face must convince him, because he says, "We'll get you home to bed, baby."

Then he has to Irish it up: "Yes, yes. We'll scoot you past the sheriff. Bed and chicken soup, baby. Okay? That'll be it, dear one. Bed and chicken soup fer ya."

A shot of vodka in this chardonnay would be more to the point, Irish buddy, is what I think at him, staring into his slightly bleary eyes.

The sheriff takes forever to get here. Finally he arrives, dripping fog off his yellow slicker and hat, and with rivulets running down his rimless glasses. He doesn't even sit down; he leans over, gripping and dripping, holding both arms of my chair and saying, "Okay, okay," meaning that he gets it how I'm half-asleep and canted sideways in my chair. Then he asks me where, when, how long we'd been out in the garden, why we went out there at all. He stares down and says, "Huh." He makes me feel he's disbelieving most of this. He says he'll see me first thing tomorrow; I should not go away from the Manor, not any place at all; do I understand?

Yes, I tell him, I understand.

When I stand up, I find I'm stiff. I look down at Susie's moon-and-stars shirt and decide that I won't tell her I was wearing it tonight.

⅃ Chapter 10

Back in my father's room Mrs. La Salle has him in bed, quilt up under his chin. She's sitting beside him with a book open on her lap and is reading aloud.

> " 'Alone, alone, all all alone
> Alone on a wide, wide sea,' "

she announces as I come in to the room. She wrinkles her nose at me. "Maybe not the best antidote for an evening of death and drama, but it was what he wanted to hear. And he does seem to be feeling better. He was worried, you know, about his *Dame sur la Plage*."

"My father speaks very good French," I tell her, somewhat crossly. I can't figure out what this handsome old lady is up to. She's not, absolutely not, one of those maternal, loving, nurturing Susie-type matrons. She's more the hard, brittle, handsome society model. Smart and well-read. But not a big-time doer of good, not a cuddler and purveyor of chicken soup. Mainly out to advance number one, I'd guess. So what does she want with my poor Alzheimer's impeded father? Does she, maybe, think he's rich?

"Well, my dear," she says, rising in one graceful gray silk motion, "I'll leave you now. Good night, Edward. You look sweet, there."

"Do I? How nice." He smiles after her as she rustles out the door. "She helped me quite a bit," he confides.

I'll bet she did.

This is a lady with remarkable savoir faire. How many other people, projected into sudden intimacy, right in the middle of a brand-new murder case, could resist asking questions? Apparently Mrs. La S. could. She didn't come up with a single one.

I sit down in the chair she's just vacated. "I'll stay in your room tonight."

Don't hover too much, I tell myself, and then issue a correction: Go ahead, hover. This frail old gentleman discovered a dead body tonight. He did a ninety-mile dash through the moonlight. And some time or other in the past he watched a woman die in a net.

He's in the middle of the dangerous action.

So am I.

I get a blanket, a quilt, a pillow, and I curl up on the window seat. Tomorrow I have to talk to the sheriff. I better be careful; if I tell him too much he'll be quizzing my father, who can't take it.

But I, myself, have to quiz my father. The time has come for me to know a few things. Find out about that net-woman. I start framing questions, oblique ones, not scary-direct.

And after that, there's what Mrs. Dexter is hiding. The lady's silence is downright dangerous. Think up questions for her, too, I tell myself.

I'll never get to sleep.

But my darling father seems to sleep perfectly all right, and eventually I guess I do, too, because Belle has to wake both of us when she comes by for the morning rounds. "Get up," she says. "I want you, the sheriff wants you, everybody screamin' for you. Come on, rouse."

"Okay." I have trouble orienting. Not the trouble where you can't figure out where you are, but the other one where you can't decide what you're supposed to know this morning. Something different from yesterday, you're sure, but what? "How is it down there?"

"Wild. Everybody talking at once." Belle is helping Daddy out of bed, and he looks over her shoulder at me. "All of 'em wondering about you. You found her, huh?"

"We both did."

"Umph." I interpret this grunt as, *Boy, are you in major difficulty.* "Lady, get down there, now. That sheriff really wants you."

I arrive downstairs for my sheriff-interview feeling dizzy. I'm starting to get a cold. I crumple a wad of Kleenex and press it against my upper lip.

The main sitting room of the Manor looks like an airport after an all-day plane-arrival embargo. People are huddled in clusters, half-asleep, where the sheriff's deputies have set up interviewing centers—islands of tables, chairs, and footstools, each with a uniformed cop and a witness. A bosomy spike-haired woman sergeant greets me, "Hey, Miss Day, we been looking for you. Sheriff Hawthorne, he's been looking. He's back there in some office."

The sheriff, whom I didn't really see last night because he was hidden under his yellow slicker and hat, turns out to be a cadaverous man with gray hair and rimless glasses and stubble. He has liberated a tapestried cubicle down the hall from Mrs. Sisal's office, where he scribbles at something for a few minutes. He tells me to sit and finally pronounces, "Okay."

"So," he says, "you found the decedent."

I resist saying *huh*? *Decedent,* I translate, equals *dead person* equals *Mona.* I agree, "Yes."

"How did that happen?"

"Well, we were walking . . ."

The sheriff tips his chair back to make it squeak. He runs his hand backward over some thin, defeated hair. He aims his glasses at me. And then proceeds into a barrage of official sheriff-type questions. Walking? Where? Why? Middle of the night, foggy, cold, you go for a walk? Your dad not so good? What kind of not so good? Why a walk? Why not back to his room?

Now, Miss Day, you just *tell* me.

It's at this point, when he squeaks his chair again and does his sheriff-challenge, *just tell me,* that I catch on. I, Carla, am the Prime Suspect. First on the scene. Discovered the body. What do you mean, body still warm, just dispatched? Of course he has you in his crosshairs.

Oh, for God's sake.

"How well do you know the decedent?" he asks.

My brain is temporarily numbed so I have to do it all over again, *decedent* means *Mona*. "I didn't."

The sheriff's eyebrow's come up over his glasses.

"I mean, I only spoke to her twice." I don't feel like telling him about my special interview with Mona. I'm not sure why.

"Like," I feed this information into a meaningful official silence, "I went to the hospital to see a friend, and she was there, and I spoke to her."

"You said?"

"I said, 'Where's Mrs. Dexter?' "

He's ready to be suspicious now. He shifts and looks at papers and says, "Well." Then suddenly he starts asking me about college. I was at Santa Cruz, did I like it? A good student, was I? Any trouble at Santa Cruz? I graduated? Oh, yeah. Uh-huh.

He shifts some more papers, which I guess confirm, yes, I graduated, and no, I wasn't in any trouble, none that shows.

"This Habitat thing. Buildin' houses for poor people, huh."

"It's a cooperative exercise."

The sheriff squints at me. I have a feeling he knows perfectly well what Habitat for Humanity is about.

Santa Cruz is a famous bliss-out campus, maybe that's what he's been digging for.

Suddenly he deflates. Almost as if he's lost interest in the project. He reads through some more of his papers and puts them down and breathes out, a walrus snort, and I get the feeling that the papers have pretty much confirmed that, no, I didn't know Mona and probably wouldn't have wanted to kill her. And that he's been kind of bluffing this whole time.

After all, I'm not his first interview of today. He must have talked to the doctor. And to Mrs. Sisal. And some of the aides. They would have told him how innocent-appearing I am.

"Well," he says, and squeaks the chair in a semicircle until it faces the window. "So. Tell me what you remember. From your walk into the dark and stormy night." I stare at him. A humorist, no less. He reads *Peanuts*, just the way Daddy used to.

It turns out he wants me to review last night's route, trying for total recall. "Anything," he says. "Anything extra."

"And," he adds, "I asked to talk to your dad, too, but the doc says he's not too good on memory, is that right?"

I send a mental thank-you to Dr. Kittredge. "That's right."

The sheriff now presents obvious questions: "When you turned at that first bend, notice anything? . . . When you went around the statue, anything at that point?" He's not too bad at doing this. I always thought the sheriff of a back-woods stronghold like Del Oro County would be the one that had bought the most people the most drinks in the bar, but now I start wondering if maybe this guy has read a book or two. "Now, beyond that turn there's a bank of white rock, remember it, did you stop there?"

And I find that just being prodded sparks one of those trains of association they write about: I see again the clusters of grass and trails of white rock and walls of moon-splashed fog and get an occasional cold warning ("Just a suggestion, I guess," I tell Sheriff Hawthorne), a hint that maybe at this curve or the next one some tiny movement has just happened. "But I wasn't noticing," I add. "I was paying attention to my father; he's kind of . . ."

"Yeah, I know, I heard. Now when you reached the lady, the body . . . anything special?"

"She was laid out too neatly, not right for a broken neck . . ." We have to stop here for a discussion (one I wish we weren't having right now; I hate knowing so much about this) of my work in the Santa Cruz animal lab and what I know about broken necks.

I don't mention about Mona's moon-and-stars cloak, how she had it earlier and then she didn't. I want to keep that fact for myself. Knowledge is power, somebody or other said.

The sheriff thinks for a while. "Her hands. She holding anything?"

"Holding something?"

"No little piece of paper, maybe?"

"Not that I could see."

He exhales loudly. That walrus snort again, the male equivalent of a sigh. "Your dad. Do you think . . . if we helped him . . . couldn't he remember a *little*?"

"He'd remember something from twenty years ago. Something that happened in Egypt. That's mostly what he talks about lately. He gets it mixed up with *now*." Jesus, I don't want Daddy questioned; he's confused enough already.

The sheriff snorts some more and hands me a sheet of paper, a photocopy that looks as if it might be a picture of something smaller, a ragged little scrap that sits lightly outlined in the middle of the page.

The scrap has numbers on it. They're uneven; maybe they were written down fast.

"Those numbers mean anything?" he asks.

I squint at them. *1028*, the *8* not very well inscribed but recognizable. It takes a minute or so, but then it clicks, and

I feel a knot in my throat and a weight on my chest, my heart goes queep. But I ask, "What is this? Where's it from?"

"The victim—Miss Mona—had it on her person."

"On her *person*?"

"Down her bra," he projects this in a funereal voice. "You *do* recognize it?"

I'm afraid my unsteady hand is giving me away, but the sheriff doesn't seem to notice. Yes, I recognize it all right. I hate being drawn into this web any closer. "That was our old house number. 1028. 1028 Klamath Avenue." I dab at my nose to deflect attention.

"Right." He looks as pleased as if he'd forced me into a confession. "Your dad's old house." When I stare at him, he says, "The first thing we did was try it on the Manor computer, and it came up a match. It was his address when he applied here. That's where he used to live."

And where I lived for a long time and also my mother. And Aunt Crystal for a while, too.

"You got an idea?" Sheriff Hawthorne asks.

He thinks I'm hiding something. I don't blame him; I am hiding several things. I shrug and say, "Absolutely none."

"This Mona lady knew your dad?" he asks, and I say the obvious: Daddy must have met her in the hospital, he never talked to me about her. I don't repeat Daddy's peculiar question about the "lady with the scissors on her belt." Why puzzle this poor guy any more than he already is?

"He knew her the way anybody here would."

"What did *you* think of her?"

"Me?" I don't understand this question.

"Yeah, you. How do you appraise her as a fellow human?"

I decide I don't much like this psychologically oriented side of the sheriff. "I only saw her twice." (*Lie.*)

"Yeah. What'd you think?"

"She was a weird, wispy little thing. Not like you expect a nurse to be. Jittery."

"Did you like her?"

"Like her?" I don't say, "What a peculiar question." I don't say, "*No*," which would be true. "I hardly knew her. I already told you."

"Yeh." The sheriff dismisses this. "But a lotta people here are sayin' they had a personal opinion, that they didn't like her. People in a place like this like to talk. They never hearda the word *incriminating*. They say Mona asked for it."

"Asked to be killed?"

"Yep." He eyes me expectantly, but I probably succeed in looking blank. Mona asked to be killed? Did she expect it? Is that what she was blathering about in the hall outside my door? Oh, my God. That poor, stupid, fluttery person.

Sheriff Hawthorne is regarding me askance (I think that's the proper word). After a while he asks what medicines Daddy takes. I start to say, "No painkillers," but decide that's too much of a leading answer. Painkillers are a danger signal: painkillers cause addiction; addiction is always bad. So I tell him that Daddy took a multivitamin compound for his general health and Aricept for his forgetfulness. "I guess the Aricept doesn't work too well," I say innocently.

While I'm talking, I'm trying to figure it out. Our old street address. What on earth use is it to anybody? It's just part of the old history of me, Daddy, and Aunt Crystal.

No wonder the sheriff is looking at me in that tone of voice. I'm beginning to feel it again—that caught-fly shiver of being trapped in an immense, insecure, quivering spiderweb—one with a lot of sticky strands that glimmer in the light and lead off into space at one end and down to a gummy center at the other. And there wrapped around with filaments is . . . I hope the figure caught in that sticky spider structure isn't my father. He's old, he's basically gentle, he's hopelessly naïve. He wants to believe good of everyone. And he forgets. He forgets a whole lot of everything, but he tries especially hard to forget anything bad. Up until now, he's sort of succeeded. It would be downright mean if fate brought him face to face with a spider right now, when his guard is down.

What has he done, or have I done, that all these trails seem to converge on us?

The Lady on the Beach, of course, that's what my father has done.

Sheriff H. is watching me. Some of this speculation probably shows in my face. And this man isn't anywhere near as dumb as I thought he was.

"Think about it," he says.

"Okay," I sit there doing that. Thinking. But nothing happens. I tell him, "No. No ideas."

"Listen," I say finally, "I *am* concerned. Genuinely, really puzzled, especially about those numbers." I present this extra-sincerely because I can see Sheriff Hawthorne suspecting about the many little things I'm not telling him. Little things that might make the sheriff try to question my father, or hypnotize him, or drug him in some weird new terror-police way. I tug down my tight black shirt where it has ridden above the top of my blue jeans. "I'll call you right away if I think of *anything*."

Probably he's not happy with that answer, but it's the one he's got to put up with for the moment.

Upstairs I'm plunged into a barrage of client questioning; every person on my schedule wants to know everything. Mr. Taylor asks, "We are doomed here, don't you think? Was her head twisted all the way around?" Mrs. Cohen says, "You poor sweetie, what a dreadful shock." Mr. Rice announces that absolutely nobody will want to stay in this place another minute. And Mrs. La Salle is philosophical: "Isn't life strange? That gushy, awful little woman. Do you really think the rest of us are in danger; I think it was just that creepy little Mona."

I don't stop to quiz Mrs. La Salle on why she dislikes Mona because the client I really need is Mrs. Dexter; I've been thinking about her ever since last night. I've saved her for now. I'll be firm with her; I'll hector her even if I hate doing it. I'm putting aside my other concerns and concentrating on my Dexter-approach.

And she must have guessed what I'm planning because she's slow at answering her door. She tries a version of Mr. Rice's "Who is it, who is it?" and then, when I say "Carla," she goes "Who?" as if she's never heard of Carla. Finally she gets the door open with a lot of clanking and banging; she pokes her head out like a little pug-nosed Walt Disney animal, blinking and half-cringing, doing the pantomime where she leans helplessly on her walker, backing slowly away and letting me loom after, forced into playing the part of the Nazi storm trooper.

"Mrs. Dexter," I say, "this is ridiculous; it's totally silly. What on earth are you afraid of? You've got to talk. This business of you not saying what you know has gone much too far . . ." I stop for a breath here, "it's your duty—you can't hide any more—you're doing damage."

"Please call me Louise." She offers this humbly, plaintively.

I don't call her Louise. "You know something," I persist. "Mona is dead. I mean, murdered. And whatever you know might have saved her *life*—no, don't look at me like that."

I'm cranking my performance up to warp speed because I'm fond of Mrs. Dexter. She's my second-favorite person in this peculiar place, right after my darling father. And now I have to be mean to her. But, yes, I have to. I feel responsible. Maybe I could have made her talk earlier if I'd been mean earlier. Maybe I could have saved silly little Mona's life.

"You've absolutely got to say what you know," I announce. It doesn't help that I'm tense about the sheriff and that my clients have said a lot of very dumb things in the last half hour. "Mrs. Dexter," I can hear myself getting even more shrill, "a woman is dead, what you know and won't talk about maybe did it. It may have caused her *death*."

My victim clunks the walker ostentatiously; she turns her back and makes a lot of metallic noise. Then, body crunched and walker rattling, she clomps across the apartment. When she gets to her easy chair, she turns to fix me with a beady little eye.

And she says, "Oh, poo." Which isn't at all the response I've been expecting. I guess you could say her attitude is somewhere halfway between defiant and don't-hit-me. "You're very unfriendly," she mentions.

"You've got to come clean," I babble. Having run out of reasonable remarks to make, I'm now relying on the movies.

"There's been a *death*. A woman *killed*." A lot of righteous energy gets into this.

"You don't know a single solitary thing, do you?" She brings the walker down, all four wheels at once.

I don't answer *No, lady, I don't know hardly anything*, though that's what I think. I simply stare while she parks her equipment and wriggles into the easy chair.

"You made assumptions," she announces.

"Of course." I'm trying not to act impatient.

"No, you *really* don't know a single thing."

I say, "Oh, for God's sake."

"You think Mona was poor, little, silly, gushy Mona, and that she was a harmless person who got killed. That's what you think."

"Mrs. Dexter, the point is . . ."

"No. The point is that *I* know—I absolutely know—I really *know*, I tell you—*she* was doing it."

That's a stopper. "*It?* What's *it?*"

She squints at me, defiant. "Why, Carla. *It*. Everything. All the bad events that have happened."

"You mean the accidents? You think *Mona* was feeding you glass? Starting fires? Leaving windows open. All that weird stuff?"

"Yes."

I say, "But." After which I add *Mona* and the words *ditsy* and *scared*. I think back over my session with Mona. She acted peculiar; she said she shouldn't have done it, but somehow I don't see her engineering the Manor's accidents.

Mrs. Dexter gestures. "What does that have to do with it? She *was*. I know it for a fact."

I say, "You have completely flipped." Normally, I'd sneak

up on an unflattering opinion like that. I'd reason, or ask intelligent, meaningful questions first. But today's been a
hard day. "You're nuts," I elucidate.

There's a silence while Mrs. Dexter rocks the walker to
make it squeak and stares at me.

I sigh and sit down on the couch. "Please tell me exactly
what you're talking about."

"Mona wasn't what she looked like." Mrs. Dexter punc-
tuates by squeaking her machinery some more. "Mona was a
person of power."

I say, "Power, you can't mean, *power?*" and Mrs. Dexter
says, "She had means," and I say, "Come on, please speak
English," and Mrs. Dexter says, "Well, not power exactly,
they say blackmailers are weak people," and I ask, "Mona
was a *blackmailer?*" And Mrs. Dexter says, "Sometimes,"
And then she adds, "Mona had the key to the drug cupboard."

"The drug cupboard," I say, and then dawn breaks for
me, and I say, "Drugs? Mona was selling drugs? Who'd she
sell them *to?*"

Mrs. Dexter tips up her chin. She's feeling better; she
smirks. She says, "Oh, *child,*" in the tone you'd use for a
four-year-old. "To *us,* of course. Do you think old people
can't be addicts?"

I guess I hadn't thought about it, exactly. Sell drugs
around the Manor? When you tell me *drugs*, I get a picture
of a Santa Cruz student flipped out under a redwood tree, or
else of a homeless Tenderloin guy in a holey overcoat. Not
an old lady with color-enhanced hair.

Drugs, I think, reviewing that confusing interview with
Mona. "I was just trying to help," and all that emotive
blather. Oh, that idiot girl. Oh, good God.

"So. Learn about how life really is," Mrs. Dexter says, smirking some more, but only partly being mean, getting into another of her Disney roles, this time the Red Queen one. "*Anybody* can get to need drugs. Old people, especially. They start out, they have to take something, and then after a while they can't not. Mona was good at finding out *who*. She loved that whole finding-out process. She loved spying and finding out and selling. She was an *evil* woman.

"And, I've told you this, she blackmailed. Her drug customers, that's who she preyed on. She didn't blackmail me, because I never did anything she could use . . . She preyed on other people. On my friends. My good friends." Mrs. Dexter stops here and screws up her face. "I hate talking about it.

"I was scared to death in the hospital," she adds after a minute. "She had drugs, and she had needles. I didn't know what she would do." She hoists herself upright, "I'm getting you a cuppa, child."

So I've gotten to be *child* now, I think. So much for my plan of standing Mrs. Dexter against a wall and being firm with her.

I feel an upwelling of something totally unexpected. Hope. Liberation. If Mona is the guilty party, then this whole train of events has really nothing to do with my father, nothing to do with me. We're just bystanders, viewers of the drama. All that stuff about the numbers the sheriff found is accidental. Peripheral. I get a wonderful feeling of release for about a third of a minute, and then common sense floods back in. There's a hole in this theory; it smells funny.

"But you see what I think," Mrs. D. is talking over her shoulder, bumping her way into her kitchen, "I'm afraid . . .

I think one of my *friends* killed her." A pot clashes against the sink board.

This idea has just crossed my mind, and I've rejected it because I don't want it to be true. I like it a lot better than the theory that puts me and my father in the center of things, but I still don't like it. "That doesn't work," I say, hopefully.

"Oh, yes, it works," and she makes kitchen noises and of-fers a list of reasons: There is motive, she says, and opportu-nity, and how cheap life seems to most people in the Manor, who are old anyway. She adds, "It's easier to say all this with my back to you." *Bump* from the refrigerator door.

That unexpectedly gets to me and makes me sad. That she needs to say it with her back to me.

"Listen," I tell her when she returns with a tray balanced on the front of the walker, "I don't believe it about the acci-dents. Your throat? Why is that part of Mona's drug deal-ing; it doesn't make sense."

Mrs. Dexter and I argue, or discuss, for half an hour. At first, she really wants Mona to be responsible for the dirty tricks. "She was mean. She would have done it just for meanness. And about my throat—she knew I was investi-gating. That glass in the oyster was a warning. I was scared to death the whole time I was in the hospital. I kept whis-pering at her, 'I won't talk. I promise I won't talk.'"

It's funny how, in a crisis, you will suddenly remember something that you knew all along was important and that you ought to have thought of earlier. "Mrs. D.," I say, "Mona *wasn't here* when you ate your oyster. She was in Provo, Utah, visiting her sister."

She at first doesn't want to believe me and claims that Mona lied saying she was out of town, and when I tell her

I'll check it with the doctor, she says that wouldn't mean anything. She really likes this Mona theory. And so would I, if only I could.

"There's something else," I say finally. "There's a reason why this is more complicated than just Mona. There was another . . . murder."

I haven't really spoken to anybody seriously about Daddy's woman-in-the-net. The old ladies know about the pastel he did in Ms. Chaundy's class, of course; they've seen it and admired it, but they didn't take it as evidence of anything *real*. It was just a picture, an imaginary exercise, the way Ms. Chaundy said. And now I start telling Mrs. Dexter that I take his drawing seriously. My poor father saw something. And ever since he saw it, the world has been getting worse for him and for me. And I'm scared. I need to share. "It was a murder," I say again. "Another murder. Or, rather, the first one."

Mrs. Dexter doesn't want to believe this, but at the same time she's very interested. She keeps telling me that I am being ridiculous, as usual, and then, in the next minute asking me why I think so. I must have evidence, she says, what evidence do I have. What does my father remember? "Well, Carla, if he's that vague, it doesn't amount to anything, does it?" At first, she's almost completely resistant. She thumps the walker on the floor. She tells me all the sensible things about how my father misses his Egyptian past and wants to recapture it with this fantasy, and "everybody does this sort of thing about wanting the past back," and I agree that yes, that's just what I was thinking, but now he's repeated the story again and again, always just the same, always with the same feeling that it matters. It matters terribly. And that it's real. He repeats it over and over . . . "And," I say, "when he drew the picture. The picture was so clear. The picture was what convinced me."

"Oh," she says. "The picture. Yes, quite frightening."

"And he acts *guilty* about it," I add.

For some reason this silences her. She stares at me, no longer looking like the Red Queen. "Poor Carla."

So now Mrs. Dexter is sorry for me. And how do I feel about that? I have to admit to myself, I hate being felt sorry for.

"Well, where are we?" I ask after a brief silence.

We aren't much of anywhere.

There's still a possibility that Mona did the tricks, or most of the tricks except for Mrs. Dexter's throat. Or something. Mrs. Dexter still likes this theory. And Mona, I guess, was one of those peculiar cases, a split or divided personality, neurotic and jumbled; you can't tell what she was really like. Someone certainly disliked or feared her enough to kill her.

Maybe there's the possibility that the events are not related, just happening simultaneously. Fat chance, I tell myself. Life's not like that.

Finally, there's the possibility, a probability according to my Santa Cruz logic teacher, who believed firmly in the pattern that underlies all randomness, that everything's related. A leads to B leads to C. Accidents lead to net-woman lead to Mona. Our spiderweb blossoms again, with my poor befuddled father in the middle, developing his talent for observing murders.

Mrs. Dexter trundles me to the door. "We'll find out what it is; I was good at watching when I did it before. You know, Carla, you've convinced me that things are worse than I thought, and I feel better for knowing they're worse.

It gives me a handle, and helps me understand a little bit better."

She stops, staring at something on the door, sucking in a corner of her mouth. "You know, the strangest thing . . ."

The pause lengthens; I have to help her out, "Yes?"

"I grew up here."

I suppress a sigh. Mrs. Dexter is talking in metaphors, and they aren't her language. I don't want to have to ask those helpful leading questions, "What do you mean, 'grew up'?" or, "How did you grow up?"

She reads my face. "No, I mean literally, I grew up here. I was a child around here."

"In the *Manor*?"

"Out there." She gestures at the scenery beyond the window. "It was all ranches. Big ranches. This house belonged to my uncle. I used to come here to play."

There's a brief silence while I think that I always imagined Mrs. Dexter coming from the East, some place in New England.

"And now," she moves the walker to indicate an encompassing gesture, "now I live here. A weird environment. Where all these unmanageable things are happening. I hate unmanageable things.

"My uncle that owned this place would have had a fit."

"That *is* interesting," I agree.

"It's strange. I don't like things to be strange."

"No."

"It upsets me. I don't like to be upset."

I agree, "Yes."

She sighs and extends her face, maybe for a kiss, maybe not. "You should get out of here for a while. Go someplace and have a fling. Learn the karaoke."

She's confused about the current entertainments, but the idea's okay. I debate whether to kiss her and finally do. Feels good, funny little papery cheek with an overlay of weird-smelling powder. Coty's Emeraude, I think it's called, or some name like that.

Some day I'll get her to talk about her childhood in Del Oro County, but right now I have to get back to my number-one troubled client, my father.

🦉 Chapter 11

I have a spiel of meaningful questions to ask my father, a pileup of meaningful inquiries about the woman in the net.

I arrive at his apartment just as Belle is returning him from the hospital. "Clean bill of health," she says triumphantly. "No aftereffects from tumbling around in the meadow. He can go out and do it again tonight. Quite a guy, right?" She hits him, an affectionate thump on the shoulder.

He looks okay, I decide, perky and just-hatched. I kiss him on the cheek. "So they examined you."

He watches me solemnly, "There are dangers so close to the sunset. Did you know that?"

I think, oh, phooey; *sunset, dangers*, not a good framework for being questioned; we'd better slow the process here. So I tell him, "Coffee," in my most phony, kindergarten voice, and sit him down with a cup and his special spoon from Istanbul and the brown sugar cubes he always asks for, and I even produce a peppermint-flavored Jelly Belly that I've been saving for a special occasion, and snuggle it next to his coffee cup. "Now," I say, "let's sit back and take things easy."

So we do. He drinks coffee, and we talk about the *Antiques Roadshow* television program; he's pleased with the estimate of seven thousand pounds for a Regency chair. "Because it had nice dark green upholstery," he tells me seriously, "that shade of dark green is very good luck."

"Now," I ask, after he has dispatched the Jelly Belly, "how are you feeling?"

"I'm feeling good. Why do you ask?"

"It wasn't too bad at the hospital?"

"It was okay." He sounds slightly irritated. "Perfectly okay. That doctor is an interesting man."

I fluff up his hair, which is flyaway textured, like an angora sweater. "You're tougher than you look."

"Of course I am," he says complacently.

I take this as a go-ahead sign and climb up after his pastel picture of the beach, which I've stored flat behind some archaeology books. First I stand it up against a chair back and admire it. Really, it's a fine picture—beach, light-washed with setting evening sun, three architectural rocks in the background, figure angled on the beach, tied with gold bindings. Eye of Horus down there in the corner. "Sweetie, let's talk about this picture."

"I can do better," he announces solemnly, examining as if he's passing judgment on someone else's work of art. "I *have* done better. In Egypt everyone complimented me on my drawing. Even your mother, and she was discriminating."

Great, I think, he remembers Constancia; he's tracking.

That little bit earlier about the sunset didn't amount to anything.

"Daddy," I say, "for this picture, where is the viewer?"

I almost expect him to go art-historian on me and tell me I'm the viewer and I'm here in his bedroom, but he doesn't do that; he points to the picture's foreground, "There's a culvert somewhere."

I get one of those cold chills of recognition that my philosophy teacher at Santa Cruz liked; she called it a *frisson*. "And you were in the culvert?" I ask, careful to keep the *frisson* out of my voice, because any sign of excitement may shut him down.

"I didn't tell anybody," he says. "I thought I better not."

I announce neutrally that caution is always good, and he says, "I like to trust people. I think I can trust you."

"Of course you can." I hear myself being especially phony.

But my answer satisfies Daddy who gives me a sweet inclusive smile. "Not telling is important. But when the spirit is weighed, it's asked if it has committed sins of omission or commission. The inability to trust is a sin of commission.

"That is a bad kind of sin," he adds solemnly.

I pick up the cue. Maybe repetition is called for. "Well, you can trust *me*."

"She spoke to me, you know. She said I should be careful."

I warn myself to go very slow here. No *frisson* is allowed. Anyway, he's probably talking about one of the aides. Or Mrs. Dexter. Or me. "*Who* spoke to you, Daddy?"

He looks at me sideways, as if I've said something I shouldn't. He says, "Oh, no."

"You said the woman spoke to you?"

"Well, my dear, there are different points of view . . ."

"But somebody spoke. You just told me." I'm handling this badly.

He's feeling threatened; his shoulders go up, his chin goes down. He turns his back slightly. "Well, I believe there was something. A shadow. I have trouble. Trouble remembering, you know.

"Carly," he adds, "it's quite complicated."

"That's all right."

But it isn't all right. He starts to fidget, the kind of moving around that involves swinging a foot and shifting shoulders. He won't look at me. "The trouble is with the sunset."

He makes the kind of arm-motions you make when you recite, " 'He saw it in the place in which it was. Do not stay on the road until evening, thinking you are sure of the houses.'

"Demotic Literature, British Museum," he identifies.

I want to shake him. We're completely off the track now, quoting Demotic literature.

I turn back to the picture, straightening it where it teeters against the scalloped mahogany chair back, "Now, Daddy, listen. Please. Where in this landscape were you?" I put a finger on the margin. "Here? Or here?"

" 'Should you hide and then let yourself be found,' " he intones, his expression flat-faced. " 'Should you leave and then return to the place where it was.' "

I think, oh, hell.

And suddenly he bolts up and stands with his back to me, shoulders straight, head tilted. He looks as if he's waiting to recite to the windowpane.

"Father," I try.

No answer. Little stubborn figure with its back turned, shoulders in that position that looks as if they have a wire hanger inside them.

I want to put my head in my hands, and then I want to swear interestingly and colorfully, and after that, if you can have three such impulses so fast and connected, I want to tell an absent Mrs. Dexter, *Okay, perhaps you were right*: he just wants to recall his glory days of Egyptian archaeology. Of course he needs to do that, he's an old man who knows he's on his way out, his light is dimming. He's failing, my own father is failing. Maybe it's the word *failing*, which I've almost said aloud, but at this point I stop this mental keening and drama and ask myself, "Carla, have you been listening at all? Did you notice anything about these quotes? Do they make any kind of sense?"

Well, they don't make much sense.

But there's something there.

Something about location, and words like, "in the place where it was," and going back to the same place.

I tell myself I'm an idiot.

Those nights near the Valley of the Kings, waiting for the Coffin Lid Tomb to be reopened, we sat around a little fire in our Luxor trailer camp. It was cold after sunset, at Qena camp, we sat around the fire, cooking our imported American foods, hot dogs and marshmallows, and reciting poetry and playing a game. The game was to invent a situation to go with the Egyptian poems we'd been saying to each other. Daddy and Robbie were very good at this, but I was okay, too. I knew some poetry then. I fish around now in my memory.

"'Great man free of baseness,'" I start intoning; this bit is Demotic also, but later period, translated into English by some German lady. "'Do justice, oh, praised one. When I speak may you hear.'"

My father says, "Ah." Then he turns away from the window and repeats, "Ah," looking more or less at me, which is an improvement.

"'Rudder of Heaven beam of earth,'" I continue. At first you feel foolish sounding like this; it seems grandiloquent. And then the rhythms get you, and you decide everyone should speak that way all the time. "'Guider to port of all who founder. Learn the Constitution of the Sky.'"

Not a bad motto, *learn*. My father seems to think so, too. He half-smiles, one of those salutes with the eyes. He sits down on the window seat and says, "'He is sad at the sorrow of your *ka*.'"

I remember when he and Robbie had a discussion about that line. The German lady, whose English may not have been that great, translated it, "He *abhors* the sorrow of your *ka*," but Robbie and Daddy were sure the correct translation was not *abhors* but *grieves at*. "Grieves, in an intensive, strong form," my father had said, biting the end off his hot dog.

"Daddy," I tell him now, feeling inspired, wondering why on earth it has taken me so long to get this far, "will you lead me to the spot?"

He nods, as if he's been waiting for this. "Lead you. You want me as a guide?"

"Yes."

"I will take the path, and you will follow?"

"That's right."

"And no part of that is telling, is it?" he asks.

"No, it's not telling."

"We will go up the path one by one," he suggests, and I agree, "Yes."

He smiles. "Why, of course, my dear. I would be happy to lead you.

"I enjoy the role of guide. Being a guide will be enjoyable. You will follow along and climb when I climb."

This must be what he wanted me to ask for all along, but he couldn't say it. Or couldn't figure out what he wanted. Maybe he promised somebody something? A not-saying promise? I'm on the verge of putting all this into a question, and then I don't.

He's happy now but not exactly relaxed. He would like to set out on this trip immediately.

"It isn't far," he says. "You won't need a sandwich."

I have to slow him down; the outside grounds are full of the sheriff's helpers measuring distances and searching for bits of rope or wire or whatever it is they look for, and decorating the bushes with festoons of yellow DO NOT CROSS tape. They would be very, very interested in any excursion my father and I made. But he's not impressed when I tell him we should wait; it's only when I say I'm really tired and want to take a nap that he responds, "Oh, my dear. Certainly. I demand too much. I understand about your feeling tired. I also will lie down for a few minutes."

He pats my shoulder and says, "That was a delicious little candy you brought me," and offers his cheek for a kiss.

I turn the television on low so he can either look at it or ignore it just as he chooses and give him a kiss, "See you later, administrator," and head off down the hall to my broom closet to brood.

Actually, I'm getting pretty fond of my plasterboard-lined cubbyhole with the IKEA bed. That bed is a good one, and it's the first absolutely brand-new bed I've ever had in my life. It still has those intrusive little NEW MATERIAL. DO NOT DESTROY THIS LABEL tags.

I prop the pillow on end and squeeze my backbone against it and pull the quilt high. I need to do some serious thinking.

I try to manage this sequentially, but I'm not good at that. The thoughts keep crowding in in a messy mixture.

Here's thought *numero uno*: My father keeps walking into the middle of this situation, whatever the situation is.

Item: Mona is dead. And Daddy found her. Well, Daddy *and I* found her. Of course, that could be accidental.

But, item: Mona had Daddy's address down her bra. Could that set of numbers also be accidental? They couldn't. Could they be someone else's personal numbers? No. I took too many logic courses at Santa Cruz to believe in random events like that. Also, I took one stat course, at which I did abysmally, but got enough out of it to know that statistically that number cannot be anyone else's number. It's his. Or, ours. His and mine.

And, further item: My father saw another murder. Which so far is confined to his head. Well, to his head, his memory, his consciousness, his pastel picture. He's been trying plenty to publicize it. And now it's part of my consciousness, because I believe in it now.

Two murders have happened along this same little random plot of seacoast.

Are they related? Of course they're related, *estupida*. How much of your life have you lived elsewhere without even one single murder?

And finally, the accidents.

Mrs. Dexter's accident seems the most dramatic because I saw it happen, but there are the other ones that I have simply heard about: the lady out the window, the beauty parlor fire, and then something about a gas heater. Dr. Kittredge says he's really worried. He says this is far too much accident for an organized place like the Manor. He says the integrity of the Manor is threatened.

I decide not to get into wondering about Dr. Kittredge and Mrs. Sisal and the suspects I've lined up for the role of who could have done all these things. I'll stick to the tangle I have now. The tangle of the murders, the numbers, the accidents. Like a Jackson Pollock painting or one of those intolerable messes I used to scramble up in my sewing kit with a mixture of red thread, green thread, black thread, and, especially, invisible thread. Aunt Crystal would open the sewing-kit lid, pull out this ridiculous snarl, and get truly cross. "I know you don't like to sew, but you don't have to be so obstreperous about it."

I try to move my mind on to something peaceful. Susie. I get up and dig out a lined yellow pad and a ballpoint pen. I'm going to write Susie a letter. She'll love that. Susie adores special attentions, and a letter from me is, believe it or not, special. I don't do it very often, not that I'm not good at writing. I am very good, but what I find hard is the process that I'm performing now: getting together paper, pen, envelope, stamp, and then sitting back and thinking it out. And then, for God's sake, getting it into the mailbox. "Hello, dear Susie," I start out.

* * *

"Okay, Superman," I tell my father, "let's go for our walk."

"I will lead," he specifies. "You will follow." He's thrilled. He's been waiting all afternoon to get this started. But the sheriff's people have only just bundled into their cortege of black-and-white vehicles and departed for the town of Green Beach, leaving the downstairs living room littered with ballpoint pens, plastic cups, and crumpled wads of notebook paper.

Outside, the yellow DO NOT CROSS tapes are still up, marking the path that leads to the Mona-discovery area as out of bounds.

Daddy surprises me by understanding the purpose of the yellow tapes. "We don't want to go there, anyway," he says, and squeezes my hand. "I am pleased, my dear, that we are doing this."

Every now and then I really get it, how much this last year of not remembering and not managing has hurt him. It was a year that yelled, "out of control," all the time. This comes out when he talks the way he does now, so proud and pleased, about leading and following. He'll get to be in front, and someone else will follow, and he will be Dr. Edward Day, archaeologist, Reinhold Lecturer, Head, Department of Near Eastern Studies, once again.

Hey, I think, I love you a lot.

He starts off now across the Manor gardens, his torso energetically crisp, but his body canted forward. He's following a course north, past the kitchens and the garbage can enclosures, beside the steam plant and the compost heaps, the nonscenic route that leads beyond the recycling bins.

"Nobody walks here," he says. He gestures, "Does it look like Egypt?"

Sure, Daddy, right. It looks like the parts of Egypt that don't get onto the tourist posters. Except that, in Egypt, those cardboard boxes would have been co-opted the minute they appeared and made into a village of houses with Hefty-bag roofs.

"Now you see," he says, "we're almost at the highway. Then we turn again. Either north or toward the sun. I'm not sure which." He waves at the horizon.

"This highway is a very old one," he lectures at me, "and quite narrow, perhaps the one Agamemnon's herald traveled on? Highways are important in art and literature. There was a highway between Athens and Heliopolis."

I don't say, "Sweetie, you're mixing it up."

"I used to know this highway's history; perhaps you can check it on your machine. Now, farther along, by that clump of coyote weed, do you see that little gap?"

I want to ask him how he ever noticed the path beside the coyote weed in the first place, and, second, how does he know it's coyote weed, which wouldn't be an Egyptian sort of thing to know, but I reject these questions. No diversionary tactics. And anyway, he's taken off, bulleting across the road, superior to the possibility of traffic.

"And here," he calls to me, "is the part where you, my dear, must be careful. *I* am very good at this."

And he wriggles his way through an opening that's hardly there, overgrown, sandily uneven, obscured by long, snaky, scratchy branches. He scrambles and dodges and dips. There's a lot of small boy in my father still.

"If we just get there before sunset," he says.

"What is it about sunset, Father?"

"Well, I really did know that, but I forgot. Sunset. The sunset and the Eye. The sunset is the death of the Eye. It was something on an e-mail."

Carla, you half-wit, you know better than to ask a question like that. "Sunset's a long time off," I say very firmly. "You're going to lead me, remember?" And I think, maybe I really should start feeling sorry for myself. Here's my father, who never exactly was much of a father and now has started acting like a child, but the kind of child that you can get to do things by pretending he's in charge. "You're leading," I repeat. "I'll follow. I'm right behind you here."

"Yes. Yes, my dear." He grabs my hand, pleased to be intent once more. We push our way through thorny bushes and high grass.

Not only is this hard work, but we're forging through major tick country, and I'll probably pick up a few little passengers. Insects love me. I squint down at my sneakers.

I stop thinking this because ahead of us the foraging aspect has gotten worse, Daddy has dropped onto all fours, vigorously endangering his elbows, knees, the crisp crease of his beautiful tweed pants, and he seems to be disappearing into a hole.

It's the culvert. Just like the rabbit hole in *Alice*.

It happens too fast for me to get seriously upset about it, but I react viscerally, that sudden cramp in the belly when you don't understand something, and then I try reaching an arm after him into the scratchy, weedy hole where I can see the bottoms of his shoes wriggling off.

He calls back, his voice exaggerated by the passageway echo, "It's all right! It's fine. You didn't know I was going to do that, did you? Just get down and try. You can do it."

Thank God, I'm wearing blue jeans. I can worry about my father's tweed pants some other time.

"It's not a very long culvert," he calls back.

And then, "See, now. I'm almost out."

My dad is skinnier than I am. My rabbit-hole trip is a tight squeeze with a lot of grief from rocks and gravel and rusty splinters snagging at my hair, abrasions collecting on my elbows and the palms of my hands. But I do see light ahead; he's right, as soon as the bottoms of his shoes disappear, there it is, flashing. This will be a short culvert creep. I marvel at the energetic scramble he's performing ahead. How old is he? Sixty when I was born; that makes him eighty-five now. I knew that all along, of course, but I can still think, *Wow.*

Suddenly the light gets much brighter. Ahead, Daddy has popped into the daytime, and in a minute, with additional damage to my elbows and the palms of my hands, I'm there, too.

We're on a cliff, lodged on our stomachs behind a barrier of high grass and seaside bushes, with a view over the edge down onto the beach that was in Daddy's picture. Clearly it's the same beach, with that exact stretch of sand and the three conical rocks at the end.

I say, "Oh." And then, "You did a great job of drawing this."

"Well, I've been trained, of course," he lowers his voice modestly.

The water's at about the same level as in his picture, midtide, I guess.

"She was down there," he points.

"And there were some other people?"

"Three people. They didn't fight at first. At first, they

just talked. They came down from there." He points to the north end of the beach.

"You were following, sort of? You were an observer?"

"Observer?" my father asks. "Oh, I don't know. Perhaps I have told too much. It was important not to tell. Not telling was mentioned. In the usual context. And I still have my token." He's begun acting anxious, moving his hands back and forth over the flattened grasses.

Token? I've got to come up with an unthreatening remark here. Repeating a fragment of conversation; sometimes that's safe. "Not telling," I say.

He has lowered his head and is resting his nose against a rock. " 'Turn away at the sentence that Isis spoke,' " he intones into the grass.

Oh, shit, I say, with energy, but, of course, not aloud.

His voice has gotten high. "We'd better go now."

I try for a lure. "You were leading. I was following."

But he has already started scrambling to his feet. He's pretty unsteady, and he's awfully close to the edge of the bluff. I get up fast.

As I stand beside him, holding his elbow, I take a last look down at that beach. It is certainly the one he showed us in his pastel picture, with the difference that it contains no body in yellow wrappings. The other people he has talked about weren't in his painting.

So what have I learned here? Not much.

I've seen the beach. My father says it's the one where a murder occurred, and I believe him.

Maybe he knows the person who was killed.

Maybe she told him something.

Maybe she gave him something.

Perhaps he recognized the people who killed her.

We stand together, looking down.

At the far south end of the beach, over by the rocks, there's some kind of a mound. At first I think it's seaweed, but then I see ropelike strands and tell myself no, it's a stack of fisherman's nets. There's a lot of salmon and herring fishing on this coast, and someone has used this cove as a storage point. Or maybe these are nets that need mending or are being abandoned, the equivalent of the derelict machinery strewn about in rural yards. It's hard to see accurately, but I squint and concentrate and decide that the net on the top is brown, the way nets always used to be, but underneath there is distinctly a glimmer of yellow, the same bright nylon yellow that Daddy used in his picture.

Beside me, he has gotten persistent. "I have to get back. I think perhaps I have been careless. I want to be careful with my token. Take me back to my hotel. I am worried, my dear, really somewhat worried."

☐ Chapter 12

I ought to be grateful that Mrs. La Salle is taking such an interest in Daddy.

She shows up nestled into a hand-woven gray tweed shawl, her short white hair topped by a gray velvet hat with mustard trim. I really like her clothes. She's a smashing-looking lady; I'm just resentful of her.

And suspicious of her.

"Whatever he wants to do," she says. "We can go for a walk. We can stay here and listen to music. We can play checkers."

When I mention *Antiques Roadshow*, she says, "Oh, but that's my favorite program. Darling Edward, what *fun* we will have."

I go off to visit Mrs. Sisal, telling myself I must find a way of convincing Mrs. La Salle that Daddy is poor. I've complained to her about prescription bills; I've stressed that I'm working at the Manor because I need money. None of that seems to register.

*   *   *

This will be my third obligatory visit to Mrs. Sisal.

After all, I more or less promised to spy for her. So here I am, pretending I've been doing that.

She greets me, "Well, Miss Day," which maybe is her standard greeting, but this time is delivered with caution and a subliminal message, understood but not voiced: *Well, Miss Day, you were supposed to report to me but so far have reported nothing,* or, *Well, Miss Day, you certainly have a talent for walking into messes.*

"Mrs. Sisal," I say, and sit down.

"That must have been a shock," she says, now aloud, screwing her face into the right mix of distaste and sympathy, since she's talking about how I found Mona. Then she adds, also aloud, all the things you'd expect, and I say back all the things I should, in the meanwhile thinking, *Lady, I'm going to have to start being suspicious of people, asking who's been doing this and who that, and you'd be high on my suspicious list, if only I could think up a good motive for you.* "Mona was dealing drugs," is what I actually tell her aloud, only not quite that flat-out and accompanied by the bland stare that means, *Of course, you've already heard this.*

Which of course she has; she evinces no surprise.

Maybe she knew all along. Maybe she was in on it?

"How is your father?" she asks.

I think at her, *You leave my father out of this. I'm getting hypersensitive about him.* Meanwhile, I'm saying aloud, with my reliable-employee's smile, "Fine. Daddy's fine."

I hope Mrs. Sisal doesn't have ESP. Basic parts of this conversation are being conducted in my head.

On her desk there is a big vase of red hot pokers, supplied, I suppose, by secretary Rebecca. Mrs. S. and I play a dodging back and forth game with our heads around these flowers, trying to look sincerely at each other while we talk. She's hunched in a protective posture in her chair, arms folded over her chest.

We've reached a hiatus in the dialogue. I've finished my report. The residents are upset. They are talking about moving. Everybody says about Mona, "Well, she asked for it, didn't she?" Or something like that. But nobody knows who finally delivered the final neck-twist. Or if they do, they aren't saying.

Mrs. Sisal unkinks her legs, which have been hunched up like the rest of her, and examines the toe of one black Gucci and says, "Well, for God's sake."

And after that, she floors me. "Miss Day," she asks, "What would you do? If you were me?"

For once I don't go off and blatt the first thing that comes into my head, which in this case is, *Are you kidding?* Nor the second, something like: *If I were you, Mrs. Sisal, I think I would move to Juneau, Alaska, and open a nice B and B.* Mrs. S. and I share a moment of contemplative silence while I debate whether she has finally and definitively snapped. But when I eventually speak it's a modified version of, "You are doing just fine." The words *capable* and *aware* and *sympathetic response* get elicited. I listen to myself using them and check them off one by one.

Why, I ask myself, do I continue to butter up Mrs. Sisal? Do Daddy and I really want to stay on in this peculiar haunted establishment? If others can sue and leave, we can do that, too, can't we?

No, I correct myself, we can't. I've got to stick it out here. I've started out to do something, and I'm going to do it.

I half-smile at Mrs. S. I'm actually beginning to feel sorry for her. Which doesn't change the fact that she seems like a good candidate for the title of Spider at the Edge of the Web, the one who waits until a quiver of the string tells her that a fly has landed in her structure of accident and circumstance, after which she races down and paralyzes him.

Motive, opportunity, means, those are the qualifications you're supposed to look for in choosing a crime suspect. The motive—well, in this case, what with the accidents, the motive has to be something about the operation of the Manor. Motive, she's got. And opportunity—she has loads of that. Means is not so good. Means would be a knowledge of how to kill, and Mrs. Sisal doesn't look to me like a neck-breaker. *So you score two out of three,* I think at her.

Whereas you get one hundred percent, I think at Dr. Kittredge when he stops by to go to lunch with me.

I wish I could get a better handle on that motive question. Why all this chaotic mess, like tipping people out of windows? Is someone purposely trying to wreck the Manor? Or idiotically, *publicizing* the place? (So far, no; no news has leaked to the rest of the world.) Getting everybody to leave the Manor? Those accidents must have some simple, cohesive purpose.

"It's tuna casserole for lunch today," I tell him, but he looks at me, one eyebrow elevated, and says, "Dear girl, I have no intention of subjectin' you to this environment one single minute more. We are goin' out, we are goin' to Conestoga, which is ten miles beyond Green Beach and is the county seat, and we'll eat in a real high-cholesterol restaurant with real plastic booths." And he takes me by the hand

and leads me out to the parking lot, to a small green Miata convertible.

I owe Dr. Kittredge one for protecting Daddy from the sheriff. Lunch in Conestoga is okay.

The Miata is a chunky little ostentatious tub with leather seats that cradle your behind and your back. It's small enough that the bulky doctor has to squeeze himself in, inch by inch. "Like gettin' a fat lady through a subway turnstile," he winks at me. He manages to make the process look sexy.

Half-fake and half-not, that sums you up, I think at him as we zip along the coast road with our hair flying.

"Ah, *darlin'*," he yells at me, and I say, "Where did you get that accent?" and he hollers, "From me mum, my darlin'," which doesn't explain why he doesn't lose at least a little bit of it, living and working in California. He sounds like an old movie about the Troubles.

In Bettie's Beach Cafe he commandeers a back booth, red formica and red Naugahyde, and settles in proprietarily to stare at me. "Whatever yer heart desires, sweet one," he says, and I tell him pancakes, and he says, "Good choice," and he himself orders a hamburger and then leans back to sweet-talk Bettie, who arrives wide and blonde and tired. "Your hamburgers are the best on the whole north coast," says he to her. "That's a hamburger made with *love*," at which Bettie comes to, giggling and with a spot of pink on each plump cheek. "A woman who knows what a man *wants*." And so on and so forth. There's nobody but me and Bettie here for him to flirt with, but he makes the two of us seem like a crowd.

"And now," he stops to put ketchup, mustard, onion

slice, and lettuce shred onto his hamburger patty, "now, Goldilocks, what news from Sally Jean?"

I ask, of course, "Who's Sally Jean?" and he says, "Oh, sweetheart, did you not know?" and then fools around with enjoying knowing something I don't. And finally eluci- dates, "That's Sisal's name. Sally Jean Sisal from Tulsa, Ok- lahoma. You'd not suspect it, would you?"

So we do the routine where I say, certainly he knows her better than I do, why ask *me* how she is? I must admit I'm surprised that the S. J. in front of Sisal's name in the Manor catalogue means Sally Jean. I would have thought she'd change it: Serena Jocelyn, Samantha Joy.

"But," I ask Dr. K., "why should I tell you what Mrs. Sisal is up to? Rumor has it you two are an item."

He manages to preen and look pleased and at the same time deny that anything obtains between him and Sally Jean. And I guess it doesn't, not right now at least, because he really wants to know what she and I were talking about. "Kind of a long conversation you had," he says. (How did he know; was he watching the door?) Finally I repeat our bor- ing interview for him, and he doesn't want to believe it. "That's all?" No, he really isn't *in* with her these days. He wishes she'd been circumstantial and told me how she feels and is she scared and what does she plan next for the Manor.

"Ah, well, you're in good with her, Goldilocks," he says, "you played your cards just fine; you are some smart lady."

And he offers more pancakes. Coffee. The coffee is awful. "Tell me about how you went to Egypt," he says unexpect- edly, without preamble. "You were just a kid, was it fun? You're smart, you're literate, are you going to write about it?"

Dr. Kittredge is not one of those people that you can feel straightforwardly one single way about. Here I was starting to get deeply bored with him, and now he asks this question which I've been dying for someone to ask: Can you talk about Egypt? Can you talk about a possible *you* after you leave the Manor? The old ladies are great on questions but they never come up with the right ones. Theirs are more like: Dear, are you getting enough sleep lately?

So I start to tell him about Egypt and then about what I would write about from that time if I were writing it. (And he was bright to mention that, because I guess I'd really like to do that some day.) "The last time we were there I was fourteen, and it seemed hopelessly romantic," I say, "even when it was dusty and hot and we were right in the middle of it. And an experience that you're in the middle of doesn't usually seem that romantic. In Egypt I got to see my father in action. He was different; that was his world, and he even stood differently when he was there. Only a couple of years off from starting his forgetting, but he was still okay. He was fun. He was decisive."

I begin to get excited talking to Dr. Kittredge about this and remembering that trip and thinking about Robbie being along and us at night around our fire and talking about everything with him: math, astronomy, poetry, death. "And Daddy was making notes for his last book," I say. "The fourteen hieroglyphs one."

Dr. Kittredge has ordered ice cream sundaes. He is slurping his and watching me emote. "Yes, dear one," he says. "I read it."

"You read what?"

"Your dad's book."

It's a known fact that no one reads a book called *The Cof-*

fin Lid Texts: Fourteen Hieroglyphs Reclaimed except another Egyptologist. Suddenly I'm cross; I've adjusted myself to too many people lately. I accuse the doctor of lying, and he laughs and says, "Ah. You look great when yer cross."

But when I say, "Jee-sus," he undercuts me by asking, "An' why should ya assume that all a doctor has is his med degree? He's got to think about other things, am I right?"

"Okay," I tell him, not the least bit convinced.

Dr. Kittredge, I am thinking, *you are under suspicion; I suspect you of everything, I suspect everybody of everything. But, come to think of it, where were you when Mona's neck was broken? They had to go looking for you, and no one ever told me where you were found, and who would be better than a doctor at neck-snapping?*

". . . back in med school," Dr. Kittredge is saying. "A hobby of mine. I had a girlfriend who was crazy about that whole ancient Egyptian scene. I read about Ramesses III in between doing gall bladders. It's interesting; there's a characteristic odor that goes with . . ."

I tell him, "Okay, *okay*," and he goes, "Sorry, baby," with a special smile that means he did that on purpose, and then he tells me, "So I knew about your dad before he ever got here. He's a very challenging man.

"Now, dear, you put that ice cream away all right, how about another one?"

This doctor is obnoxious; I'm right to be suspicious of him. And of everybody else in the Manor; Sisal, Daddy's aides Belle and Kellee, Rebecca the secretary, even my darling cross and peculiar old ladies. I'm suspicious of every single one of them. I wish there were somebody here who was smart and funny, and I didn't have to feel wary of them.

The doctor is back now into talking about Daddy, about

just how daffy he is. (He uses the term *confused*.) Is it constant? Does it come and go? Affected by diet, temperature, phases of the moon? He pushes a bit on this. Have I seen signs that, if Dr. Day's memory were tweaked a little, is there any chance that some memory would . . .

I get mad. "Don't talk like that. That's a human being, my father, not some damn computer that you can stick a paper clip into, don't you even think about *tweaking*."

And right away he's apologetic, "I didn't mean really . . . sweetheart, goddamn, no, I'm just interested in the mechanisms of memory, how it all works, speculating on what *you've* observed; you're a damn good observer, y'know?"

"Quit speculating."

"Oh, dear, we, that is we doctors, know so damn little." Delivered with a big dose of aw-shucks charm.

Damn right, you know so little. And lay off it about my father, everybody in the world is interested in him. "Hey," I say, "you've got *other* Alzheimer's patients."

All in all, Dr. Kittredge has proved to be an irritating lunch companion and has moved to first place in my list of people to feel edgy about. But just the same I have to stop myself, as we climb back into the Miata, from confiding in him about thinking Daddy's at the center of all the action lately. I open my mouth to talk about this and, mouth half-open, think better of it, and don't.

🐦 Chapter 13

Mrs. La Salle decides just from looking at me that I'm worrying too much. She stops me at the door to the dining room and caresses my wrist with a small manicured finger. "We've decided you need an escape. And so does Ed."

"My father has an escape. He escapes into himself."

She shakes her head, the one amethyst earring catching the light. "He needs to get away. We've discussed it."

We is the trio—Daddy's fan club of herself, Mrs. Cohen, and Mrs. Dexter. "You shall have dinner out," she proclaims. "Someplace away, far from all this." A wave of her hand takes in the Manor scene—the sheriff's interviewing team, still camped in the main lounge, the yellow tape scraps still dangling around the garden, the luggage in the main hall waiting for departing residents.

"Justine's Restaurant," she says. "On the highway. Very elegant. I can get a reservation. I know many of the people in restaurants. From my gossip column."

I agree, "Yes," remembering Mrs. La Salle's glamorous past. But I tell her I'm not sure about this; I better think about it. Daddy's and my last attempt at a party didn't turn out too well, did it? Then I catch a wave of high-pitched sound from the lobby—irritated voices, luggage scrape, wheeled suitcase squeak—and after that another, different wave, this one of dining-room smell, not exactly bad, just starchy-bland, mashed potatoes and a whiff of that kind of gravy that stands up all by itself, and I think, *Gourmet restaurant—classic food, deft, assiduous waiters—it's been a long, long time. All the way back to Egypt, maybe.* So I tell Mrs. La Salle yes, gourmet restaurant sounds great.

We set out toward Justine's in a gray-and-yellow van. The ladies are excited by this ride, and so is my father. A little too excited. He clutches my hand and says, "Many wrongs will be righted."

I just tell him okay. I don't want to start a long conversation for the old ladies to listen to.

"I received another e-mail," he says, and I agree, "Okay," again, wondering, *E-mail, where did he even pick up the term?*

"No secrets in the back," Mrs. Dexter snaps in our direction.

The cab belongs to someone named Henry, a potbellied gentleman in a checked shirt and beard, who tells us our outing is "A-OK. Good for you, get out and see the world," although he thinks we should go to the Supersteak at the Conestoga Best Western. "This Justine's has a real snooty reputation." But he's cheerful about pointing out sights: "Over there's where the seals come." "There's where some

English explorer discovered something. They left a sign, some kind of brass sign."

My father is interested in the brass sign. He tries to stick his head out the too-small window to see.

Justine's perches on a cliff out of sight of the highway and over an intensely blue Pacific; it's a Neanderthal-Modern building with a white cement front spotted by oval portholes. Henry is astonished, "Jeez Louise, looks like the women's facility at Santa Rita. You'd think a snooty place would do better about how it looks, huh?"

Inside, an austere lobby stretches out, green glass on two sides, a hall where fish swim irritatedly back and forth behind pebbled walls. My father moves close, muttering something that sounds like "The horns of water."

"I have a duty," he says. I'm alarmed and reach for his hand, but he's okay. As we walk farther along, he stops to admire and tap and comment on a whiskered fish, "A scavenger, you know. Entirely necessary for the balance of their city, you know."

Beyond the lobby, the restaurant opens in a long prospect of thick white plaster and recessed alcoves with occasional lights and clumps of people.

The whole thing looks like a spread from *Architectural Digest*—some Saudi Prince's new scatter on an island off the coast of Africa, where, the caption says, "The integrity of the fabric resists the encroachment of the terrain," meaning that the inside of the building is as different as possible from whatever is outside. At Justine's the outside shows up only down at the far end of the room, where three large windows open onto a wild marine view: miles and acres of blue water and u-shaped huddles of cliffs, overwhelming, but hard to see because the windows are so deep.

Mrs. Dexter squints into the restaurant and says, "Good God." Mrs. Cohen squeaks, "*Intriguing*." Mrs. La Salle calmly offers that, "The architect is famous, you know," and Mrs. Dexter thumps the walker, "They always try to *confuse* things."

My father seems interested but maybe a little alarmed. He touches me on the arm. "It reminds me of something. What would that be?"

I don't say that I know what it reminds him of, but I do know. The inside of this building reminds him of a tomb. An old empty one. The kind we used to joke about, back in the Valley of the Kings, joking especially loudly if the place was spooky or damp or funny-colored, maybe green or that wavery acid blue. Robbie and I were way too cool to say *haunted*, but I at least half-thought it.

I have my eye on those three window tables and am planning to ask in my most winning way if, possibly, we can sit there, when the hostess tells us to, "Follow me," and, surprise, it *is* a window table she leads us to. Before we sit, I stop at the window to stare down and marvel at the direct drop, straight along the side of the building into a boiling ocean. Our table is the best one in the house; someone, Mrs. La Salle I guess, has tipped management a lot. Mrs. La Salle, with her on-target elegance, projects *rich*. Most of the Manor ladies project *comfortable—once*.

The hostess smiles her struck-dumb hostess smile; she has a lot of wiry curls scooped to one side and held up by airplane glue. "My dear," my father tells her, "you look like an houri." She blinks twice; I'll bet that's a new one. Now she'll have to go home and look up *houri* on the internet.

Houris are beautiful virgins of the Koranic Paradise. I want to get Daddy away from these Egyptian associations, so I change the subject by spreading out his leather-bound menu and handing it to him, "Look, purple writing." And this works. "Of course, my dear," he says, "purple; in all the best hotels it's always purple. I have forgotten the name of this hotel but that's all right. . . . The purple writing," he tells Mrs. Dexter, "is known as a hectograph process."

"An' damn messy it was, too," Mrs. Dexter agrees.

So my father lectures about hectograph, and Mrs. Dexter and Mrs. Cohen reminisce about getting hectograph all over your hands. And Daddy turns the crinkly pages of his menu, and although he looks kind of lost, we're getting into the spirit of things. Mrs. Cohen says, reading the purple French, "*Homard*, that's lobster, *n'est-ce pas*? Oh, my, lobster would be so wonderful, let's all have lobster."

And Mrs. La Salle goes, "And a wine, white, very dry, two bottles," and Mrs. Dexter asks if two bottles will be enough, and everyone thinks that's hilariously funny.

So I decide, okay; he's forgotten about e-mails, this is going to be a happy outing after all.

Of course, the ladies need to talk Manor gossip. "Mr. Rice is leaving," Mrs. La Salle says, and, "No, I beg your pardon; he isn't," Mrs. Cohen says, and finally they're down to some conversation about Mona, where I marvel again that nobody takes her murder seriously. Mona has become a historical figure, as if she had died a hundred years ago. "She had a false cupboard full of addictive substances," Mrs. Cohen announces. Apparently that's safe to say since nobody jumps or looks scared. I guess no one here is an addict.

Mrs. Dexter talks a little about her childhood in these parts. "A beautiful place? I suppose so. Children don't think about beautiful. Children think about each other. About their families. About whom they hate."

Mrs. Cohen giggles. "Louise, you're being bad."

My father has been edgy ever since we came in; now he's doing it again. He stares at the window and then back into the dining room. "Perhaps there was something over there?" he gestures into the receding set of white alcoves.

Yes, I think. Maybe in a different time, a different country.

The alcoves look like the abandoned tomb of the merchant Intep. Intep's was the tomb next to our coffin-text one; it had recesses like these and that same heavy, hangs-over-you feeling. The tomb was empty; it had been stripped of treasure two thousand years ago. But very faintly on the walls you could see where the painter had inscribed part of the *Declaration of Innocence*: "I have not caused pain. I have not made to weep." You didn't usually put thoughts like that on your tomb wall; usually you had pictures of your happy life in the world, drinking wine, hunting birds on the Nile. "Poor chap must have had a guilty conscience," Daddy had said as he deciphered the hieroglyphs.

The ladies are now on the subject of Mona's childhood, which they're guessing was unhappy.

My father is watching the window. "Is there," he asks, "a beach down there?"

Several voices tell him, "Sure," and "I guess."

"If someone could have stopped something and didn't and they have regret for it afterwards . . ." he begins.

These ladies are really sweet. That proposition must seem to come out of nowhere, but they can still be comforting about it. Mrs. Cohen pats his hand, "We just can't tell, can we?" Mrs. Dexter says, "Everyone always wonders."

He says, "What I'm thinking is, the *Declaration of Innocence*."

I think, *Oh, God, the Declaration of Innocence*. And, of course, the guilty conscience. I try to send *stop* and *quit* mental messages at him. Don't rehash it. Please. What could you have done? If you were up on the bluff and it was happening down on the beach?

Our time waiting for lobster is occupied eating dabs of food on gold-rimmed plates. My father continues staring at the window, a wide arced expanse of glass that begins at waist height and stretches two tables across. "Let's open it," he tells the waiter.

"Oh, I can't, sir. Here's your wine sorbet, sir."

"It doesn't open?"

This waiter, in his tux and black pants, looks generically continental, but when he talks he's more Central Valley. "Well only to wash it, sir, swivels out, kinda, hard to manage, practically takes an engineering degree." He hands Daddy a dish of tan-colored ice, "Here's to cleanse the palate, sir."

"Amazing," says my father.

I start playing with the gold-rimmed dishes and then with the silver candleholder, and discover that I can see the whole restaurant in the shiny candleholder surface. The room in the candleholder appears long and wobbly, stretched in the middle and disappearing at the edges, with white tables and a low, rounded Moorish ceiling. That skinny place in the middle is an attenuated front door.

"I don't care about her unhappy childhood," Mrs. La Salle is saying, "she was a *bitch*." She pronounces the word precisely, as if it's one she appreciates.

Daddy is still dividing his time between the room,

which he doesn't like, and the view, which he wants to watch. I move to see it, but with the window starting at waist height the view is mostly sky; just a line of horizon, and then the sweep of heaven where the sun is squat and fat and getting lower.

Mrs. La Salle is saying that there's a reason for the split between Mona's visible smarmy personality and her underlying evil scheming one; people with an ego split have a recognizable psychic illness, and Mrs. Cohen says, "Oh, tell me, Daphne, you're so informed," and I return to my candleholder where there is somebody in a blue dress gesticulating and crossing the room, and now someone with red hair, coming from the opposite direction, wobbling because the reflective surface is bumpy. And now arrives the hostess, undulating away, recognizable because of her scrambled hairdo. And finally . . . I stop here. I call a halt. I simply won't start the game of recognizing old friends in this mirror. But, yes, there is a man now, waiting over by the door, who looks familiar. How silly to think you can identify someone reflected in a candleholder, but just the same I do recognize him.

"The sun is getting ready to depart; I need to speak to her," says my father. He's right about the sun; I can feel over my left shoulder that the sky is growing very deeply crimson.

Now there's a chorus of gasps from my table mates; the lobsters have arrived, paraded home by a matched pair of busboys. "How totally gorgeous," Mrs. Cohen exhales and, "Well, I do love all the nonsense." That's Mrs. Dexter.

I leave my candleholder. I am firm with myself. Quit being silly; quit pretending you're the Lady of Shallot or some damn stupid thing. How often lately do you get to eat lobster?

There's a several-minute hiatus while napkins are arranged and silverware jostles. Mrs. Cohen says, "You know, I never could do this when I was a child. Because of the dietary laws," and Mrs. La Salle tells her that those Old Testament rules are admirable, entirely sensible.

I am fussing with lobster claws. Pretty soon I have broached the small claw and eaten the meat out of it. And that, I decide, makes it okay for me to sneak a sideways peek into my magic mirror.

The person I think I know is crossing the restaurant. Over my shoulder the sky has gotten a deeper red.

Now the figure is circling in my mirror, and the walk is definitely familiar. There he goes, led by the hostess, into a cubicle at the edge of my view. I don't think he sees me. If he did he'd be here in a minute; there's nothing subtle about him. *Him* of course being Rob, in case you hadn't guessed. And it *is* Rob; he goes into a cubicle, and there's someone with him. You don't come to a place like this alone.

If I want to put an end to this childish mirror-watching, all I have to do is get up and speak to him. That'll be a perfectly straightforward, ordinary encounter. "Hi, Rob." "Well, *hi*, Carly." "Hey, *you*." "Well, hey, yourself." Anticlimax times ten.

He's here with a date, and I am here with my father and three old ladies.

I won't let Robbie feel sorry for me. I'll wait before I speak to him. Maybe I'll never speak.

The ladies have moved from discussing Mona to debating eternity and God. People talk like that over wine and lobster. Mrs. La Salle says, "No, Louise, it's not that there aren't atheists in foxholes . . ." and Mrs. Dexter says, "If I were in a foxhole, I'd show you an atheist, all right."

My father isn't eating his lobster; his eyes are glued on the window where the sun, enormous now, is spreading itself, ready to flatten, which is what it does just before it sets. The setting of the sun in the Egyptian religion equals the descent of Re, sent underground for his dangerous journey. "Don't stare right at it, Father."

He's rapt, not moving a muscle. I don't like this much. "Daddy?"

It does something to your retina, I've read about that; fries it. Maybe I should tap him on the shoulder.

"Why, dear." He smiles his chairman's smile but keeps on looking past my shoulder as if I'm not there.

I sit back and examine my hands, my napkin, my fingernails, and a spot on the knee of my good black pants. Mrs. Dexter is saying, "What makes it interesting, we're the only species with the foresight of death."

Mrs. La Salle talks about Heraclitus and something about the sweet and the bittersweet. Mrs. Dexter moves the walker an inch, for emphasis maybe, she says, "Daphne, now, you must listen . . ."

I can feel with the side of my face that Robbie is just a couple of dozen feet away. Maybe I should simply turn and smile, straightforward, nothing to it.

"But death is a going over," Mrs. Cohen is saying, "a translation, a passing into the next stage of life . . ."

From some place near me, maybe right beside me, yes, from my father; he's the one that's doing it—there's a scream, a skull-splitting shriek, a gargling, ferocious noise wrenched from stomach, lungs, throat, gut, to make you grab for your chest, put your hands over your ears. Voices say, "My God," "Where is it?" "What?" and "Who?" A glass clangs, sets of plates crash, a metal stand collapses. And Edward Day, screaming, is on the window ledge. He has somehow, without fuss or muss, in an instant, got the magic window open and is trying to climb out of it into the setting sun.

This window opens onto nothing at all. Below it is one hundred and fifty feet of building side, cliff side, rocks, then ocean.

Carla, for God's sake, for *God*'s sake, get up, don't just sit there.

He has one knee up on the white cement casement sill; his head is out, his body bent, he has kicked over his wineglass, pushed his lobster plate onto the floor. What is he saying? Words. I can understand them; "Tell her . . . I'm supposed to . . . help."

And I'm beside him now, which has happened in one motion without my thinking. I'm on one side, and somebody else is on the other side. I can feel that other person though I don't really look, only with the side of my vision; there's a dark jacket and an arm, and my father is half out the window, knee flexed, body bent, rock him the wrong way and the whole man goes end over end into the view.

"Careful, careful."

"There, darling, there."

"I did not help," he is saying.

It's only the setting sun, a brilliant red streak across the black of the blackened mind. Life, strength, force, reason, and all those things you've lost. "Watch it. Slow . . ."

"Careful . . . he's a lot stronger than he looks."

"Without scaring . . . try it without scaring him."

"Watch out, don't tip that way. Back . . ."

My God, for a minute there I thought he was going through, tipping and teetering, old fragile kneecap on rough white sill, old man balanced insecurely like a toy. *Oh, Jesus.*

The sun is almost gone now, and there's nothing left except a purple glow and that green streak they talk about. Then careful and slow, let's get him back down without catching his arm. He's coming willingly, maybe he's a little scared, looking down into that vastness and the sea blue and hard and the rocks brown and hard.

We pull him in slowly, his shoulders still partly out the window and one shoe catching on something. We push the table back. There, now. Sit down. Gently, gently. It's all right, dear, really it is.

Rob says, "Dr. Day? It's Robbie. Hey, now, it's me, Dr. Day. Robbie Ackroyd."

Out in Justine's parking lot a small crowd of subdued people has collected. First of all the Manor ladies, then Justine's hostess dabbing at her makeup with a restaurant napkin, then Rob and his girlfriend and Henry the cabdriver, his bearded face screwed into a question, and finally Daddy and me, with my father the most subdued of us all. Cabdriver Henry is patting him on the shoulder, saying, "Heard about the mess in there, good thing you had me wait, not the right place for you people, I coulda told ya." Daddy is shaking his head. He looks puzzled. The hostess says to me,

"You're sure now?" and I say, "We'll just take the cab home."

The hostess is worried that something happened in the restaurant—a rat or a bat or a cockroach—to make my father behave like that. I let her think this.

Daddy tries to tell her that he had an e-mail. He says, "E-mail," and she says, "Oh, don't do that."

Rob and I have had a six-sentence conversation in the lobby. Now he tells my father, "Ed, I certainly would like to take you back and examine you."

I stare. I'd sort of forgotten that Rob is a doctor.

Daddy says, "That is so good of you. But not at all."

Rob's girlfriend sticks her hand out. "Hi. I'm Arlette."

Henry says, "Hey, everybody almost ready?" Unlikely as it seems, our outing is going to end as it began, with a quiet taxi ride. Henry will probably point out some new shoreline sights.

Rob asks am I sure? And I say, yes, yes, and he says, "I'll come with you," and I say, "It's all right now," and he tells me he'll see me tomorrow. Meanwhile, the ladies start piling up into the cab. My father shakes his head. "Carla, I must have left something in that restaurant." That's the way he looks, a little troubled, the way you are when you think you've lost that ad you were saving for the shopping expedition tomorrow.

I tell him, "No, Father, I'm sure you haven't," and he says, "Well, now, if you're sure, my dear, you always seem to know, and I will once again sit all the way in the back," and he's up the van steps and has started wiggling past the middle seats.

I say, "Robbie, thank you." I remember to tell Arlette it

is good to meet her. I look up into the cab after my father who seems okay, just a little bit, I suppose you'd say, quenched. I thank Rob one time more and climb up the van steps after my dad.

♔ Chapter 14

"Carly, if you've been here for a month, why didn't you call me a month ago?"

It's the day after the Justine's Restaurant evening, and Robbie and I are in the Manor garden, bench-sitting near the mermaid statue.

"I don't know," I say sullenly, staring down at my hands as if I'm eight years old.

Actually, I do know pretty well why I didn't call him.

"Carla," he says, "we're friends. Good friends. You're my *oldest* friend."

Oh, Robbie, go climb a tree.

The Manor old ladies are very excited about the lovely young man who appeared out of nowhere to help me last night. Mrs. Cohen says, "I recognized him, dear, did you know that? He was our doctor last summer when Dr. Kittredge was away. So young and energetic, I thought then.

Just what you've been needing. And you can tell, that little person with him, she doesn't mean a thing."

Mrs. Cohen, darling, climb the other tree.

"Maybe," I tell Robbie now, "I expected Susie to tell you. About my being here."

"Well, she didn't."

Rob is just the same, hardly any older, still sturdy and energetic, with slightly broader shoulders and lots of wavy brown hair. He's a little taller than me. He doesn't like to sit still. Right now he's scuffing a foot back and forth, tracing patterns in the pink dust of the mermaid path. "How long has Ed been like this?"

"It's worse lately."

"Well, listen, I'm really, really sorry, and it's awful to see him this way, and I'll go do a lot of research. Maybe there's something they haven't been trying." Rob's field isn't Aging or Alzheimer's or anything even remotely like that; he's an intern in tropical medicine because he wants to return to Egypt and do good for the populace. You wouldn't think they'd have a tropical medicine clinic at North Coast Hospital, but they do because of the workers who come up from Central America to pick artichokes and lettuce and asparagus in our farm fields.

"None of that medicine will help," I say. "I know because I've been researching, too. Come on, Rob, let's go for a walk." I take his hand and think, sixteen hours he's back into my life and he's already revising it.

Daddy is fine today; right now he's taking a nap. He doesn't seem to remember anything bad about last night. This morning he was cheerful, welcoming Robbie. "Hello there. We really know you're one of us when we see you looking like that, don't we? Now, the name's on the tip of my tongue." He was okay about letting Rob listen to his chest and thump his back, and during lunch he was so relaxed and funny that I think if Rob hadn't seen him last night he would have been telling me, "Carly, nothing much is wrong with him; that's just normal fatigue, not Alzheimer's. All old people are like that."

Rob and I start walking, hand in hand like the good friends we're supposed to be; I'm leading him along the nonscenic route, past the Manor garbage cans. I want to show him the net-woman beach. I've told him the story about that; I've told him most of our stories, and he's been horrified and says we've got to move. And doesn't remember about the lifetime clause and the full lifetime payment to the Manor and says, forget about that, you have to move anyway. Rob likes to take charge.

We approach Daddy's beach by walking along the top of the culvert; I've decided Rob is too broad to squeeze through the inside. So we scramble precariously over the top and then through the weeds and bushes and finally down into Daddy's viewing place where we're in a standing position, not lying on our bellies the way Daddy and I were.

Rob says, "Wow," and "Uh-huh," and "Yeah, I see, yeah, I get it."

The beach looks the same except that the tide is halfway out and the pile of nets is smaller. "It's funny," I say, "I'm getting used to thinking he saw something here, and now I can start asking questions, like, *why* was he here at all? How did he know there would be anything *to* see? There are the steps where he says the people came down." I point to the north end of the beach and the ragged seacoast structure of sagging steps and rickety balustrades. "He knew they were coming; he'd been observing for a while.

"And, Rob, he keeps repeating about secrecy. Or not talking. Except that last night he thought he had to talk. He said he got an e-mail."

"E-mail?" Rob asks. Both of us are silent for a minute, chasing the idea *e-mail*. What does Edward think that is?

"Existential-mail," I suggest, and, "Evaporating mail," Rob counters.

We waste some time giggling and telling each other how funny we are.

One of our local long-legged hares pops out of the bushes and looks at us, standing on his rear legs like a kangaroo. Rob knows the scientific name of the breed: *Lepus townsendii*.

He then offers the opinion, which irks me, that most of my dad's vagueness is Alzheimer's. Of course I knew that. I act cross. Rob says, "And furthermore . . . furthermore . . . well, you know that, too."

So I have to persuade him. "What, already?"

After a minute's silence he says, "Know what the big question is, Carly, the big, big question?"

I tell him no.

Robbie's single-mindedness seems conceited sometimes, but that's not accurate. It's more that he jumps on his horse and rides enthusiastically off in whatever direction he sees at the moment.

He waves an arm around. "If they wrapped somebody in a net until she stopped wriggling, where is she? Where's the body?"

I point. "In the ocean. They dumped her."

"Okay, right, sometime she'll wash up. But meanwhile, somebody is missing. Her relatives are looking. She's on a list someplace."

I say, "Ye-ah," trying not to sound too contemplative. *Estupida*, I tell myself. Not believing Daddy's story kept me from getting this far in thinking about it.

We're silent for a couple of heartbeats, and then I say, "Probably someone from around here."

"Most likely."

"Daddy does seem to sort of know her. He saw her, and he watched them going through the Manor grounds, and he sort of followed—he's good at that little boy stuff, hiding and peering . . ." This fantasy begins to trickle away, and I say, "Or something," and sit in the weeds where Rob has already hunkered down and is unwrapping a protein bar, which he hands me half of. "Apricot flavor," he explains.

"Who's Arlette?" I ask. It's Arlette from last night that I'm asking about, and I mean, of course, what sort of a person is she; does she like Yo-Yo Ma and *The Sopranos*; where did you get her? He tells me, all enthusiasm, that Arlette is a great girl, smart and, well, *simpatico*, "You're going to love her." I look sideways to see if he's being ironic, and he isn't; his square face is flushed with pleasure.

There's a brief pause, after which he changes the subject, "I came by here to see Ed three times since your aunt moved him in. Did he say anything?"

"I'm not sure. Maybe." After a minute I add, "That shows how he's not such a great witness; a couple of times when he talked about a nice young man who went to Egypt. I guess maybe he was telling me he'd seen you and I didn't catch on."

"Lately, he has a new one," I add. "He's started talking about his token. 'I have my token. Through all this I kept my token.' What's a token?"

Rob says a token is whatever you want it to be. Like a sign. Or a word. Something that stands in for something else. "A bus token is a stand-in for money."

I want to tell him he sounds like my philosophy book, but I know he's trying to be helpful. Instead I say, "I'll get my old ladies on about the missing woman; they'll love snooping around," and right away feel guilty calling the trio the old ladies and talking about them snooping; they're my good friends whom I like and who've helped me ever since I arrived here. So I make up for being mean about them by being mean to Robbie. "We've wasted all afternoon, let's get going."

Yes, he and I are back to normal; each of us wants to pilot the plane. I take his hand and squeeze it for apology and think, *Oh, hell*.

The rest of the week has various ups and downs.

I start inquiries about the net-woman. Here I run into a brick wall at first. Everyone knows my father's beach-murder story and thinks it's Alzheimer's. Even Mrs. Dexter, whom I tried to persuade that it was real. "Oh, but we can't take that tale of his seriously?"

And then, after pressure from me, they do begin to take it seriously. "You mean it was *real*? That scene he painted? How awful. Dear, what makes you think so?"

"Just because his picture was so specific? Oh, you've seen the place? And he's been talking about it, too? A lot? Oh, poor Ed. Poor you. How awful. So gruesome. Wrapped in gold cord. Yes, strange, terrible."

"But, darling, do you *really* think so?"

I partly—or maybe mostly—convince them.

Mrs. La Salle is the only one who continues unpersuaded. "It's such a standard fantasy. Legendary. All those Greek stories with the woman tied up at the water's edge, an offering for the sea god." She touches her feathered white hair.

For some reason I ask her about e-mails. "What's an e-mail?" I ask.

"E-mail." She seems to welcome the question. "E-mail is magic. The air must be warm with those things." She makes a flapping motion, as if she's swatting flies.

"Is that what my father thinks?"

"Ed? Does he think about e-mail?" She stares at my face for a minute. "Ed's probably afraid of them. I understand your father very well, you know."

"Did you send him an e-mail?"

Her tone so far has been bantering, but she now sounds cross. "Why, Carla, of course not."

Daddy's net-woman problem becomes something for the ladies to do. A topic to check back and forth on. Has anyone left the Manor suddenly? Gone for a trip and not written? Even Mrs. La Salle, who is extra dubious, starts searching. "Truly, I think that story is Alzheimer's. But yes, I'll ask around." Mrs. Dexter is great; she's like a little terrier, ears up, nose down. She chases down staff members who've quit or been fired, and she racks up a nice fat phone bill, which she won't discuss with me. "It's interesting, and what else can you do parked in front of a walker?"

Rob buys me a cell phone, with six months' of calls paid up in advance. At first I tell him, "No, absolutely not, too expensive," and he says, "You got to," and I say, "I haven't got to anything." We carry on this way for a while with me emoting into the standup public phone in the hall until I realize that several entranced old ladies are listening. Robbie tells me, "Carla, honey, it's a gift of love."

So I accept. Actually I like the phone a lot. It's a black clamshell-type and feels good when you hold it.

Of course, the first person who calls is Rob himself. "Hi, how are you? How's Ed? Listen, I've been reading up some more on Alzheimer's and about that excitation he had in the restaurant, the way he carried on and tried to get out the window. I think his problem is two different things, one is memory and the other is chemistry, but interdependent, you understand, interlocked and related. Did you know there are plateaus, times when the patient just stays the same for months? Then sometimes he goes back, gets better. And in Germany, they've been using special drugs that jack you up—make you a *lot* better for a while. But these may be dangerous. Fascinating stuff. Wow, what a lot of info, more than three thousand items; my mouse-hand went numb."

My old ladies telephone, even though they're just a few feet away and could yell their greetings if they wanted to. All of them love telephoning. "Hello, Carly, how are you today? You know, I heard, and it may not amount to anything, that there's a woman over in South Building hasn't heard from her cousin . . ."

Mrs. Cohen has met a lady whose brother visited a month ago. But since then he hasn't written and hasn't called; the lady is very worried. "Now I know Ed thought it was a woman, *however*, we hear so much about false memory and altered perceptions, and I just think it would be so very interesting if it turned out to be a man instead of, as far as

Ed's memory of it went . . ." The lady with the brother is named Mrs. Goliard; I take her phone number.

"Oh," Mrs. Cohen adds, "she's the one that went out the window. I don't think that figures, do you?"

Mrs. Dexter has been talking to Rebecca, Mrs. Sisal's secretary, who tells her that someone named Idora left the office a month ago and hasn't been heard from since. "Not that I'd be heard from, either, if I'd worked for that Sisal woman," Mrs. Dexter says. "But she *is* a Disappeared, and they seem to have hired her without any records. I think you should check."

Also, Arlette telephones. Robbie's girlfriend, Arlette. She has a message for Robbie and thinks maybe he's here with me. The fact that Arlette looks for Robbie at my new phone number cheers me up a lot. I am, I tell myself, really mean.

Daddy wonders if I can call Cairo on my new telephone, so I do. He asks the operator, in Arabic, what time it is, and gets told, in English, that it's two o'clock in the morning. Then he holds the phone against my ear and tells me, "Carly, this is absolutely wonderful, isn't it?"

He plays with the phone for a minute, flipping and unflipping it. "It reminds me of something. What would that be?"

I think my father is a little better these last few weeks. Asking me what something reminds him of is a sign of this; the buried messages are crowding closer, trying to poke their snouts out.

I settle down into some new detective work, which gets me nowhere. First, I try some chasing and tracing with the secretarial agency that sent Idora. I call her former employer, the Portland Chamber of Commerce, after that I move on to Pacific Bell's World Wide Information Service, and finally I'm calling Idora's sister, who says, yes, of course she's heard from Idora, Idora is having a great time with her new boyfriend. They are in Bermuda now, why am I asking?

Mrs. Goliard is the lady with the missing brother. She lives at the far end of the Manor, so I call her but to no avail; she has birdcalls from three different birds tweeting at you for her answering message. Her own voice comes on the tape afterwards to say what kinds of birds they are, but they all sound alike to me. I leave her a message.

All this time people are packing up and leaving the Manor. The hall is full of their stacked-up luggage.

Mr. Rice on my corridor is going. "But it's not your fault," he says, "you really tried." I'm touched by Mr. Rice's compliment, since he's been the most complaining of my clients. "You helped," Mr. Rice says, "you and Belle. You two were responsible. You listened to my concerns."

None of my trio of special old ladies is leaving. "It's much too interesting here," Mrs. Cohen says. Mrs. Dexter tells her it's damn boring, if you must know, but she'll leave only when she feels like it. Mrs. La Salle just shrugs and says, "What for?" She has come around to take Daddy for a walk. "I'm not afraid of falling out a window," she says, and pulls her fur hat down over one ear. Her white hair fluffs out on the other side. "I'm not troubled much by fear."

It's funny how, in a time of tension, you can have periods of feeling good, thinking life is almost normal. So I'm not prepared when I discover that my room has been trashed.

It takes me a minute to get it, to understand. I stand at the half-open door.

I do a double, then triple take. This doesn't make sense. What happened?

The place is a mess.

Clothes on the floor.

Hand-lotion bottle on the floor, uncapped, big puddle, perfume smell, other smells.

Broken mirror shards, glinting and reflecting, bits of china, mascara, lipstick, ripped-up underpants, unfurled rolls of toilet paper.

Upside-down dresser drawers, rug in a heap, books, pages ripped out.

Scattered papers, letters, newspaper, magazines.

Something's on the bed, lodged high in a hill of bed-clothes.

A heaped-up bundle, red stains on it.

I don't want to see this.

I'm going to back out of here, close the door.

I don't back out, I cross the room to the bed and the heap of blanket and sheet.

The sheets are red-smeared, like butcher paper. I pull them down.

There's more red; it smears my hands. Inside is some-thing. A red slimy object.

It's not meat exactly. It's an object. An animal.

I have trouble thinking. You saw a lot of animals when you worked in the animal lab, Carla. Never one like this.

But you know what it is. You've seen something like it. At the butcher shop. Something red and bare. With the skin pulled off. This is an animal that has been skinned. All the natural, expected covering peeled away except at the head and the paws.

The head is how I know what it is. Was. It's one of our hares, those long-legged guys, scared eyes and upstanding ears. The ones that hung out in the meadow or near the mermaid statue.

I pull the sheet completely off. Here it is. A body: red, oozing, muscles outlined. When the sheet moves over it a muscle twitches.

That can happen after death. I know that's true. A latent reaction. It doesn't mean the animal's still alive.

I tell myself this several times.

But that doesn't work, and finally I have to do it. I don't want to. But I have to. If there's a chance this creature is still alive. I act fast. I put a hand at the back of its neck, grip firmly around flesh, bone, bloody fur collar, bend the head back, firmly, sudden, hard. And snap.

Clouded brown eyes are staring at the wall. Surely you were dead anyway. You were dead, and you couldn't feel. There's a prayer for this. I can't say the prayer. Something about *Go in beauty*, or some crap like that.

I sit down on the floor. I'm crying hard, but I manage to pull my phone out of my pants pocket and call Rob. I leave sticky smears all over the push buttons.

"I can't stand it," I tell Rob. "I don't want any lunch." He and I are sitting in the weeds at the far border of the Manor grounds, right next to the highway, which is a quiet thoroughfare, with a car only every ten minutes.

Rob says. "You need lunch."

I pick up a sandwich and pry it open and look at the filling. "What do they want? For me to get scared and get out of here?"

"Maybe."

"For me to stop poking my nose into things?"

"Very likely."

"Why should they care? I haven't found out a single thing. Just . . . nothing."

"Carla, you have to leave the Manor."

"I'm not leaving."

"You've got to."

"I'm not. They can't make me."

"The person who did that is crazy. Deranged. Dangerous."

"And wants to scare me."

"Yeah. You better be scared."

"I won't be scared. I'm not going."

"Be sensible."

"No." I can hear myself being unreasonable. I can feel my inner me doing a weird set of parallels: My mother went away. She got scared off. She was a quitter. Now my father's going off someplace. A place very far away and unreachable. He's scared; he's backing off, afraid of life. He's quitting. Not me.

"They can't force me," I tell Rob. "I'm staying."

"And subjecting your dad?"

"He'd want to stay . . . if he could understand."

"Oh, for God's sake."

"I'm just starting to get some answers. All kinds of little pointers. One of them will pan out. That's what they're afraid of, one of the things I'm turning up being real."

Rob says, "Oh, for God's sake," again.

"I have to stay. You can understand."

"I understand you're being stupidly stubborn."

There's a pause. I say, "I keep hoping it wasn't still alive."

Rob says, "Huh?" and I say, "The rabbit."

And he corrects me, "Hare."

A car comes along the road and pauses. Children in the backseat are waving.

Rob has called the sheriff, who is waiting for me at the door to my room when I get back.

"Well," says Sheriff Hawthorne. "Big mess. Don't touch anything. We'll fingerprint."

He surveys me. I can't decide whether his gaze is accusing, inquiring, or maybe triumphant. (You got into more trouble, like I knew you would. You had to come to me.) He's chewing gum. "Come on down to my office."

He is still in his tapestry-paneled hidey-hole down the hall from Mrs. Sisal. It's clearly his office now, with stacks of papers, green-and-tan boxes. A bosomy lady cop clutching a notebook shares it with him.

The sheriff tips back his desk chair and stares at me some more. "So why'd they do this to you?"

I debate being smart-alecky. *They don't like me.* Or just dumb: *I don't know.* I debate confiding my father's net-woman story. Then I think again about having my father questioned. This sheriff has been okay so far, but with those slit eyes and those midwestern-dentist practical glasses and that set to his chin, I don't trust him much. I imagine him grilling Daddy. Insisting on drugs, hypnosis. I picture a whole lineup of bosomy lady cops with notebooks.

So I try to answer reasonably and humbly. "I must have done something. I'm not sure what."

The sheriff scoots his chair farther back. "Let's think, sweet cakes."

Bosomy is poking away at her notes. Maybe drawing pictures.

I make several efforts. "I did do a couple of things. I checked up on Mrs. Dexter and the oyster. I discovered Mona. Maybe I noticed something then. Before that. Afterward. My father fell in the garden. I was confused. I have trouble remembering."

Sheriff H. and I keep this up for a while, with me working hard to stress the two H's—humble and helpful. I don't think the sheriff trusts me for a minute, but he finally lets me go and says some of his guys will watch out for me until he leaves the Manor—"Just a coupla more days, sweet cakes. You better rilly watch it. That's a mean summabitch did that there." He chews gum and gestures upward in the direction of my room.

I'm glad to have Sheriff H. say he'll watch out for me. My father and I can use all the watching that's offered.

⅃ Chapter 15

I sit staring at the mermaid and thinking—a peculiar mixture of *Why am I here* and *What have I done with my life so far* and *How very odd, to be my age and have had such disparate adventures.*

Disparate is a good word. I think my life would be different if I'd had a mother. Even when Constancia was around she wasn't there, and then when I was ten years old, she left for good.

I don't miss her, although there are times I think I ought to. I mean, I remember how handsome she was, straight back and calm perfect profile, and how she stood shoulders-erect, better than most people's mothers. And how she wasn't at all, not a bit, interested in clothes. She'd go into whatever store was nearby, Ross Dress-for-Less or Neiman Marcus or whatever, and buy anything they had; it always looked fine. I had a struggle with myself about the way she looked because I would feel proud of her and not want to.

But then she'd stare at me when I came near, an expression like deafness across her face, as if I were a homeless person asking for a dollar, and she didn't want to shut me up, so she'd wait to be polite and listen, then eventually maybe give me that dollar.

Anyway, she was away eighty percent of the time. Well, seventy-five percent. Conferences in Jeddah, Haifa, Tehran, Istanbul. Teaching positions in London. Even in Vancouver. You wouldn't think they'd want to know about Phrygian bowls in Vancouver.

Susie says there was a lovely lady named Mrs. Esposito who got me through my infancy, and although I don't remember Mrs. Esposito at all, I do understand some Spanish—that comes when I'm not expecting it, all of a sudden I'll understand what the guys behind the counter in Subway Pizza are telling each other. And one of my lifetime projects is to go to Oaxaca, where Mrs. Esposito is living now, and get to know her again. Maybe she can tell me about myself when I was a baby.

Susie was the other person who helped me through. And of course Daddy. Though I have to admit it, my father is vague. But I do love him.

Oh. And Aunt Crystal. Much as the idea of Aunt Crystal makes me cross, I have to state that, yes, she cared about my life, too. Aunt C. would come up from Southern California and march into our house and exclaim about how peculiar it all was, with my mother gone and my father never answering the mail. He liked getting mail and liked reading it. He just thought answering was too much trouble and took energy away from his archaeological studies.

On the archaeology I think he was pretty good. Maybe very good. His book, *The Coffin Lid Texts: Fourteen Hiero-*

glyphs Reclaimed caused a stir in archaeology circles. After it came out he went to Egypt a lot. Which was okay, because when he was gone I stayed with Susie and Robbie. And sometimes he took me with him. Twice he took both Robbie and me. Rob discovered Egyptian archaeology in our library when he was fifteen; he was crazy about it. That was a really good year, the first time Daddy took me and Rob to Luxor. We rented a little tan stucco house with tame cockroaches and a big fan in the middle of the living room ceiling; we went every day to the Valley of the Kings, and I wrote things down in notebooks while Daddy and Rob dug. Maybe it was the best year of my life.

But you hate to think you had the best year of your life when you were twelve. That makes you feel like a child gymnast, too old to do those quadruple flips any more. *My future is behind me. The future is prologue.* And all that depressing stuff.

I sit on the bench by the mermaid statue thinking about all this long enough to eat four peppermint Jelly Bellies and to murmur a final salute to the mermaid circle's former tenant, the long-legged hare, whom Rob has promised to bury beside a clump of wild iris in one of our cliffside meadows.

My telephone rings. "Carla? You better get over here right away."

"Who's this? Where's here?"

The voice says, "*Who* is Mrs. La Salle and *here* is your father's apartment—well not his apartment exactly. Outside his apartment."

Mrs. La Salle sounds upset, which is not like her, and also confused, again atypical. "Hurry up," she says.

Outside my father's apartment Mrs. La Salle stands, clutching the ends of a purple-and-blue cloak and looking up. She is making sounds, negative monosyllables like "No," and "Don't." And, twice, "Ed." Just that, my father's name. "Thank God," she says about my arrival, and then, gesturing and flashing bits of chunky jewelry, "Up there."

Up there and ahead, along a brick walkway and some mossy stairs, is one of Green Beach's fake Norman towers. At the top of this tower there's an arched opening onto a projecting Romeo-and-Juliet balcony; this balcony holds a large terra-cotta flowerpot and a man on one knee balancing a rifle on the balcony rail. He is squinting along the barrel of the rifle and looks as if he's getting ready to shoot it. The man is my father. He wears his best tie, a navy blue one, his Johns Hopkins tie. The rest of him is complete in a tan tweed suit and vest. Over his right shoulder there's some kind of a rope or sling. Both he and the rifle look insecure; they wobble and vibrate.

Mrs. La Salle is perhaps safe where she has hidden herself under the overhang of our bay window; she's still bravely calling up, "No, Ed!" I ask, strangulated, "How do I get up there?"

She points at a door half-hidden in ivy in the base of the tower. I start toward it fast, trying to run unthreateningly so as not to scare my father, who is watching. Meanwhile, I'm talking up at him. "Now, then, just stay put . . . don't move your finger . . . it's going to be all right . . . *you're* going to be all right." And whatever other feeble-minded cheery thing I can think of to yell as I pull the tower door open (it sticks) and squeeze through, and, feet stumbling and getting in the way of each other, scramble up the metal stairs that circle the inside.

The stairs ring under my feet. Around and around. The wall of the tower is lined in brick, the sort of checkerboard pattern that makes you dizzy when you run fast in a circle. "Daddy, don't move."

At the top of the stairs is a circular landing space floored in shiny gray material; its major feature is a view of the balcony with my father framed, dramatizing Shoot-out at the OK Corral.

"Daddy," I say in the calm voice you're supposed to use with rabid dogs and small children in danger, "Put the gun down . . . on the floor . . . in front of you. Don't move your finger. Then step back . . . little steps . . . one at a time. You can do it."

My heart is pounding so drumlike that I can hardly hear myself. And my father looks like a traditional madman, his normally neat, brushed hair scraggly from the wind, his eyes red. He's wobbling that weapon. Pointing it off someplace down the road.

"It's not a gun," he shouts into the air, "it's a rifle." He starts a rhythmic gesturing, he chants: "Here is my rifle, here is my gun; one is for fighting, the other . . ."

This is the second time I've seen him look the way an Alzheimer's patient is supposed to look, that is, crazy and dangerous. "Father. Put it down."

"Down? Why? They promised me. An e-mail. They need my token." He waves this out into space; he semaphores.

"Listen. Please."

"Please? What kind of a word, *please*? They promised." More space gestures, rifle up, rifle down. I'm behind him, halfway out of the hole at the top of the stairs; I resist an impulse to grab him.

"I could shoot them," he says. "All of them . . . Good idea," he adds. "She needs me."

"Just put it down. We'll talk."

"But she *needs* me."

"Father, *I* need you."

"Then why is she dead? I knew her. The woman in the net."

"The woman in the net is over, Daddy."

"And the woman on the beach. The woman in the net and the woman on the beach. Woman in net. Woman on beach." He makes a kind of chant of this, gesturing with the rifle to keep time. "Beach . . . net . . . beach . . . net. They said it. My token will help." He has slid part way back into the room now. "Did you know? They left me a hangman's noose."

His gesturing has got the rifle caught in the scalloped balcony rail design. He struggles and tugs.

"Father," I squawk. "Stop. Don't pull." Now I'm up and out of the circular staircase and almost behind him.

He says, "Oh, no," in a heartstricken voice, as he braces one foot. "Caught," he wrenches something.

A shot discharges; there's dust, noise, a sharp dusty smell, and he tumbles backward into the room. Particles settle. A metallic clatter from below signals that the rifle has landed.

My father lies on his back. He says, "Woman in net. Dead, and I couldn't . . ."

"Father!" I blurt out. I've had it. A mixture of fear and irritation overwhelms my social-work approaches. "*Stop* that. I can't *stand* it."

And this works. He shifts; he's lying on his back, half on

the balcony, half in the room, a haze of dust and plaster set-
tling around him. He shoves up on one elbow, thinking
about this. I can see his mind starting to partly clear; it's almost two images at once, like a montage in a movie. Slowly
his shoulders realign, he straightens, he sighs. And then he
pushes entirely away from the balcony. "Well, now." He almost sounds like Edward Day again.

Which doesn't help me much. I'm still scared of him and
for him.

"Sit here," I say. There's a ledge around the inside wall of
this landing, I pull him up and shove him on to it. He's still
hanging on to the rope across his shoulder.

"I *didn't* see her," he says. "I saw you. And that lady. That
particular lady. But I didn't see *her*. That was a terrible
thing. Did I frighten you? I'm so very sorry."

Yes, you frightened me. I guess this craziness will get
worse from now on. "Where did you get that rifle?"

"That? I hope it's all right. It was a gift. It was sent to me
in a package. Wasn't that nice? It's quite a good one. Did I
frighten you?"

My father isn't a gun nut, but he knows how a rifle works.
He had a rifle in Egypt where it might be useful against jack-
als and looters; I never saw him fire it, but I guess he knew
how. "Yes, you frightened me. Who sent you the rifle?"

"Some friend. A nice gesture."

From below Mrs. La Salle's voice wafts up: "Are you all
right up there? I have your firearm." Mrs. La Salle knows
enough not to call a rifle a gun.

My father reaches up and touches my face. "I'm truly
sorry, dear."

And all this time, the sweet man has been waiting underneath. That fact mixes with the panic I've been feeling, and I get a surge of anger. What business does he have being sweet during a crisis like this? "You must promise me you will never, *never* . . ."

"Oh, but my dear." His voice is mild. "They sent me an e-mail."

"Who's 'they'?"

He shifts his attention to the floor. "Curious. Linoleum. Not suitable."

"Daddy. Someone *told* you?"

He's still examining the floor, bent over and scratching with one finger at the crusty surface. "Yes, they. It's important that it was *they*. Several people. More than one, I believe. I'm an archaeologist, you know. Interesting. Two different layers of time." He lifts his head. "Here, would you take this rope? It's beginning to scrape." And he pulls at the tan rope hanging over his shoulder. The way he's had it, over one shoulder and down his side, I couldn't see the back of it, but now that it's free I recognize that it ends in a kind of loop with a knot at the top. Heavy rope, the kind you'd want for tying a boat to its dock.

He stretches it out and examines it interestedly. "A hangman's noose. Hard to make. Do you know, I think it was for me?" And he stretches the loop wide, puts his head inside, rests his chin on the knot, and makes a horrible face, eyes crossed and tongue extruded. "Awwk!" he chokes.

I tell him, "Stop it. You're showing off." Which is true. It feels good to tell him that.

"Nevertheless, I wasn't scared," he says. "And I still have my token." He crosses his eyes some more, "When you do this they don't stick, though some people say they will.

"But I wasn't scared. It seemed too bad, with such a nice rifle. Do you know, I've just realized, it might be teatime. I want scones. And vanilla yogurt. I'm *hungry*!"

He *thunks* the rope over to me. Yes, it is a hangman's noose, no question about it. Made of rope so heavy that the whole arrangement must weigh almost four pounds.

We take Mrs. La Salle to tea with us. She carries the rifle, hidden under her cashmere cloak, and I carry the rope with most of the noose part under my jacket.

Over the tea table I try several times to elicit details from my father. "Who sent the e-mail? Who said what?"

"It was to help her, you know."

"But someone sent you the rifle?"

"My dear, apparently."

"And the noose was in the same package with the rifle?"

"I think he doesn't want to talk," Mrs. La Salle observes.

Daddy is breaking his scone into small pieces. I've combed his hair and he looks like Edward Day again. "It probably wasn't very safe. That end board, the one on the edge there, was unsteady."

"Listen, you *must* remember."

"Perhaps I tied that knot myself."

"Let's just eat," says Mrs. La Salle. She herself is managing fine, with three cucumber sandwiches and a cappuccino, and the rifle placed crosswise under her chair. She has promised not to talk about this adventure; she understands that management may still want to send Daddy off to the special facility. "You silly man," she says to him now, approaching a firm, pink-tinged cheek for a kiss.

"It was a symbol of something," my father says.

* * *

I take him back to his room, where I try to find a place to stash the rifle. I finally decide to take it back to my broom closet and stash it behind my cardboard dresser. This isn't a good place, but nowhere is. A rifle is an inconvenient shape.

The rope can be untied; I can keep it. A lot of people save rope.

"What in hell was that all about?" Rob asks when I describe the scene to him.

"Trying to scare him," I say.

"Trying to get him to tell them something," Rob says.

"Trying to get some object. Find some object." I say.

"To persuade him to give it to them. The token." Rob suggests.

"Trying to scare him," I repeat. "A threat. A hangman's noose. But he doesn't seem really scared."

"He has Alzheimer's. The response synapses are different."

"You mean you don't get scared when you have Alzheimer's?"

"You can be plenty scared. Really frightened. Obsessive about it. But often it's irrational. Scared of stuff that isn't there. Of different things. Not the logical ones. *Hangman's noose* didn't connect for him. He knew what it meant, but it didn't really matter, wasn't part of his personal mythic history. Now if it were something Egyptian . . ."

"Well, *I'm* scared."

Rob latches on to this. "Good. Leave. Pack up. Come stay with me."

"We did this already. No."

Rob says, "Oh, hell," and kicks at the dirt near the mermaid statue.

"Were they trying to make him fall?" I ask, after a prickly silence.

"No. They can't want him dead. Not now. He's got something they want."

"Jeez Louise," I say, imitating Henry the cabdriver, "It's giving me nightmares."

"You *should* have nightmares. You're the stubbornest human being in captivity." For a minute I think Rob is going to walk off and leave me sitting there, but he doesn't do that.

🦉 Chapter 16

Mrs. Goliard, the lady-out-the-window, the one with the birdcalls on her answering service whose brother doesn't communicate, finally phones me back.

We have an entirely confusing conversation in which I am saying, "I wondered if you had heard from your brother," and she is saying things about me being Dr. Day's daughter. "Is that possible?" she asks. "Are you related to Dr. Day? In that case you're related to . . ." and her voice starts trailing off into the atmosphere. She has one of those indistinct whines that gets more inaudible with confusion, but she seems now to be talking about my Aunt Crystal.

So at the same moment I'm saying, "Aunt Crystal?" and she's saying, "My brother Kevin? Oh, yes, Kevin wrote to me, of course he did. I was so foolish; I worry too much . . . But your Aunt Crystal . . . I'm afraid I must have offended her."

It seems she was working with Crystal on some kind of project.

I try to remember when Aunt Crystal was at the Manor last. About a week before I left Berkeley, that's when I got the postcard with the mermaid statue and the spiky message: "Service fair; breakfast waffles leathery; yr fr. adjusting v. well."

"So your brother is all right?" I'm asking, and Mrs. Goliard keeps talking about Aunt Crystal, "Your aunt, how wonderful. I was working with her.

"That is, I *thought* I was working with her," Mrs. Goliard talks in a high bleat. "You simply must—oh, I would appreciate it if only—please *do* come to see me."

She and I make a date for later that afternoon.

Mrs. Goliard is a skinny lady with dyed red hair who leans her body to one side and fidgets with her face, one hand pulling at a cheek, an ear, a chin sag. She hovers in her doorway, looking dazed.

"Oh, my goodness," she says. "Oh, Crystal's niece. She mentioned about you, but I had no idea until Belle told me. I mean, that you were *living* here . . ."

"Maybe we should go inside," I say, since it looks as if she won't be able to get out of her doorway unless I give her a shove, and she says, "Oh, my goodness, oh, yes," and leads the way into a dark, overheated apartment full of brocade drapes and a lot of those little porcelain dancer figures up on one toe and with lace flounces baked into their porcelain.

I get seated on a red velvet couch with an impossibly hard back, and she sits facing me in a flowered chair and

stares and says, "Oh," and "Please," and "Oh, my, do you
have any idea—well, you wouldn't have, would you? Anyway, why did Crystal never get back to me? Was she angry?
I didn't do the research, but I couldn't, could I, not knowing
what it was supposed to be?"

"I'd really like a cup of tea," I prod, not because I really
would (I wouldn't; I've had enough tea since I joined the
Manor to float myself all the way back to Berkeley), but in
order to give her something specific to do, and at this she
says, "Oh, dear," and "Oh, of course," and starts to fluster
gratefully toward her small kitchen.

Meanwhile, I'm trying to put together my idea of Aunt
Crystal, so organized and precise, and asking myself what
on earth would she want with this chaotic little lady, just
the kind Aunt C. can't stand. She must have an extra-special
reason.

Mrs. Goliard dithers out with apple-cinnamon tea and
Pepperidge Farm cookie sandwiches that get displayed on a
pink marble table, and while we sip and munch, her story
slowly emerges.

Aunt Crystal had looked up Mrs. Goliard because she,
like Aunt C., used to be a librarian.

"Not that I was in her class," Mrs. Goliard dithers. "Oh,
not at all. Your aunt, before she retired, was head of the
main branch of the Ventura library, and she even taught a
course at—where was it?"

"USC," I say. "University of Southern California."

"*So* prestigious. And I was just the weekend person at the
downtown branch in The Dalles, Oregon."

Her voice fades here; she's losing track of her thought. I
jump-start her, "Aunt Crystal came to you . . ."

"Oh, yes, yes. Though I must say for myself, I *am* trained in research; I do know about that. And your aunt had a research project.

"I was so excited to be asked, because, you know, here at the Manor, it's all very, very nice, or at least it was before all these accidents started, but still . . . well, anyway, you do start to feel, even though it's so nice . . ."

Here she begins a session of chin-pulling that makes me feel I'll be doing it too unless I rescue her. "It's nice here, but you were glad to have something to do."

"Oh, yes. Oh, absolutely. You're so like your aunt. Such an incisive mind."

Aunt Crystal, I am saying in my head, *this will never work out.*

"But," Mrs. Goliard continues, "I never found out what exactly your aunt was researching. She was coming back to tell me about it more fully. And then she didn't." *Tug, tug* on the chin. "And I wrote and got no answer. I blamed myself, of course. But it *is* confusing. What she wanted with me, here. Because we aren't near a good library, now are we? Of course there is the little local library in Conestoga and then the historic mansion outside of town—maybe there's a library there; I never asked . . ."

I'm starting to feel some sort of cold warning, a clutch of danger deep in my belly. I try for a minute to identify it and can't, so I grab back into the conversation, "But she didn't give you any idea at all?" Aunt Crystal likes to be busy; I know that. She's a volunteer teacher of reading and math, she visits hospitals. Those are great things to be doing, though I can't help feeling sorry for the people she helps, having Aunt Crystal leaning over their shoulder like a witch out of *Macbeth*, tracing their mistakes with a bony finger. Research, I never heard about that.

"Research on what?" I ask, stifling the cold feeling. Mrs. Goliard tugs and looks flustered.

"Something about California history," she suggests. "I mean, she didn't exactly say it. Only that it's important. And it's local. I got that California-history feeling."

At the back of my mind somebody erects a large sign: WHAT DOES THIS HAVE TO DO WITH MONA? WITH THE AC-CIDENTS AT THE MANOR?

I am saying "Accidents" to my subconscious at the same moment that Mrs. Goliard is telling me, "And then I fell out of the window."

Fell, I go. More like *accident*. Not saying it aloud, just thinking. I had pretty much forgotten that this was the out-the-window lady.

"So very stupid," Mrs. Goliard dithers on. "You know, I liked to go to the window and stand and look out; it gave me a feeling that I was getting out of my problems. Then, suddenly there wasn't any glass, and I got dizzy. That's one of my things, in a situation like that, if I'm up high and if the light comes from underneath, well, I get dizzy."

"So very foolish," she adds, looking to me as if I will agree, yes, foolish. "If the new chef hadn't come by and caught me . . . And it's really only these last few days . . . I mean, it's taken me four whole weeks to get over being scared about it."

"Four weeks?" I ask.

My subconscious has turned into an echoing mess. That word *accident* still clangs around there like a ball in a pinball machine that can't find its pocket, but there's also this new word making its own noise. About something else, something cold and really evil.

Mrs. Goliard is still talking, "I told myself that was what I got for being so pleased about your aunt. Something bad always happens right away if something good does. And then I just waited to hear from her and when I didn't, well, that was all right at first, and I could tell myself not to be silly. But now that it has been almost a month . . ."

That's it, that's it, I think. *When,* that's the cold word. A month. A month since *when.* I open my mouth, and I can't speak. I close my mouth, and I try again. "Mrs. Goliard," I say finally, *"when* was Aunt Crystal here?"

Mrs. Goliard thinks I am accusing her of something. She says, "When," and "My goodness." She drops a cookie. "It was . . . I can't remember the date exactly. Just about a month ago. Just before I fell out the window."

Somehow I get out of Mrs. Goliard's apartment and home to my cubbyhole, where I call Aunt Crystal in Venice, California, and listen to her answering machine greeting: "This is Crystal Day. Please leave a message." Then I rifle through my things to find my address book, and remember that, yes, I had it in my pocket when my room was trashed, otherwise I wouldn't have it at all. And there under Aunt Crystal's name and in her handwriting is her next-door neighbor's name, address, and phone number; how like Aunt C., to worry about me some day needing that information.

The lady's name is Mrs. Bascomb.

I reach her right away.

She's the cheerful sort, at least at the beginning of our

conversation. "Crystal's niece? Yes, of course, you're Carla, yes, I heard about you. So glad you called because I must say, I had begun to wonder . . . I mean, I'm glad to go on with the watering and all that, but the garden is getting out of hand and the mail is piling up and some of it looks like bills and . . .

"Well," she asks, pausing for breath, "when is Crystal coming back, anyway?"

I find myself going breathless and oddly unwilling to tell Mrs. Bascomb that I have no idea where Aunt Crystal is. "When did she leave Venice?" I ask. And Mrs. B., sounding surprised, says, "Why, last month . . . yes, maybe in the middle of the month. She was going to stay at her brother's place, a very nice place—oh, he would be your father, wouldn't he? Then you know the place, that's where she would be staying. Do you mean, are you telling me, you're not in touch with her?"

Mrs. Bascomb hasn't put it together that I live at the Manor and that I don't know where Aunt Crystal is. And when at last we connect on this, she is quite horrified. She does the acting out for me. I am sitting holding the phone, feeling all kinds of heat changes and freezing changes as if a new temperature-altering substance has been invented and applied to me from head to toe, but especially in the gut area. My personal alarm system is going: Yes, I knew it, I could feel it; Aunt Crystal is missing, she's the one, she was here at the Manor. She's the woman who went away and didn't write home.

Mrs. Bascomb of course doesn't have all the history I have, and after her initial shock wants to believe various harmless things until finally I manage to say, sounding all right and in charge when I say it, "Thank you, you are so good to worry. I'll take care of it; I'll look into everything, and I'll call you back. You'll hear from me."

Then I hang up and think I'm going to be sick. I waste about ten minutes in the employees' bathroom down the hall, hanging on to the enamel toilet bowl and feeling dizzy and weak. I can't throw up; all I can manage is staring at the white enamel and then fixing on the stainless steel handle and feeling awful. When I finally stagger out into the hall I meet Belle who says, "Hell's bells kid, you look like shit." I squeeze by her not answering and make it back into my little cell, where I lie down for a few minutes before I call Mrs. Sisal's office.

Rebecca, the Sisal secretary, acts surprised. "Sure, Miss Day was here visiting her brother, just a while before you came. We thought you knew."

She stayed a week, Rebecca says, and her bill was paid by Dr. Day's account.

Skrrtch, skrrtch over the telephone, it's Rebecca turning pages. "Left something, I guess," she adds. "We mailed it to her. Doesn't say what."

I hang up and make my way to the bathroom again. But I don't throw up this time, either. Then I come back and call the sheriff.

Sheriff Hawthorne is downstairs and can see me right away.

He's standing by his partially dismantled desk, surrounded by cardboard cartons and rolls of sticky tape. He, with his crew, is leaving us tomorrow. He's only moderately happy to see me. "Came to confess, I guess," he says, projecting irony. He's not at all interested in my most recent wild story. "Your aunt? You have an *aunt* that doesn't write to you?

"Tell me something useful for a change," he suggests. "You remembered a fact. Your dad remembered a fact.

"And cut it out with this bullshit about a missing aunt who doesn't send postcards. Lissen. We got a murder. The lady had your house number down her bra. Somebody tossed your room. You're into this mess, in like Flynn."

On the Aunt Crystal question he tells me I'm being a female overreacter. "You got a lot of things to think about lately, right?" After which he walks around, slapping Scotch tape onto packages. "Right in the middle of leaving here," he mutters. "Kee-reep. . . . Just tell me, back to basics, why were you in the meadow that night, huh?"

When I don't give up and keep trying to convince him that my aunt is *missing*, and it's his responsibility to *do something*, he snorts his walrus snort, "She was an independent kind of lady, right? Traveled a lot? Librarian, you say, teacher. Yeah, your dad maybe hasn't heard from her, but your dad forgets, correct? . . . Hey, on that, have you thought about it, how about . . . could we jump-start him? You realize, it looks pretty suspicious the way these pointers keep aiming at him.

"Okay, okay," he says, in response to a semihysterical outburst from me. He sits down. "Of course if you insist, I'll fill out a form, but listen, Miss Day, you'll see, this'll be one of those times when the lady shows up with a suitcase full of souvenirs from Yosemite and talks about the wonderful time she had and that impulse just to climb on a bus and explore . . ."

I am sitting in Sheriff Hawthorne's temporary office, one of our Victorian type of Manor rooms with the whipped-cream ceiling molding. I am shifting back and forth in a cerise velvet Manor chair and looking at his collection of cartons containing details of the Mona murder, and I'm fighting down a tide of anxiety and going *Yes, no, yes, no* at myself; the question being, do I finally have to tell Sheriff Hawthorne about what Daddy saw from the cliff top? ("Listen, Sheriff Hawthorne, my father thinks he saw this murder where they rolled the woman in a net, but of course he's not a very reliable witness, and I don't want him questioned at all . . .")

"We have these things all the time," the sheriff is droning on, paying no attention to my projected thoughts. "People are goddamn stupid; they go away, and they just don't make sense. Now, Miss Day, why don't you try to concentrate on the murder you walked in on, remember? Let's not let some other damn thing make us go off half-cocked."

"Listen, Sheriff Hawthorne," I break in, "I do emphatically want you to list my aunt as missing. She left some stuff in her room, the Manor had to send it after her. And she was close to my dad. She had special information about him that might help us now."

Maybe the idea of Aunt Crystal knowing things about Daddy interests the sheriff. The left-behind objects certainly do, because he asks what she left and is disappointed I don't know. He snorts his walrus snort, "Her toothbrush, that's what it always is, toothbrush.

"But, yeah," he concedes, "okay, okay, we'll list her." And he locates a half-empty box and digs around until he comes up with a paper that he proceeds to write on. And I sign it, watching my hand write my name and thinking, *That hand is going to start shaking in a minute*. But it doesn't.

On the surface I guess I seem pretty calm. I even get another helping of sympathy from the sheriff, who looks at me sideways and says, "Hey, well, I guess you've had a pretty tense time of it these last few days, huh?"

On my way back to my room I stop by Daddy's apartment, where he is asleep in his preferred position, the good little crusader, quilt neatly arranged, head slightly propped, hands crossed over chest. His face is pink and smooth, his breathing regular. I look at him and think, all this time you remembered that murder. You saw it imprecisely from above. You were afraid maybe you'd recognized her, and you had. She was your own younger sister: Little, cross, difficult Crystal, that you loved even though she followed you around and tried to boss your life. Your own little Crystal-sister, you saw her murdered. But could you be sure? You didn't want to admit it. You wanted to escape any shreds of memory that came to the surface. She wasn't just the lady in the net, she was your sister in the net. Daddy, I'm so sorry.

I want to reach down and clasp one of his loosely positioned hands. But I don't do that because it would wake him up, and I figure he needs his sleep.

When my mother went off I felt a mixture of emotions. I wasn't too young to do that and to recognize a lot of them. So I made a mental list: *regret* (Why weren't you a better mother? Why didn't I make you be better?), *confusion* (What happened here? Books say it's not supposed to be like this), *irritation* (You've always let me down. Now you're doing it again), *disbelief* (To Turkey? A Turkish archaeologist? I can't tell people. Everyone will think it's a joke). The disbelief was a big part of it. Disbelief and a muffled kind of surprise. Not straightforward emotions. Even though I was only ten, I thought I wasn't feeling enough.

And now that I've decided Aunt Crystal is gone and that she was the woman in the net, my emotions are all direct and forceful, emotions of love and loss, a surprise to me. Maybe they're the thoughts I didn't have when Mother went. Maybe displaced feelings, a textbook case. Think of all the times I complained about my anally retentive Aunt C. About how she bossed me. But now I'm remembering her again, very specifically, my thorny, brisk, bossy aunt; the one who came up to Berkeley and criticized my hair, my homework, my bedmaking, the way I washed the colored and white laundry together, and then said, "Well, at least you do try, Carla. I give you that." Wasn't she, together with Susie, the only mother I ever had? Shake them up together, Susie, Crystal, Susie, Crystal, and you get . . . some kind of a mother, maybe.

Oh, shut up, I tell myself.

Mostly, I seem to be lying on my bed seeing that scene of Daddy's, the woman rolled in the yellow binding on the edge of the tide, the three people around her poking at her. A scene out of an old picture of hell—what was the artist's name? Breughel? But this isn't a scene from someone's imagination; it happened, and who it happened to is real. My own crusty, difficult, pain-in-the-neck aunt.

If I could cry I would feel better. In a while I'll call Robbie; at least I finally have someone I can talk to. For now I just want to lie here on my flat hard IKEA bed and think about Aunt Crystal and project words at her in whatever new space she's gotten to. Aunt Crystal, I'm sorry. Hey, Aunt C., I'll get even with them, honest to God I will.

I'll nail whoever it was did that to you.

꒕ Chapter 17

My phone call to Robbie is confused by the fact that Arlette answers his phone and I try to be polite and not to sound panicky or possessive, as in, "Come on, Arlette, get off the phone, I need Rob now." Anyway, he isn't there. I attempt *polite and strained*; Arlette attempts *polite and strained*. I'm glad Rob is at the hospital. I don't know whether I could tell him my news with Arlette hovering in the background.

Rob at the hospital takes a while to pick up his phone. He seems to be with a patient; from the sound of it, at the patient's bedside. He hears my story, at first with grunts and then with exclamations of "Jeez" and "Holy God" and finally with an outburst of, "Oh, Jesus Christ, Carly. Oh, that's awful. No, no, Leona, nothing to do with you"—this last apparently to someone behind him—"Oh, Carly, that is so goddamn awful, of course you're upset, it's dreadful. Listen, honey, I'll be over as soon as I get off; late though, after eleven. Can you wait up? Okay, chin up, honey." He starts to hang up and then says, "Listen, call Mom, she'll hold your hand for a while," and then he signs off to comfort Leona, whoever that is, and reassure her that his phone call wasn't the news that she had a terminal something.

And I do call Susie, but I'm hampered by the weirdness of my story. I simply can't bring myself to drag that nightmarish medieval torture-net scene across Susie's bright horizon. Although what's the matter with me? Susie is a lady from the sixties, she knows all about drug nightmares and bad trips. Nevertheless, I just say that Crystal is missing and her neighbor thinks . . . and here I supply a few extra false details to strengthen my case: Crystal promised the neighbor she would call every week. She was supposed to deliver a talk on computer systems at the local library last Tuesday. She owed the neighbor-lady money. This last false detail is convincing to Sue because both of us know that Crystal would never owe anyone money for more than a day.

So Susie is worried and immediately starts out being comforting. She promises to call me every night. She'll think of me, she'll hold dear Crystal, and me, in her best thoughts. "And, Carla, isn't it possible that Crystal—no, no, it's not possible. She wouldn't suddenly give in to impulse and go off somewhere; that's the way *I'd* behave. Oh, dear, Carla darling, I'm so sorry. Have you talked to Robbie?"

I depart for work on my aide's rounds grateful that I have a job to report to and clients that I have to be cheerful and competent for. I've decided I'm not going to tell my trio of old ladies anything yet; all I have so far is suspicion, not any actual certainty about Aunt Crystal. Heavy suspicion, of course, but still.

Actually, I'm not being fair. I asked the three ladies to pry and inquire and search, and they have been doing that, and now I've found out something and I'm not telling them what I've found.

Maybe the truth is that I don't want to talk about it.

I'm sitting in my room that evening reading *Sophie's World* when Rob finally arrives.

Sophie's World is an innovative and straightforward philosophy book. The good thing about a book like *Sophie* is that it juggles lots of ideas but at the same time is clear and absorbing; you can read it in a crisis, getting pretty much intellectually involved, and then sometime later in another crisis be perfectly ready to read it again. Robbie knocks when I'm halfway into Heraclitus and his idea of the way up and the way down so I dog-ear the page and go to the door for a hug and a "Carly . . . My God. Hey, baby, it'll be okay."

I hold on to him, "It isn't okay, it will never be okay." I probably say some other stuff about how the world is barbaric, life is barbaric, and how can there be a world where things like this happen. Although maybe I don't say any of this; it's hard to remember afterwards whether you've really said something aloud or just felt it. After a while Rob and I are walking down the hall with our arms around each other; the hall is big and wide and spooky looking. The sheriff's crew left this afternoon, and there aren't any people here unless you count the Renoirs. The one I'm looking at now is a seminaked lady holding a white kitten; I hate her for it. She's a fake Renoir. No real Renoir would have a white kitten, since he would know that the lady and the kitten are too much alike to share a painting.

I've noticed that when you're depressed you hate things like that more.

I call Mrs. Dexter and ask her if she'll sit in Daddy's room while Rob and I go for a walk. I tell her he's been having bad dreams, which is a lie. I'm the one with the bad dreams, but I'm afraid to leave my father alone.

Outside, it's an absolutely clear night (I just stopped myself from thinking *crystal clear*), with no fog, no wind, the air almost warm, which it practically never is on the northern California coast, and about eight million stars lined up overhead, so tight you feel there just wouldn't be room for another one.

Rob talks about a patient he had this morning—not the Leona who was part of our phone conversation, but a more seriously ill patient—and how she told him she'd valued her family and she'd had a good life, and she was ready to die now and it had all been worth it. "She looked great when she said that," he reports, "as if she really meant it." He can talk about things like this and not sound sappy. It has to do with an unforced enthusiasm, a tone of absolute commitment. He doesn't have to try for this; it's just there. Which is another reason why I look at him and think what a great guy he is, then look at him again and get cross.

We make the mermaid-circuit talking first about his patient, then about me and how totally awful I feel. After that, about him, how he feels guilty and thinks that he should have guessed Aunt Crystal was the one in the net, though why he thinks that I haven't a clue. I take a minute to smooth the mermaid's red—or pink—bronze hair, touching her seems like a hopeful act because she's such a special favorite of Daddy's.

After a while we turn and go around the buildings in the other direction, toward the county road. Then finally we head up into the hills and woods on the north side of the Manor complex. There are hiking trails up here that I've been intending to explore ever since I arrived, but I've never quite gotten around to it.

It's dramatic scenery because suddenly, without what I usually think of as the border between one kind of coastal foliage and another, we're in the middle of a forest primeval: thick, soft-looking, hairy, shedding redwood trees mixed in with twisted bent-over cypresses. Underneath this tree canopy is a soft mat of leaves, pine needles, and roots. We walk for a while, climbing slightly, holding hands. The feel of the pine-needle floor giving under my feet sends up a kind of comfort, and so does the smell of evergreen, cypress, redwood—tree-essence perfume. Rob squeezes my hand as we stumble uphill into the almost complete dark, with just an occasional glimmer of light. The path wants you to follow it; it feels different, firmer than the yielding rest of the terrain.

Rob says, "Carly, what a pileup of scary pain." I get the feeling he's trying to look at me, but I can't really tell. I just have an idea of where the side of his body is.

We keep on walking up and up, half-feeling our way, the night so heavy and dense it's like stepping into somebody's sauna. With that smell of cedar chips that's a sauna-thing, too.

Suddenly I stop and say, "Oh, God."

"Yeah, I know."

"You don't know. I was going to say, 'What happens when he *gets* it?'"

"Hey," Rob says, then again, "Hey," after which we stop, teetering because it's hard to stay straight when you've lost your visual guides about up and down. He puts out a hand to support me. The hand stays for a while at my waist, big, warm, comfortable. I can feel myself letting go—leaning into it. Now both of his hands are there; big thumbs and fingers, substantial hands, and I'm pretty slim. A single hand can almost half-encircle me. It feels nice. A minute later the arms are up and around. And mine, too. I think, *Yes*, as my hands go up. We've got an interlocking deal here, a nice pretzel-puzzle. This hug gets substantial and real; squeeze and gasp, it becomes a genuine hug. We hold it; we rock back and forth and lean. Maybe I even say, "Mmmm." After that we do a kiss.

The kiss, though, is a just a halfway job. Halfway between a lot of things—sad, scared, brotherly, loverly. Mouth only half-open, so to speak. After all, Robbie and I were brother and sister for a while, and then lovers for a while.

There's a muffled crash in the underbrush over to the side of us. The sort of noise you get if you step on a stack of twigs and it gives way. We jump. Rob heaves back, and I lurch in the opposite direction. The whole kiss effort gets stopped. He's holding me off at arm's length and saying "Wha . . . what?" and then amending, "Oh, sure, *deer*."

He tries to gather me in for another kiss, but it turns out to be an aborted effort, one of those European cheek-salutes.

I listen hard and think I hear the retreat of the observer, or Bambi, rustling off among the poison oak. If I were all alone, I'd feel pretty damn scared. Rob and I teeter and attempt to look at each other, which we can't do because it's too dark to see.

So we let go. And I try to figure out where we are. We seem to have arrived at a wooden structure that tilts or tips loomingly into the trees, and that also maybe has a jutting-out platform scraping our shins. Rob coughs, one of those embarrassed cover-up-a-situation coughs, then he bends and dusts off part of the platform with his jacket sleeve.

We sit down. Wooden things squeak. I don't say anything about the kiss. I say, "My father's been brooding. I know he has. Ever since."

He agrees, "Right."

"Knowing and not knowing. *Does* he know?"

"Search me. Jeez, I *hope* not."

I try talking fast, for something to do. "I'll get this Mrs. Bascomb to send me Aunt Crystal's mail. That'll tell us something."

"Good idea."

Muffled responses from Rob.

Part of that piled-up mail to Aunt Crystal will be a post-card from me.

Another moment of silence.

"He's started in again about his token," I say.

"A small thing that stands for a bigger thing."

More silence, then some sneaker-toe-scraping from Rob. The mixture of pine needles and decayed bark makes a funny, gentle, abrasive rustle when it's scraped.

I'm telling myself again the terrible story about how Crystal, my own aunt, was the woman on the beach.

They rolled her in a net and tormented her and then

killed her. *They*. That's a powerful, amorphous word for me now. They can do murder, they can do cruelty, they can do action, any kind of action. Whatever they think they need, they'll do. I don't say all this to Rob; he knows it, anyway.

Now I look up at the wooden thing we've been sitting on. Maybe my eyes have gotten used to the dark, or maybe the moon has grown brighter, but I can sort of see it. First there is the wooden platform that sticks out and gets you under the knees, and then there's a dark open wallow, what appears to be a big empty space. And finally, right above us, looms a sort of mast or derrick.

"What *is* that?" I gesture up.

He doesn't answer right away. He leans over and picks up something, bounces it around in his hand for a minute, and then stands up. Pulls his arm back; he can aim, even in the dark. And does one of those neat masculine overhanded throws. There's a distant, echoing clunk. "I think it's a well."

The idea of a well seems strange and, somehow in tune with this whole dislocated evening. We sit looking up at the superstructure for a while. At last, we stand up and go off slowly, holding on to each other, tripping over roots and fallen tree limbs.

⏻ Chapter 18

You'd think then I'd have more sense, the next day, than to go for a walk along the bluff that features in Daddy's pastel painting. The bluff above our net-woman beach.

Here I am though, making myself miserable, trotting along the route past the garbage cans and across the highway and over the meadow and doing a running commentary with myself, like, *Let's watch how Crystal got there.*

I just feel I have to see it.

It's the day after Rob's and my evening session in the woods. I've turned Daddy over to Belle with sharp instructions about *Please, please keep a good watch on him; he's not reliable, and things are weird here.* And I'm going out to think and figure, how does it all connect?

She came along this path, and then went off onto that other path that heads south toward the steps.

She went with three other people.

My dad decided he had to watch her. He knew to keep

his movements careful and quiet. He crawled through the drain pipe. He was cautious. He went this way, and here I am also at that same place, the entrance to the culvert. I'm not going to shimmy my way inside that pipe, I'll walk along the top. And I start out, feeling the grass under my shoes and below that the metal of the pipe.

That was an okay walk up to the forest last night in spite of how awful I was feeling.

I'm thinking so hard that I'm pretty startled when I realize someone's sitting just a few feet away from me, on the ground at the end of the pipe, someone crouched on the bluff, a figure with its feet up, jacket looped around shoulders, a bulky figure. It looks like a man.

Danger, I decide, and am half-turned to get out of there, but too late. He can see me better than I can see him because for me he's just a shape against the sun. He raises a hand. "Hi," he announces, cheerful and perky. He adds something that sounds like, "Long time no see." And maybe, is it possible, "Gorgeous lady." Yes, all right, I get it. This person is Dr. Kittredge.

I stop, still standing on top of the drainage pipe, which puts me higher than him. I say, "What in hell are *you* doing here?"

"Why, darlin', what a way to greet an old, old friend." I bet he's smiling, but I can't see that because of the sun-haze. Now he moves a hand, he pats a piece of grass. "Come sit. I've got a bottle, and I've got a book by our new poet laureate who writes pretty good, and I've got, coming up, a nice sunset, and all I need is a lovely lady. In this interesting spot. Because that is an interesting beach down there, did you know that?"

Of course I don't answer, and he goes on, "Because maybe

the famous Sir Francis Drake beached right down there, on that very beach, on that golden strip of golden sand." He pats the grass beside him some more.

Can I get away from here in time, I think, with no idea of in time for what, and decide I can't, and then think, *Probably you came to admire the place where you murdered my aunt, and now you want to murder me*, and then I speak aloud and say, "Belle and Mrs. Cohen both know I came out here; Mrs. Cohen is going to phone in a minute.

"I asked her to check up on me," I lie, reinforcing things, in case I've not made myself clear. And then I add another thought-dart: So, if you're planning to push me off that cliff don't. Now is not a good time. I've got friends. They're almost here . . .

"*What* is the matter with you?" Dr. Kittredge asks. He has shifted position so he's no longer backed up against the sun, and now I can see his face. He has that big, florid, phony actor's face that's great for showing emotion. He contracts his brows and pulls down his mouth-corners. Looks hurt and puzzled. "You act . . ." He seems genuinely to be trying to sort this out. "Hey, darling, you look as if I *did* something. I mean, sweetheart, *really*. I've been a gentleman with you, Carla. Always. You can't say I haven't. Never so much as a single pass."

I say, "Oh, shut up." I'm not expressing myself well today, that's for sure. Suddenly this isn't a potential murderer but only Dr. Stupid Kittredge, over-testosteroned and over-buttressed by his corny male charm. Probably not a murderer because he's much too certain he's God's ultimate gift to women. I don't like it one bit that he's here ahead of me at Suspicion Beach, but that doesn't mean much.

I climb off the top of my drain pipe. "Move over," I say, "and share what you've got in your bottle."

Don't tell me alcohol isn't an antidote for misery. For a little while, getting drunk will make you forget even things like your aunt, rolled in a net, face-down on the sand, bound round and round with gold nylon cord.

What he has in the bottle is Italian red, which is okay with me.

"Well, here's to you, *bella donna*," Kittredge says, wiping the neck of the bottle off on his sleeve. I'll say this for him, he's not completely obtuse. He looks at me sideways and asks, "You okay, child?" And then hands me the bottle and says, "Wish I had a glass." And then asks, "You sure you're okay?"

"Absolutely not." The wine is the kind that back at Santa Cruz we called milk-bottle red, because of those cardboard milk-bottle–type containers.

"Did you know you were being followed?" Kittredge asks without preamble. "When you walked along the path?"

I take a swig of milk-bottle red and ask, "Followed? What do you mean?" And then stop because of course I understand the word.

"Somebody about forty feet behind you. Diving behind bushes."

I say, "Um."

I make a conscious decision. I'm paranoid enough already. I won't listen to this. That's Kittredge talking. He wants to scare me, he wants power over me.

After a pause he tries some more, "You sure lead a busy life. You gotta be careful of that stalker stuff. I had a patient whose husband . . ."

I halfway tune out his story about a broken cheekbone. Thinking "The Ride of the Valkyrie" at the back of your brain works sometimes for tuning out.

Kittredge notices I've gotten silent. "Okay, okay," he says. After a minute he asks, "How's your dad?"

"*He's* okay." I think about it and have to confirm, yes, Daddy is moderately all right; I'm the one that isn't.

"I've got a whole new batch of memory-enhancing drugs," Kittredge says. "Arrived last week."

Are we on to this again? "No memory enhancement. Don't even think about it."

"They're doing good things all the time."

"Not to my father, they're not."

"Tests on one of these are real interesting."

I hand the bottle back and make myself speak very slowly and firmly with space between each word cluster. "Leave him. Alone. Don't. Give him. Anything new."

"All right. Absolutely. Sure. But why?"

Because there's too much talk about this lately, and I trust almost nobody, and especially not you, you sexy fat oaf. Because everybody is trying to interfere. Because I'm suspicious. *Why* do you want to enhance my father's memory? Aloud, I say, "He's hit a—what do you call it?—plateau. He's doing fine."

"You're right, absolutely. A plateau. Like I said to you before, that's what makes it so sad. I mean, he's almost there. He and I had a real good discussion just the other day about that phrase in Spell 122, 'I have gone in as a falcon; I have come out as a phoenix.' The falcon, you know, a bird of prey that dives, bang, and the phoenix, a being that rises from the dead, except your dad doesn't think the ancient Egyptians saw the phoenix like that. Carla, I wish I'da known him in his prime; he must have been something. Well, I just think maybe a little prompting with some medication, keep it real mild at this point . . ."

Kittredge is cuddling the wine, and I really need it.

"Cut it out. Don't mention it one more time. And hand that bottle back."

He wipes the neck again on his sleeve and asks, professionally plaintive, "So, what do I do to get this lady to call me Patrick?"

"*Dr.* Kittredge," I underline his title heavily, "what's going to happen next at the Manor?"

"Well, dear, it's good you asked because I been worrying about that, and I think, an' I'm sorry, really sorry to say it, because I love the idea of the Manor—did I ever tell you that?"

"Yes, Dr. Kittredge, you told me."

"Jesus, will I never be Patrick to her at all? Well, I love the Manor, an' I love the idea of it, an elegant, dignified place for older folk. I was one of the big fighters for a Manor even existin', but times change, and we change with them, and maybe, I'm thinkin', we're all going to have to jump ship. Close the whole operation up."

I say, "Urp," and feel a lurch inside. First we've got a Manor where my father can live, but we're scared to be in it. And now, ahead, no Manor.

"There's a group," Dr. K. goes on, "wants to buy everything."

"Somebody wants to *buy* it?" I almost drop the milk-bottle red, which of course isn't in a cardboard milk bottle but in a real glass bottle that would shatter. But this buy-out plan seems like the last thing I'd have suspected.

"Yes, love. Fork over cash. Take possession."

"But, why? It can't be *profitable*?"

"Nope. Right now it's not profitable one bit. These purchasin' folks are real estate. Gonna make everything over. Build a model town or some garbage. I haven't kept that good track, I mean, as a director I knew they were out there, but I just never took it seriously, couldn't believe it, idiotic idea, model town? A million miles from God? Anyway, now, with things so bad, some directors are dyin' to sell. Hard on the residents."

"Yes," I agree. "Right."

"Believe it, hard on me, too. Incidentally, dear, where're your friends?"

"What?" It takes me a minute to catch on. At first, I think he means Rob, and then I remember that five minutes ago I told him Mrs. Cohen or Belle would be calling me. "Oh," I say. "Mrs. Cohen? Forgets. You know." Kittredge and I are comfortably silent around this lie. I give him back his bottle. "Tell me more about selling the Manor."

"I don't know any more. It's been in the background for six months, maybe, but I never took it seriously, and then these accidents and lawsuits started piling up, and now I guess it *is* serious. I mean, the deal might go through. I feel bad, even though I, personally, got other possibilities for my future. Sisal, though, really wants to hang in. Not sell. Die on the barricades. Strong-minded lady." The doctor's voice holds a smile, reminiscent of happy office-couch afternoons with Mrs. Sisal.

"I wish we had something to eat," I say. "Have you got a sandwich? Or crackers? Some cookies?"

"No, I don't. I'm being unprecedentedly generous with this bottle." He makes a noise by blowing into it. "An' you do have to admit," he goes on. "The whole thing with this buy-out proposal looks peculiar. We been having a kind of industrial sabotage, so to speak, for months now, accidents, lawsuits, dirty tricks all over the place, got everybody scared shitless—excuse me, dear—get the clients starting to leave and sue, and the Manor set up for bankruptcy, and then, bingo, enter the evil real estaters to buy it up for a song."

"What about Mona?" I ask. "*That* wasn't industrial sabotage?"

"Hey, Jesus, no. Have you asked around about that busy Mona bee? She was another, different story; dealt drugs, and profited big time, and screwed everybody. With a little blackmail for extras. Mona was not a nice lady. Careless, too. But she wasn't part of this buy-out deal. Anybody coulda killed her.

"We are almost finished with this bottle, dear. One teeny hit left inside for each of us."

"Thank you," I reach out my hand. "Thanks for sharing, like we say."

"We do, don't we?"

For a minute I debate confiding in Dr. Kittredge about Aunt Crystal. Lying in the grass beside somebody you're sharing a bottle with is a bonding experience, even if you halfway suspect the person of a major crime. The combination of grass and sea air and milk-bottle red dulls your perceptions. I think about this for half a second and then mentally shake myself and return to normal.

Tomorrow, I announce to myself, I'll get serious about things. I have to rethink my whole position here.

I climb to my feet. "Thanks for the wine."

He groans. "Honey, I'm stuck here. Flat on my back. You're gonna have to give me a hand up."

"Boy," he says, when he's halfway standing and my hand

is in his, "boy, I sure yearn to see that Coffin Lid Text of your dad's. Talkin' to him an' readin' his book some. Fascinatin' stuff. Around here some place, isn't it?"

"It's at Egypt Regained, a museum in a place called Homeland," I say shortly. I don't know what to make of Kittredge's interest in Daddy's Egyptian studies. I think it has to be phony. Everything else about the doctor screams phony, or at least half-phony.

And I tell myself again that I've never met anybody except another archaeologist who would read a book about fourteen obscure hieroglyphs.

Just the same, Dr. Kittredge and I walk companionably back to the Manor, with him being good and only making his hand stray into the small of my back twice or maybe three times, and me swatting at him and saying absent-mindedly, "Cut it out, will you?"

I have just seen Dr. Kittredge to his back door. He pauses there—he has that apartment behind the hospital with a metal seabird on the door—and does another Kittredge-charm attempt. "Hey, come on in, Goldilocks darlin', enter and schmooze some more. I promise total safe-conduct, and I got another bottle of the really good stuff this time." And so on and so forth, at which I just laugh and start to wave good-bye, until he shrugs, "Okay, babe, next time," and disappears inside, *clunk*.

So I am standing there, a little drunk, thinking about our grassy session and wondering if I've picked up any deer ticks, when the door across the steps from Kittredge's opens to emit Mrs. Sisal.

"Well, now," she says.

I say, "Hello, Mrs. Sisal."

She repeats, "Well." She is looking as she always does, high-end expensive, but casually so, for at-home living, in a simple, little wide-pants outfit with a simple, little, hand-woven silk shirt and some chunky beads. Her asymmetrical haircut glimmers, straight and shiny-black.

I'm waiting for a crack about me and Kittredge and about how I reek of red wine, and what am I doing here anyway in the better residential part of the Manor, but what she says is, "Has he been feeding you his fairy story about the takeover?"

I stare and make unintelligent noises, as in, "Huh?"

"I guess he really believes that," she says. "But mostly he made it up. Patrick likes to invent."

It occurs to me that Mrs. Sisal is drunker than I am.

"Patrick the giant killer," she says. "Did you have a nice, nice walk?"

"It was okay." I'm wondering how in hell I'm going to get out of here. A jealous Mrs. Sisal could be a major problem. Even the hair-pulling, assaultive kind.

But she doesn't seem interested in that side of things. She wants to talk about the takeover. Or what she describes as the nontakeover. "Don't believe him. All that garbage about somebody buying something. He made it up." She tucks a strand of the straight, very black hair behind an ear and leans against her doorjamb. A little unsteady but handsome, like a *New York Times* fashion spread. "Makes him feel good. And he's a liar. He'll talk endlessly about what . . . oh, hell, who cares?" She fixes on me as if she has just noticed me. "So how are things for you, Miss Dutiful Daughter?"

Yes, Mrs. Sisal is pretty drunk.

"I'm okay."

"Not enough dutiful daughters around here. You are a model. An absolute paragon. The morning stars will warble about you. Is that your own hair or a wig?"

I stare.

She analyzes, head on one side. "You're young enough," she decides. "Probably you just get up in the A.M. and shake it around, and all day your hair looks like that. Well . . . don't believe anything Patrick tells you. Not a damn thing.

"And listen." She wobbles against her doorjamb. "You and I have got to talk." She raises a finger at me. "Because I know what you've been up to.

"No, no," drunk as she is, I guess she can read my expression, "it's all *right*. *Somebody* needs to poke and pry around here.

"But you and I should talk. I have something to tell you. Something important. Things aren't always what they seem. Come see me tomorrow, you hear?

"And have a nice, nice day.

"It *is* important," she adds, and she exits abruptly back behind her half-open door, which, instead of a bas-relief of seabirds like the doctor's, has an elegant stained-glass panel.

♟ Chapter 19

Rob comes by that night.

I discover that I am expecting a visit from Rob, that I've mentally set aside eleven P.M. as Rob Time. I wait for him on the settee down the hall from my dad's door. He's gone to sleep, but I'm keeping guard from here. I'm reading Alice Munro, which is okay for right now because she's simple and straightforward and a marvelous writer and slightly depressing. I'm about to finish that great story where the woman leaves the kids to run off with the summer-theater director, and she tells us near the end that the children didn't forget and didn't forgive, and finally she lets slip at the very end that the romance didn't last anyhow. It was several romances ago by this time.

"So what's up?" Rob asks.

I tell him that I want to wait here outside my dad's door. Just because I feel uneasy. So he kisses me and sits down on the couch and takes Alice Munro out of my lap. "Anything new?" he asks and I tell him about Dr. Kittredge's buy-out story and then about Mrs. Sisal's drunk act. I put in plenty of local color about Sisal and how unstable she was leaning against her doorjamb, about how, if I were feeling well enough to think some things were funny, that would be one of the funny ones. But I don't tell him that I also was drunk, and Kittredge, too, was drunk along with me. I'm interested in myself for not saying this.

Robbie says he wouldn't trust Kittredge and he wouldn't trust Sisal, so where does that leave anybody?

"Sure he's in my hospital, but I still don't trust him," Rob augments. "He projects *phony*."

Rob and I usually agree about people. It's on how to live our lives that we don't reach accord.

"Listen," he leans forward, looks at his knees, picks at something on his blue jeans, "you know, Carla . . . this isn't your problem, it's my problem entirely. I hate to dump on you, but . . . well, I'm feeling bad about Arlette."

I exercise self-control. I don't say, "Thanks a bundle."

"I mean," Robbie says, "there's a kind of *understanding* between me and Arlie."

Now I do say something. "Oh, shit." And, "You're right, it's your problem." And then, "Okay, verbalize, say more, how *do* you feel?"

Rob shrugs. "I dunno. I mean, like, you're my *oldest* friend."

I say, "Sure." I settle back on the base of my spine.

I must have been expecting this statement for a while without knowing it, because now I only need to spend a few minutes of being surprised and jealous before I'm able to get mad and talk pretty fast. "Listen, everything on earth has happened to me this year: my father's crazy and my aunt got murdered and I'm stuck in this weird place and I don't have any money. You having a girlfriend is nothing, just a blip on the screen—everybody has a girlfriend, give me a break. I had a *philandering boyfriend . . .*" I'm about to go on with a *who also* about the Habitat guy, and then don't.

Robbie says, "Yep."

I think back over the list I just gave him. "You didn't need to dump on me."

"Yeah, I did. 'Cause otherwise it's cheating."

I think, cheating? If he's worried about cheating on Arlette, how does talking to me help?

I guess he means it would be cheating on me not to remind me of Arlette. Noble-minded, a Robbie gesture. Revoltingly so. Really wrong and almost right. It helps to get mad at him; it's good for my soul, cleans out the sludge. "Let me give you a Boy Scout badge," I say. "Our new decoration, the nobleness merit badge; you do seven noble deeds . . ."

He says, "Hey, cut the crap."

Suddenly I'm yelling, "Crap? What's crap about it?" I realize that we're in the hall of the Manor and will probably wake up half the aged populace. I take a breath. Then I begin a three-minute low-voiced squawk about how pious he is and back in my life now after almost three years and acting as if he has voting privileges, "Look at how you try to order me around, ideas for my future. Yes, I do think you're bossy, and yes, poor Arlette, I do agree. You and I should totally stop seeing each other. Right away. Now. This minute. Good-bye. I'll go one way, and you go the other." I'm half-standing, prepared to dive for my room and leave him sitting here.

He reaches out and grabs my wrist. I don't much want to sit back down, but I do.

"Listen, Carl . . . Oh, God, I guess I *was* pious. Sweetheart, let's give it time." After a while he adds, "It's been a godawful week, just let it be. I know, everything's awful. I'm sorry."

I wait to stop ventilating. "I meant it."

"Yeah, I know."

We're both breathing hard, and suddenly we just drop the subject.

The window's open; outside it's a nice night, not much wind, smell of salt and kelp.

"So, okay," I tell him, "you're my oldest friend."

And somehow for the next ten minutes we get into a big discussion, trying to remember when was the first time we saw each other. A long time back. "You were about six," Rob says, "sitting on the steps going up to your porch, and you had some kind of a book open on your knees. You were drawing in it. Not that I really paid attention. You were just this little kid."

That's not the way I remember it. What I remember is Rob out in front of Susie's practicing his yo-yo and my dad coming over to watch, with me right beside him. After a minute Daddy asked to try it out; in about four minutes he got pretty good.

Finally, we stall into a moment of silence during which Rob looks toward my father's door and says, "Y'know, maybe we better check on him."

"Check on him? I've been *here*. Except for a few minutes, bathroom and stuff." But meanwhile I'm up and halfway down the hall toward the door, thinking, well, *estupida*, your

father's a target, what's the matter with you, and Rob likes
to be directive, good quality, so let him.

When I look back he's following, his wide flushed face
screwed up into what I guess is a worried frown.

The door to Daddy's apartment is locked, that is, locked to
someone who might try to get in from the hall, but okay for
him if he needs to get out. I fumble around with the key
and throw the door open and then have to stand for a
minute blinking, because the room is dark, with only a
small glow from the night-light at the foot of the sleeping
alcove.

It takes me a minute to discover that my father isn't in
his bed. The bed, nestled in the alcove, is a bit scrambled,
covers disarranged, but there's no old gentleman there. I
dally in the entryway making amorphous questioning
noises; Rob, from behind me, turns on the light.

The room isn't particularly messy, but it looks, with the
tumbled bedclothes and a displaced chair, as if someone has
left it suddenly.

The bathroom door is open, and he's not in there.

Rob is the one who finally notices. He points to the space
under the window seat. This little cavern probably once had
a cupboard door, but that door has been removed, leaving
the molding that would fit around it and a space inside suitable for storing things like bedding.

Right now it contains a hunched-up figure, a round
shape unidentifiable except for one sleeve of a tweed jacket,
one pants leg, also of tweed, and the back of a head.

My father is curled up in there like a fetus, his head

against his knees. His feet are side by side with their backs to us; one of his nice brown leather shoes has come untied, the lace dangles across the cupboard threshold.

Rob and I dash and kneel close. He's breathing raggedly. I say, "Father, we're here." Rob says, "Hey, Ed. Hey, buddy." I say, "Darling, it's okay," and Rob says, "Come on out and let me look at you." And so on and so forth.

At first there's no answer. Finally we get some twitching and a slight shoulder-muscle movement from inside the tweed jacket.

Rob says, "Attaboy," and "Come on," and "Let's get out of here, shall we?"

Nothing more happens.

Rob mouths, "Catatonic," at me, and I agree, "Shock."

I murmur into the cupboard, "Daddy, did something scare you?"

Rob tells me, "Traumatic shock—they come out of that."

"Who's 'they'? This is my father."

Rob says, "It's short-lived, usually."

I say, "Oh God, how dumb I was." I've started crying. The tears are mostly frustration and anger, all aimed by Carla at Carla. I'm thinking, I knew I had to get him out of this place. I was being stubborn, I wanted to disagree with Rob. It's my fault this happened, I'm to blame.

Rob says, "Hey, Carla," trying to make it sound comforting.

From inside the cupboard a voice emerges. It's cracked and rusty-sounding, but recognizable, "*Carla?* Did somebody say 'Carla'? You know, I had a *daughter* named Carla."

"I'm here." I put my hand in the cupboard with him and pat his knee.

It takes a while, but finally he turns enough to peer out.
He says, "Oh, of course," in a very ordinary voice. And in a
minute he's scrambling on his hands and knees over the
closet sill and onto the rug.

He doesn't look too bad. His hair is messed up, and he
blinks at the light. He's clutching a piece of paper that has
gotten folded and spindled into a baton.

We descend on him with soothing useless chirps. Rob
says, "Come on now," and I say, "Now, now, just sit here."
Rob says at me, "Drugs, maybe." I say, "He hid. Not drugs."

My father gets positioned onto a chair. He is still holding
his rolled-up scroll of paper. He seems insecure about sitting on the chair; he plants his feet flat and his back straight
and angles his baton upright. He looks like one of the little
Egyptian guardian tomb-figures, a *shabti*.

"Father, did something happen?"

"I got an e-mail." He gestures with the rolled-up paper
baton. He seems to want to hand it to me and to not want
to. Finally, he extends it.

Straightened out, the baton becomes a big piece of paper,
clearly labeled, "e-mail," in red computer-printing. With a
message, all in caps:

> THIS OLD AND USELESS KING WOULD NOT HELP THE
> JUDGES AND HAS BEEN CONDEMNED TO THE FAR-
> THEST PUNISHMENT IN LONELINESS AND DARKNESS,
> WHERE THE KA IS CONDEMNED TO DRINK FILTH AND
> EAT FECES.

"An ugly message," my father says.

I suppress an impulse to crunch the paper up and throw

it away. To rip it into little bits. To tell my father it doesn't matter. "Where did you get this, Daddy?"

"They usually just drop them through the transom."

Rob and I exchange looks. My father's apartment doesn't have a transom. I don't think any of the quarters at the Manor do.

"And then they come and get it." Daddy looks at me and apparently decides he hasn't answered our question. "She brought it. The lady with the scissors."

I stare at him, completely stopped. I always thought the lady with the scissors was Mona.

"With the moon and stars."

Mona again. I mouth at Rob, "Tell you later." I'm still holding the e-mail. "This is evil."

It's evil, and it has truly upset Edward Day. I have to acknowledge the authenticity, the Egyptian-ness. All that stuff about wandering in darkness, drinking filth. Straight out of *The Book of the Dead*. Some parts may even be quotes. Guaranteed to abrade my poor Dad in the vulnerable parts of his psyche.

But in *The Book of the Dead* we have straightforward ways of dealing with evil.

"I'm going to destroy this now, Father. You watch, and I will completely destroy it."

I set the paper afire by holding it against the element of the little electric kitchen stove. Rob supplies a saucer to catch the ashes, and together Rob and I, with my father witnessing, flush the ashes down the toilet.

"There now," I say. I even add the childhood formula, "All, all gone."

Daddy seems better after this exorcising ceremony. He

talks about how upset he was. "I didn't like that. It bothered me. That was a bad paper. I'm glad you came."

Rob and I give him tea and put him back to bed. And he seems happy when I say I'll spend the night here on his window seat. "Yes, wonderful, dear. Truly thoughtful. I would appreciate it."

He still claims it was the moon-and-stars lady who brought his e-mail. "Oh, yes indeed. In a cape like yours, you know.

"They want my token. But they can't have that, not the token, I've hidden it. Hidden where no one can find it.

"I think it possible that's why they cursed me."

I decide he's right. Yes, that's why they cursed him.

"Well, obviously not." I scratch that message on a long yellow pad and shove it at Rob. He and I are in my father's kitchen discussing, via whispers and notes, the Mona question.

"It wasn't Mona. But Kittredge wrote the curse."

It takes a lot of yellow notepad and ballpoint pen to explain why I think this, after which Rob nods, yes.

"Lock the doors. Lock the windows," he scribbles.

I try to picture Dr. Kittredge disguised as Mona. And fail.

"But why Mona?" Rob writes.

I have an idea, but I don't try to explain. It's the sort of ridiculous, fanciful thing that practical Rob doesn't go in for, but I can imagine that a certain kind of sick person would get a charge from dressing up, pretending to be Mona, dead Mona, Mona gone now for several days, Mona with her neck broken. I can also imagine that maybe Mona, in her original form (nurse, hospital worker) is someone my father thinks has a right to come into his apartment when she scratches on the window.

Because that's how it must have happened—entry through the window, which is almost floor-to-ceiling height. I've bolted that window in two different places now and leaned a chair against it.

⌐ Chapter 20

"How are you this morning? Are you better? You slept well, I think? Does that make you feel okay now?"

My father, of course, can't answer all these intrusive questions. He looks at me confusedly and drops his toothbrush.

Our tête-à-tête is broken up by Mrs. Dexter, who bangs on our door and nails me with an accusation: "What on earth are you doing in your father's apartment so early in the morning, and in your pajamas, for goodness sake?"

Mrs. Dexter has been consistently cross with me lately. Perhaps it dates from my doing the Heimlich on her after the oyster-glass. Everyone says I saved her life then, and there's a legend about how the saved person always resents the one who butted in and took over. Something about indebtedness.

I mutter a couple of words about Daddy not feeling well, which she ignores. "I came by to show him my new car."

My father says, "New car!" and I say the wrong thing, "I didn't know you could drive."

Which totally riles Mrs. Dexter, who wants to know why I thought that; did I think she had always been an old lady with a walker? She's only had the walker for ten years, she grew up on a ranch; how could she not know how to drive?

"I got the walker after I fell off a horse. And then the bastard kicked me."

My face probably gives me away. I also didn't imagine Mrs. Dexter on a horse. I didn't imagine her using the word *bastard*. But my father, thank God, enters the conversation at this point. He has new-car questions. "I like new cars. What kind of new car?"

The new car is a Lincoln.

Daddy completely approves. He thinks that a Lincoln is the best kind of car. "Didn't I see you recently? You didn't tell me you had a Lincoln."

Mrs. Dexter recomposes herself and smiles at him. She offers him a ride in her car. Now. After breakfast. As soon as Carla has gotten herself out of her pajamas.

I'm not the least bit sure about letting Daddy out for an excursion right now, what with e-mails and traumatic withdrawal episodes, but then I look at his face, washed with pleasure and seeming alive again, and listen to him saying, "Does it have leather seats?" and think that an hour's drive with an old friend would be good recreation. And Mrs. Dexter, although crotchety, is reliable. I don't question her motives, the way I do Mrs. La Salle's.

"I'm going to eat breakfast with you," Mrs. Dexter announces, obviously making a concession. "Go ahead now, Carla, get dressed."

*   *   *

Over French toast Mrs. Dexter mellows into conversation and talks about the horse who kicked her. "Burly old brute. Just like my uncle, who owned his dam. My uncle lived here, you know."

"You told me earlier."

"In this house. He was rich. He lived *here*, in the Manor."

I look around me, at the high ceilings, chandeliers, redwood walls. "It seems so overwhelming. So institutional."

"Always did. He was filthy, and he was filthy rich, and he owned the Manor. We were his poor relations. Used to come over here to play. And sometimes ride. It was a role we acted, poor relations. And he did the rich act . . . Pulled out all the stops . . . Lord of the Manor. Edward, are you almost ready?"

"Kicked by a horse," my father says. "That would be hard on the *ka.*"

Mrs. Dexter asks, "But did they have horses in ancient Egypt?"

"Of course they did. I would like another piece of French toast."

I've been wanting to congratulate Mrs. Dexter on her purple suit with the fur collar, which looks new, but she glares at me so peremptorily that I decide to stuff it.

"They have an exhibit on California history," she says after breakfast; she's speaking of the Conestoga Library. "That'll interest you, won't it, Edward? Things they dug up, like arrowheads, pots?"

"Perhaps." He seems more interested in the car and its leather upholstery. He climbs in and leans his head back. "I need this drive. I have serious concerns. Things to travel to."

I start to tell Mrs. Dexter to be careful with him, to watch him, and then don't say it. I start to caution that he's been feeling bad lately, and don't do that, either. "Call me as soon as you get back?"

And she snaps, "Of course." She backs up in a whirl of dust; she's a decisive, if demonstrative, driver.

And I go off to work only about one-eighth there. I'm worried about us. I've decided, maybe during the night, maybe while I was asleep, the way you sometimes decide such things, that Rob has been right all along and that my father and I absolutely need to get out of here. Are we in danger now? Is my father in danger now? How much of a real threat is a mean, nasty note? Should we, today, pack up a little stuff and call Henry the cabdriver? "Yes, of course," I tell Mrs. Cohen, "I'll get a new inhaler for you. Coming right up." Noble of me to come to work this morning, but I hate to leave the old people stranded before they even get out of their bathrobes.

Maybe I can borrow Mrs. Dexter's Lincoln to exit the Manor. Maybe I can steal the doctor's Miata. The point is, make a plan, a simple, step-by-step plan, and leave.

I'm not helped by meeting Ms. Deirdre Chaundy in the hall, poking through the bottles on the prescription shelf of my cart. I say, "Hey, good morning Ms. Chaundy, what's up?" and she says, not turning a hair, of which she has plenty (and this big fat teutonic braid down the middle of her back), "Good morning, my dear, I was simply wonder-ing what exactly got onto these carts. I am a director of the Manor, you know, and I thought I should be more informed about what goes on every day; the daily experience is so im-portant, isn't it? Such a responsibility for *you,* the aides, hav-ing serious medications for the patients out here in the hall. Unsupervised."

"Yes, indeed," I say heartily, as if she's just given me a compliment, although what she has done is to adroitly turn a situation where she's been caught snooping into one where she accuses me of laxity.

"Great that you should want to investigate," I say, re-couping some control of the conversation. And she comes back, "You know, I think about that strange, strange picture of your father's. Such an example of, well, disturbance, don't you think? How is he now? Is he better?"

Ms. Chaundy and I smile at each other, lips stretched and lots of teeth, and I tell her, "Oh, my goodness, I have to get back to my rounds."

Finally I'm done and on my way down to Mrs. Sisal's office where I'll find out what she thought she wanted yesterday. She was pretty insistent. She needed to see me. A lot has happened since then, so the tense tone in her voice has faded from my memory, but now it comes back. Insistent: "You and I should talk . . . It is important." Amazing, Sisal con-fiding in me. Everybody's changing lately.

Well, one thing I'll do; I'll tell her I'm taking the after-noon off. Maybe the rest of my life off. I won't ask her; I'll tell her. My father is being persecuted and has episodes and needs me, but I won't say that, either. I need me and I'm quitting and I won't tell her that, too. If seeing her drunk yesterday doesn't give me some extra perks, what does?

Mrs. Sisal's door is partially open, and I push it in and enter, full of determination. Her office contains a wide official-looking desk which faces the door; behind it, with its back to the window, is her chair, also facing the door. There are various oriental rugs and books and pictures and mahogany bookcases. To the left is the cubicle where Rebecca does her typing; that's empty now. A handsome bay window behind the desk throws too much light on everything and makes it hard to see. I stand for a minute, blinking.

But after my sight adjusts I still find it hard to see. Mrs. Sisal seems to be here. In her chair. She seems to be asleep, head on the desk. She's turned to the left, cheek against the desktop, one hand beside it, fingers outspread against the desktop. She wears a spray of red geraniums in her hair. No, they're red orchids. How peculiar, how un-Sisal-like. I give the image a minute to subside.

There's a funny smell.

Orchids. Geraniums. Some red flower. Mrs. Sisal has a red rose over her ear. Some flower or other.

I step forward. Confirming what I knew all along, really. Not red orchids or geraniums. Mrs. Sisal lies with her head on her desk and a blossom of blood above her ear. More blood, a trail of it, is down her cheek. Her half-open mouth has oozed a path of silvery drool onto the desk surface, the eye that's visible stares, wide open, canted up, a blue iris with red lines across the sclera, lashes stuck high, gaze aimed at the ceiling. There's a big splash of blood and some other stuff behind her head, on the other side. And there's a heavy, throat-clenching smell.

I know that smell; we had to get used to it in the animal lab. Sometimes the just-killed animal lets go the contents of its bowel and bladder. Poor Mrs. Sisal, so elegant and precise.

I start reciting a mantra. *No, no.* And, *You won't.*

No, you won't be sick. No, you won't throw up. You won't throw up, you won't pass out. You won't let the walls go black. You will stand here until your hands and ankles stop shaking. Your fingers will be okay. Move your fingers. Your head is starting to clear. You can stand okay. You can think. Try to think.

I can stand without starting to fall over.

I can think about what to do.

I am not going to call the sheriff.

I am not going to page Rebecca.

I am going to get out of here.

I reach to feel the pulse in Mrs. Sisal's outstretched arm. There is no pulse.

Again, I repeat, I am getting out of here; I am not telling the sheriff I was here. I am in enough trouble already. If the sheriff knew I had discovered Mrs. Sisal, he would be suspicious. He would draw conclusions about me and my connection to the deaths at the Manor. He would put me and my father on a short leash, and he would keep us around forever as witnesses.

And my father and I are getting out of here. We're leaving the Manor. We are going to do this now.

I concentrate on removing all traces of me from this room.

I've seen enough movies to know the usual things. I don't think her wrist will show my fingerprints. Maybe I touched the desk; I wipe the edge of it with my shirt sleeve.

I pull the sleeve over my hand to open the door and use it to polish the doorknob. I back into the hall. There's no one there. I polish the outside doorknob. Then I go away, fast but not too fast, toward my cubbyhole room.

I think I've just committed a crime, that of fleeing the scene of a crime.

I liked Mrs. Sisal. Well, sort of liked her. I had gotten used to her and admired her and thought she was a classy dresser.

Nothing about her made me think I was going to find her dead.

The sheriff and the murderer would both be interested.

The sheriff would be deeply interested if he knew that I'd found Mrs. Sisal's lifeless body. Did I check on that thoroughly? Do I know for sure that no little spark of life lingered in her? No, I don't. Refusing to give aid to a dying person. That may be my big crime, probably a worse one than fleeing the scene.

The murderer would like it that I fled the scene. He/she wants me to be scared. He/she wants to scare me first, so I'll be ready to give up whatever information I've got that I don't know I have. After that, he/she will kill me.

I start to do a little chorus in my head of "Oh, good God, good God," and then stop myself. I don't have time for that.

There are several halls and stairways before my room. I remember not to run. I move circumspectly, turn corners carefully. I've stopped shaking. I watch my feet; they're moving okay. There's a clot of something rancid stuck halfway up my gullet. I swallow hard. No. I'm not going to be sick.

The picture of Mrs. Sisal with her head on her desk and part of her scalp blotted by a red blood-flower and a trail of drool across the desk follows me. It's traveling along with me.

My phone, which is stashed in my pocket, rings. It's Mrs. Dexter. I have trouble figuring this out at first, and then I realize, yes, okay, Mrs. Dexter. Here, on my phone. She's calling me about my dad. She said she'd do that. She probably has him back in the Manor now.

But she sounds upset, not at all like herself. "Well, I am sorry," she's saying, "I just can't explain it. He wanted something or other. He's so vague, you know. I couldn't figure out what he wanted. Something about a cue? A koo? He wouldn't explain, and I couldn't persuade him. He insisted. He got quite frantic. So I stopped and let him out. And then when I'd reparked the car—we were on a blind curve—I don't know how to say this . . . it's hard to believe. After I got out he wasn't there."

I lean against a chunk of tapestried wall with a gold-framed picture on either side of me and try to understand.

"I went back and forth," she says. "It was hard, of course, with the walker. I went down some lanes, as far as a couple of fences . . . all of that, several times. I don't see how it's possible, but he wasn't there. He just disappeared."

I'm beginning to get this.

Mrs. Dexter has lost my father.

She has lost him some place on the highway.

"About a mile from here," she says. "I've looked and

looked. I've been driving back and forth. I got out and scrambled around on the side of the road . . . with the walker . . . among the bushes . . . for a long time, and nothing. I shouldn't have let him out, but he was so frantic. I don't know how to explain it, how could he just vanish?"

To my surprise, my mind seems to be working. I tell Mrs. Dexter that I will handle it. I hang up. I lean against the wall.

I think I understand the situation.

It's simple.

Two things have happened. Mrs. Sisal has been murdered and my father has disappeared.

The sheriff is going to be here in a few minutes, as soon as somebody else blunders in on Mrs. Sisal's body with the blood-orchid across her scalp.

The sheriff is going to do a lockdown. No one will leave the Manor.

My jobs are simple. First I have to get out of here, and second I have to find my father. Those are direct and basic tasks.

I rest my shoulder against the wall for a while longer. Time is closing in.

🐦 Chapter 21

Henry the cabdriver and I are in Henry's taxi; we are driving toward the Conestoga bus station. I haven't told Henry that we'll be going there slowly and looking for my father along the way, but that's what we're doing, and Henry seems to understand. "You think he got off and explored?" Henry asks. "Wonderful old gent. Loves to explore."

We take two hours and twenty minutes for the half-hour trip. We make stops at Ms. Chaundy's painting meadow, at the meadow with the picnic tables, at the meadow from which Daddy observed them slowly and quietly murder my aunt, at several other fields and lanes, at one abandoned farmhouse. And no trace of a lost old man. "Wants to be off on his own," Henry surmises. "Independent old gent."

I'm clutching a piece of paper that I found in Daddy's room along with a Greyhound bus schedule. "The Eye has been broached," it says. "The *khus* have fallen into darkness." This is in his own handwriting, some of which is quite legible, almost normal. I guess he wrote it just before he went off with Mrs. Dexter.

In addition to the bus schedule and the note, there's a map of the town of Conestoga. All of this makes me think that Conestoga, especially Conestoga's bus station, is a good place to start looking for him.

I hold Daddy's note in my hand and crumple it. I recite the facts: Mrs. Sisal is murdered. My father is lost. The *khus* are fallen. My father is in danger. I'm in danger.

Who did all this? Dr. Kittredge. He's the one I should watch out for. Kittredge perfectly fits the profile of my murderer. Strong. Good eyesight. Good physical shape. In on everything at the Manor. Smarming up to me. He would have known when to shoot Mrs. Sisal, what it was she wanted to tell me. He knew how to break Mona's neck.

After a lot of palaver, Henry agrees to let me off in front of the bus station. He doesn't want to. He wants to go in with me, help me, offer advice: "Nice old gent. I understand." I have a hard time dissuading Henry, but I finally succeed. Because he's so anxious to help, I give him a note for the sheriff saying I'm in Conestoga. Suddenly, I'm developing some sense; I want the world to know where I am.

An hour later, where I am is down at the end of Conestoga's main street, turning into an alley. I've been to the bus station, the diner, the library, the bakery, the drugstore. *Have you seen an old gentleman, very polite? He gets confused. He was wearing a tweed suit and vest. He might ask . . .* Here I run into trouble, imagining what he might ask. (In the bus station, maybe: "Where do I catch the bus to Haifa? To Jeddah?") But no one in the bus station remembers him at all. (In the library: "Have you a book on the *khus*?") The librarian frowns, chomps the end of her pencil, thinks maybe she remembers an old gentleman who wandered quietly, touching the spines of books and murmuring; he didn't ask questions. The bakery lady suddenly remembers him because he bought two currant scones. A neat-looking old gentleman who paid in dollar bills and asked about her mother. "Hey, that was real sweet."

I have no idea where he got the dollar bills.

And the drugstore lady remembers him well because he wanted to buy the eyedrops display. "Big picture of an eye, it was. He got upset. And he said something about koos? Cues?

"He said something else weird, 'I need to lie down under a date palm.' An' I told him, 'I don't think we got any date palms here. That's farther down the coast.' But he went off anyway. Maybe down the alley?

"You'll find him, dear," she adds. "My grandpa used to do that. Down that alley, that one there. I think I saw him turn."

The alley has a couple of garages and two pink cottages, and it leads to the backside of Main Street. Across the street from the backside of Main Street stretches an open field with occasional orange splotches; those could be California poppies. There is no date palm, unless you think the oil derrick looks like one.

Daddy likes alleys. In Egypt it was always the back roads that attracted him.

But there's no white-haired gentleman here, nobody sitting on the steps of the cottages.

Nothing except a handsome, uneven field of wavering silver-green April grass with, maybe, poppies. Staring at it, I remember what that silver-green is called: California ryegrass. Blue mountains in the distance. I stare some more and try to feel with the back of my neck if I'm being followed.

That's always possible. Yes, I'm paranoid these days.

In the middle distance of the meadow is the oil derrick, a tipsy one, and closer in is the ryegrass, silver-and-green, with orange for the poppies. And then comes a dark splotch that could be nothing; grass comes in different types and colors, maybe it's a patch of special growth with one of those other grass-names like Blue Fescue. But maybe something else. A place where somebody has mashed everything down by sitting or lying, and that person is still there stretched out or bent down below the grass heads.

Give me strength for the journey home.

If that splotch is made by my father, huddled up, he's going to be feeling peculiar. Deserted, puzzled, lost.

I start out across the field. One of the Prayers in *The Book of the Dead* is about crossing a field of high metal wheat; that's one of the dangers the poor departed *ka* has to go through.

In another section, the wandering *ka* gets a few minutes' respite; it can lie down and get comfort for the rest of its journey.

This meadow has been baked by the afternoon sun; the rye seeds bob invitingly.

* * *

It takes me five minutes of wading; the stems are thigh-high and pull at my jeans. I am sort of seeing something ahead of me that looks like an old gentleman camped among the weeds. And sort of not. I'm thinking that I hope he's here and is all right while part of me hopes he isn't. That some miracle made him feel enterprising enough to go back to the bus station and climb on a bus (even without money, maybe somehow he'd find a way).

But nearer that dark place in the field I decide yes, okay, something is indeed there. The grass has been mashed down; around the edges it makes a wavering high wall.

And, yes, I reach the depressed place in the field and look down, and there he is. I think, *Oh you poor darling.* He's curled on his side, buried in the tall stems, arms bent up beside his head. He's in the fetal position again. I drop on my knees beside him.

"Father," I say. No answer. I say, "It's all right, dear, really it is, it's Carla here." No answer. I take one of his hands, which is clenched into a tight little fist, and undo it, and chafe it the way you would for cold or exposure. Although it's warm in here, he's been lying in partial sun. The hand finally relaxes some, so I pat it smooth and start on the other one.

Meanwhile saying over and over, "It's all right." Which doesn't seem to be working.

I sit, simply holding and stroking. Watching for watchers. Saying an Egyptian prayer. Or a Susie prayer. The shadows across the field get longer. It's beginning to get cold.

"Father." A slight squeeze from his hand, but no answer. It's an accident that I start the humming. I'm not really aware that I'm doing it, but I hear myself making a drone to accompany the hand-chafing; it's a tune that he likes: "Get up, Darling Corey."

A bluegrass tune: "The revenue-officers are coming/ Gonna tear your still-house down." My dad is a real Renaissance man; back in his glory days he had lots of interests, and folk music was a sweet one of those. He could even plunk a few notes on a banjo.

There's a stirring at my feet. Grass squeaks and clicks. He moves an arm. "Why, Daughter . . ."

See. Like I was thinking. Sweet.

"Well," I say, "hello."

He rolls over and squints. The setting sun shines right across his nose. "I must have lain down for a little nap."

"I guess you did."

"I think I was scared. Do you think so?"

"Maybe."

He sits up and bends over, resting his forehead on his cupped hands. "I do not enjoy being scared."

"Me, neither, Daddy."

"If I could figure out why . . ."

I tell him don't worry. I put my arm around him. "Do you want to stand up? Okay, let's try it." When he's on his feet, a little unsteady and complaining that the light dazzles him, I say, "Listen, there's a nice hotel back there, let's go in and get a room. Maybe they have the ones with the little refrigerators, and maybe we can get a Coke . . ."

"A cup of tea," he interjects.

"Right." I gesture toward the back of the Best Western. "Over there. Can you walk okay? All right, honey, a cup of tea . . . lean on me then, let's go."

We set off diagonally across the meadow, pushing through the grass.

I don't think anybody else is in sight down at the end of Main Street.

The Best Western scarlet neon sign is on already and is blinking.

My father is shaky but can still be interested in this sign. "I wonder how they keep it going? Some kind of clockwork? Hydraulic power?" His attention is all on the sign; he doesn't seem to understand the hotel.

Inside the lobby he concentrates on the clerk, a bored male in a wide-lapeled jacket with brass buttons, who pays no attention to us until my father comments on his cuff links. "Nice. Jade?" The guy warms up immediately, swipes my credit card, tells him, "Yeah. Right. Oriental jade, the good kind," and blesses us upstairs, "Real good room. Terrace room."

And upstairs I have the chance to see that Best Western rooms have two beds, two pictures of seacoast, one television, a cubbyhole with a hot pot, and outside of all this a fenced porch, which I guess is what the clerk meant when he said "terrace." I get my father out of his jacket and bundled onto the bed, against a stack of pillows. He's shaking slightly. I, when I look at my hand, am also shaking slightly. But he's still himself. He says, "I was upset out there. But you came." I hand him the TV remote, and he says, "You do usually. Come when I need you." After which he gives me his Elvenfolk smile and settles in to watch a TV domestic dispute, where the guy says she nags, and she says he promised to buy her a Dolce & Gabbana Light Blue perfume set. "Dear, dear," my father says to them, chidingly.

My cell phone rings.

Should I answer it? Of course I shouldn't. I do.

It's Rob, who is as close to hysterical as Rob can get. "Carly? Jesus. Have you any idea what's been going on here? . . ."

Rob is at the Manor. I tell him about us. He's horrified to hear how I discovered Mrs. Sisal, keeps interrupting with exclamations of "Carly, darling. Oh, Jesus." But he's not exactly surprised. He remembered that Sisal wanted to see me this morning. He says there are cops ten-deep around the Manor. Nobody connects me with anything yet. Their world is much too hectic; they're not thinking about me.

"Stay put, honey; I'll be right there. No, don't try to tell me. I'm coming, don't argue, this is nonnegotiable. I'll be there in forty minutes; the Best Western in Conestoga. Is there anything you need? Hang in, chin up, oh my God. Good-bye."

I don't try to talk Robbie out of it. For once I'm pleased with his take-charge attitude.

Daddy has fallen asleep. His head is sideways on the pillow, mouth a tiny bit open, hair mussy and dandelion-fuzz-like across his forehead, a blade of grass in it from his meadow stay. He looks vulnerable and sweet. And surprisingly young.

I settle down to fumble through the Best Western's guide to Del Oro County.

* * *

My father is still asleep when Rob arrives. We do a hasty kiss at the door and a whispered discussion that quickly escalates into almost normal volume because Daddy shows no signs of waking up. "He's all right; he's all right?" Rob keeps insisting/asking.

"It was bad at first," I say. "He wouldn't move, couldn't talk. Like last night."

"Catatonic," Rob looks murderous.

"But then he woke up and talked some. I think he's okay."

Rob surveys the rag-doll shape of Edward, slumped against the pillows. He turns and puts both hands on my shoulders. "And you, baby?"

I'm proud of Rob. He's holding himself in, trying not to be too big-brother patronizing. Of course he shouldn't call me "baby," but old habits die hard.

"Not great." My voice goes down into my gut at this point, and Rob says, "Okay, okay," and massages my shoulders. He gives me a muffled hug. "Come on, let's sit here," and he positions some furniture to face the window.

I say, "Tea." I've been too long at the Manor. If you're going to sit and talk and cry and look at a view, you need tea. I establish myself in the alcove.

"Shit," Rob pushes his tea bag around.

I say. "Yeah."

I fish up and squeeze my tea bag and watch myself drop it carefully onto the Best Western's wall-to-wall. The carpet is one of those indestructible fiber-constructs that invites this kind of treatment, and I'm not feeling like a good member of society. "I guess we're in real danger, huh?"

"Sure."

After a minute I say, "Mrs. Sisal looked as if she had been violently killed."

Rob doesn't answer this, so I go on, "Mona didn't. Mona could have been asleep. But Mrs. Sisal looked as if her life had been stopped short in anger and upheaval and retribution. All that biblical stuff."

We're silent for a while, with Rob blowing his breath out and making a noise like "Who-ee."

I pick my tea bag up off the floor and mash it from hand to hand for a while. "You ever think that everything, flowers and grass and sunsets, the whole gorgeous panoply of it all, is pretty damn pointless?"

"No. Cut it out. And you don't, either. What you mean is—"

I interrupt, "Okay, I know what I mean. I want all this that we're in now to stop. I want to be the one that stops it. I want to grab Dr. Kittredge by a tender spot. Get back at him. Do something major. This trailing around and waiting and lurking . . ."

Rob just says, "Yeah," but something in the way he says it works, and I start shutting up. "You don't really know it's Kittredge," Rob says.

"I do," I come back. I talk for a while about why I think so.

There is a fairly long silence. I slurp cooling tea and can hear Rob doing likewise. "Carly," he says finally.

"Uh-huh?"

"It's funny what bad luck and life's trials and all that will do."

I hold out on saying "Yep." I think I can feel where this is going. Not someplace I want to go right now.

"Well, I think you and I have been getting closer."

I don't respond.

"I feel as if we need each other. I mean . . ." Here Rob, usually so ebullient, able to grab any situation by its tail, has to fumble around. "I need you, and you need me," he elaborates not very sparklingly. "I mean, we really *are* a couple. We were before, and we've been getting that way more and more again. I mean . . ."

I've lapsed into complete nonmovement, the lady congealed into a statue, so he goes, "Carly?"

Oh, what the bloody hell, I tell myself, a phrase borrowed from some British movie. Why does everything have to get so complicated?

Confess it, Carla. You wanted him to say that. Or something like it. But without any consequences, like a cartoon-strip comment floated in the air above his head. Not causing any repercussions in the real world, not needing an answer.

Now I feel as if I've swallowed a large, round intractable object. A tortoise, maybe, complete with claws.

What I say out loud, sort of desperately, is "Hey, Rob, you're my *brother*!" Boy what a cop-out, but still fair, because he's used it on me.

He doesn't answer at all. His shoulders slump. I want to comfort him, and I absolutely want not to do that, and I want to be free of this mess and the other ones I'm neck-deep in. And someplace at the meanest cockroach level of my personality, I'm pleased that Arlette now seems to be out in the cold without her mittens.

After a very long wait I tell Rob that we should put this on the back burner. Then, slowly, I watch him get some of the starch back into his shoulders. After all, he's a truly resilient type.

What he finally says is that we should send downstairs for some steak dinners, which seems a perfectly all-right idea.

"I know something," I say. "Know it for certain, even if it's not provable. That token Daddy has, the one he keeps talking about, is from Aunt Crystal."

Rob agrees. "Yeah, I think so."

"She gave it to him just before *it* happened; maybe in his room or maybe on her way down to the beach, she handed it to him and told him it was important. It was her last chance, she had to get through to him." I wait a minute and add, "Maybe it's what she had discovered, some special knowledge that she had and they wanted."

"Sounds good." Rob doesn't seem quite as convinced this time.

"Hey," he diverts, "they do pretty good steak here."

I agree; the steak is fine. The paper plates aren't the world's most elegant, and these plastic knives . . . the sawing motion has to be terrific for the upper arms.

We're sitting at the little round table that Best Western provides. The table rocks when you saw steak with a plastic knife.

Rob is cheerful, or at least moderately so. He doesn't seem to need to brood about our anti-romantic conversation.

My father is starting to wake up. There's a flurry over at the bed; he lifts his head, subsides, then tries it again, peers out, baby bird in its nest, covers up under his chin. "Why, hello, my dear, what a pleasant place you have found. What is the name of that object there?" He's pointing at the round fire alarm unit in the ceiling over his head. "Sometimes when I sleep I dream that I am under a date palm. It is warm; it would be warm under there, wouldn't it? And I am refulgently happy. I always liked that word." He shifts himself more upright and spots Rob, gives him a nice, welcoming smile. "Hello, there. I dreamed you might be here; that was part of what I dreamed." He's up on one elbow now, feeling around with his feet.

I'm beside him. "Take it easy, dear. Maybe you'll be dizzy."

Which makes him cross. "Why, now, tell me, should I be dizzy. *There* we are."

But I've been distracted. Sitting beside him, I can see directly down into the meadow, and I'm seeing a wobble at the edge of my vision, right on the edge of the circle of light cast by the back of the Best Western. The sort of flicker you think might be made by someone dodging around among the California grasses. Someone trying to see up into our lighted window and then deciding not to be too visible.

A resident of the back of Main Street wouldn't be dodging around like that. A back-of-Main-Street person wouldn't be walking there anyway; that grass is hard to navigate. I gesture at Rob and make faces, trying not to alarm Daddy.

"Sweetheart, how about some steak?" I ask.

When he says yes, I manage, while cutting steak and arranging a table setting, to huddle and whisper with Rob. Who is cool, only flicking a glance sideways at the window.

The whatever-it-is out there stops. Creepy thought: It sees Rob and me huddled. And disappears, not even leaving a snaky trail.

I remember that the more people who know where we are, the better, so I call the Manor, leaving a message for Mrs. Cohen. The person at the Manor sounds besieged and says, "Yes, yes," vaguely.

"This is good," my father says. "A tasty steak. You did well."

He eats for a while, appreciatively.

"You know, it's a curious thing," he waves a scrap of meat skewered on a plastic forktine, "I was lying out there in the grass. Did you think I was sleeping?"

"Sort of."

"I was *thinking*. Down in the meadow, among the deep grass, a fine, good place for thinking. And what did I think about?" He waits, fork upraised. "I thought about my daughter. And how good you have been. And how I should trust."

A moment for chewing. "Trust is important, don't you think?"

Rob and I stare, each of us quietly willing this to be a turning point.

"Especially in time of trouble, don't you think?"

Come on, dear, get to the point.

Is my sweet, forgetful father playing games with us? Maybe so, because the next thing he says is, "Do you know, I'm remembering better. It comes and goes, but I truly believe, yes, I think I am."

Another beat, another mouthful of steak, "I think I should prove my full trust in you. Prove it entirely. Do you think?"

Rob says, "Absolutely." I say, "Wonderful. If you want to."

Rob scowls at his hands, says, "Of course." I say, "Yes, you should."

There's a moment of silence, which my father breaks by saying, "My token."

He waits about ten seconds while Rob and I hold our breath; he smiles sweetly. "Yes, indeed, my token. I'm going to entrust you with it. You helped me, you know. Out there in the meadow. I was lost among the wheat. And you found me. That was important. Anyway . . ." He stops eating, lays his fork neatly on the edge of the plastic plate and bends over.

And takes off his right shoe.

After the shoe is off, he lifts it up and looks critically at the lining. Which, a minute later, he peels up. It's still partly stuck to the inside of the shoe and makes a ripping sound as he pulls. "There!" And he comes up with a small piece of paper, which he hands to me.

It seems to be a receipt from a Walgreen's drug store, $25.03, dated March 12, 2004. About five weeks ago. "*There*," he announces again, in the tone that the geometrician uses to proclaim, "This has been demonstrated."

A receipt from a Walgreen's drug store.

I am staring down at this paper. My first thought is, *Oh, for God's sake, of course; it had to be something like this*, and my second is, *Well, you should have known*, and my third is a lecture to myself about how my father has Alzheimer's, had I forgotten? Meanwhile he's saying, "No, no, darling, the other side! The other *side* of the paper."

Rob is being enormously disciplined and not scrabbling for control or saying "Let *me* see."

So I move to sit beside Rob in the armchair, and together
we turn the Walgreen's receipt over. The other side has writing on it in pencil. And also some kind of a drawing.

First of all, the writing. This writing is important, and
actually says so. Like, the first word is *important*, underlined.
Here's the way it reads, "<u>Important</u>. Edward. Go there."

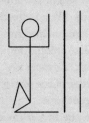

And the handwriting of this message also is important.
Because the handwriting is Aunt Crystal's. Her tight, no-
nonsense, slightly slanted script. I'd know it anywhere, if an
example floated by my airplane window at thirty thousand
feet.

Rob asks "What the hell?"

I say, "Oh."

Rob asks, "It means something?"

I say, "Sure it does. Of course."

My father says, "Didn't I do well to keep it in my shoe?
They do that in spy novels, you know, but nobody would
have thought I knew about spy novels and it was a lot of
trouble. I had to keep gluing it back with rubber cement;
we used rubber cement in Egypt on the lesser artifacts, it
peels right off afterward, you know."

Rob asks, "Carly, *what* does it mean?"

"It's a hieroglyph, sort of, and hieroglyphs started out as

pictures of something and ended up being words. So it's a word or maybe a couple of them. But not necessarily a word that has much connection with the original picture. Is it a little person, do you think?"

Rob squints. "No."

"The little person gets into hieroglyphs a lot. It indicates 'me,' or 'men,' or 'people' or a lot of other things." I stop, feeling hopeless.

I hold the unfolded paper under my dad's nose. "Tell us what it means, Daddy."

He smiles.

Rob says, "It looks like a tadpole to me." In Egypt, he was principally interested in jumping down into dark holes and digging; he didn't pay much attention to the written end of it.

My father appears to be off on his own trail of association, murmuring about rubber cement, but he pops up right away, "From my coffin lid. That has hieroglyphs. Up one side of the lid and down the other. That's what it's from. I need to go see my coffin lid. It will tell us. Can we go right away to see my coffin lid? Please? Oh, it would be such a fine treat to go see my coffin lid."

Outside the window it's starting to get dark, but I can spot again, over by the oil derrick this time, that little shred of movement. Someone has followed us; someone is watching.

Rob has taken a room across the hall, but he spends the evening in Daddy's and my room. Rob and I draw hangman games on the back of the Best Western hospitality book, and we eat popcorn.

My father watches *M*A*S*H* reruns. He likes them; maybe he remembers the program from its first time around. Though he's vague as to where and what the soldiers are. "It looks like California," he says, accurately. "Are they fighting some place in California?"

Robbie turns off his phone and won't even check in with his hospital. "I've got a standby. Let them sweat."

We act like my idea of a normal American motel evening.

With no murderous folk out there. No weird Gothic situation. And you wouldn't think Rob and I this afternoon had a conversation that was sort of about marriage, and ended with me sort of telling him to get lost.

For a couple of minutes there I worried that I'd hurt his feelings irrevocably, damaged him some way, and now it seems that my worry was unnecessary. Rob is okay. He recovers fast, not only because he's ebullient, but also because he's attractive and knows it. A man with plenty of fallback. He's got ladies to apply comfort. Maybe Arlette will still be around, and if not Arlette, a new somebody.

One of the things I liked about the Habitat guy was the need. He needed me. Damn flattering, that. I look at Robbie's nice sturdy reliable meaty shoulders and feel like swatting him.

Daddy pipes up in the middle of a Kicky Ketchup commercial.

"It's meaningful," he says. "Really meaningful. What she told me. Are you listening?"

Bam. Yes, we're listening; you bet we are. Competition stops cold at the hangman contest.

"She said it very slowly. She called me 'Edward.' 'Take good care of it,' she said."

Robbie and I watch each other. *She*. What does he re-member? Should we push?

"She was in a hurry," my father says. "On her way down there, you know." He stops and rubs the side of his face. "I didn't know. I wasn't sure." Here he seems to be getting up-set, and I decide that's dangerous and I should change the subject; I dive into my backpack and resurrect a pack of peppermint Jelly Bellies, "Sweetie, break it open, don't spill them all."

After that, though, there's nothing more for a while. We don't get back to the token again until after *M*A*S*H*.

"That was very good," my father judges the last episode, which ends with the nurse kissing somebody.

He goes on, no preamble, "I sort of think I knew her, you understand."

Rob and I look at each other, then I look down. I make a quieting motion with the flat of my hand; let's not push. Let it act itself out.

But this is the last thing he says about the *her* of his to-ken. The only other remark like that is, "We have to look there, you know."

This time Rob piles in and tries to pry. "Where, Ed? Tell us. Guide us." That gets us no place. Daddy's eyes get that curious Greek-statue hooded look. "I need to see my coffin lid," in a whiny voice.

Half an hour later my father is in bed, half sitting up, but with the lights off. Rob has persuaded him that archaeolo-gists can sleep in their underwear. My father knows this isn't true, but is willing to give it a try. "Good night, then," he says, and Rob answers, "Good night, then." After which

Rob, instead of going off to his own little room, opens the door onto my porch and hunkers down at the edge of it, with his nose against the railing.

I wait until Daddy's deeply drawn breaths tell me he's asleep. I follow Rob outside.

Have I mentioned the stars? There are many of them, and quite low.

Rob responds to my presence with a shoulder-quiver and a motion that means, "Come sit beside me," which I don't do. "So what do you think?" he asks.

I settle in near the door. "I think like before. He met her. He sort of understands that but doesn't want to remember. She was in a hurry. Crisis, danger. She gave him this little note. She made it Egyptian. Put it in a form he'd value."

"And if we translate it, it'll tell us something?"

I shrug. "He tells us, 'We have to look there.' And she says in her note, 'Go there.' So, if we can figure out where *there* is, I guess something in *there* will give us a fact. Or show us an object. Papers, isn't that what it usually is? Aunt Crystal was into papers. Bits of record." I've been thinking as I talk, and add, "I've just remembered, she wanted to work with Mrs. Goliard. Because she was a librarian."

Rob says, "Yeah," in a thoughtful voice.

And now we're both silent for a while. I move in closer. It's cold at night in our part of California.

"What's this place where the coffin lid is?" he asks. "This Egon person?"

"Egon Rothskeller is an Egyptology nut. You know."

Robbie nods. Both of us know lots of them, the Egyptology addicts, people who're sure ancient Egypt contains The

Answer. Ancient Egypt is where they lived their life sixty incarnations ago. Where they'll go next time round. Where they'll find the message about Armageddon. And discover a rocketload of treasure. And regain the knowledge that drowned with Atlantis. Not to mention the proofs of interstellar travel hidden in the pyramid tip or under the pyramid base or inside the blue beads scattered in two thousand holes in the desert. Or in the wrappings of Tutankhamen's decaying feet.

"Except," I say, "unlike most of them, Egon Rothskeller is majorly rich, and he built this museum that is more Disney than E. Wallis Budge." E. Wallis Budge is a big-time, dead, white male Egyptian scholar.

Rob lies down on his back and rests the back of his head on his cradled arms and looks up at the stars.

"Rothskeller," I tell him, "called his place Egypt Regained, and it has everything. Everything except a pyramid. Mummies, statues, vases, pots, papyri, stelae, bracelets, beads. Mummied cats. Stone statues, clay statues. Some stuff four thousand years old, some new. Egon can't tell the difference."

After a pause I add, "Daddy could tell the difference. But he didn't care. He was glad to have his coffin lid nearby. And that museum has climate control."

"Are you in love with somebody else?" Rob asks.

I say, "Oh, shut up," and scrunch forward a bit and bend over and kiss him.

Maybe it's the same idea as making love on the train track when a train is due. The danger is two-thirds of the thrill. Down there, maybe, is a bunch of murderous hoods who want to wrap us in a net and chuck us into the ocean or shoot us in the face or snap our necks like Mona's. And up here are just little old us, hanging out under the stars. Plus the fact that I've just told Rob we're not an item makes the relationship more interesting. Puts everything in perspective. All is transitory.

Behind it all is a picture of Mrs. Sisal with her brains shot out.

Actually, I kind of liked Mrs. Sisal.

Actually, it's a good idea not to think.

We settle in to a very good kiss. None of the tentative indecisive stuff of our walk through the woods. A genuine lips-teeth-tongue exploring, deep and fully, and then the hands moving and getting busy, and then the bodies shifting and pushing close.

And, good God, who knows what would happen next, except for some jostling and bed-creaking from inside at just the right time to remind us that my parent sleeps within and could wake up any time at all. *Pow, bam,* poor little defective father in the doorway, staring baffled.

He doesn't, but it's good for us to be reminded of the possibility.

We break apart, and I say, "Oh, go on to bed, Robbie. In your own bed." And I unsteadily pull myself up, grabbing at the porch railing.

ㄱ Chapter 22

It's eight-thirty A.M., a bright, assertive morning, sun and breeze briskly attacking the eucalypti and grasses of the California countryside, as Rob and Daddy and I drive along a rutted road in Rob's Honda. We're en route to Egypt Regained.

"Homeland?" Rob has said. "*Home*land?" That's the name of the post office/gas station near Egypt Regained. "I feel peculiar about this," he adds after a minute.

"I feel peculiar, too. Have a sweet roll." We've left the Best Western without eating our complimentary breakfast, but I have it in my backpack. One roll for Rob, one for my father.

"Did you sleep?" I ask.

"Not worth mentioning."

"Me, neither. Anyway, Egon's expecting us. He said he was thrilled. He said he'd put out the red carpet. That's what he said. 'The reddest red.' He's sort of affected. He's proud of Daddy."

"Red carpet?" My father turns around, arm over the back of the seat. He's in the front, beside Rob. Rob and I decided the front was less isolating than the back.

"We're going to see Mr. Rothskellar."

"Rothskellar," Daddy broods, dubiously.

"Where your coffin lid is. Remember? We're going to see your coffin lid."

"Oh! I am *so* glad."

"Mr. Rothskellar is the man who has it."

"My coffin lid," my father says. "Yes. I am very glad."

"He's the one that used the climate control, darling." For some reason I want him to remember this.

"This Egon," Rob says to me, low-voiced. "Does he . . . Has he *seen* Ed recently?"

"It's okay," I tell him. "Egon won't notice. He refuses to notice. 'Your father is a genius,' he says. The day Daddy delivered the lid, they had a lightning storm that knocked the cross off the Homeland church. Egon loved that. It was a sign, he said. He thinks Daddy's magic."

We pass a roadside stand with a tipsy array of *raku* pots, "Made by a Local Craftsperson." My father is intrigued. "*Raku.* An old system, *raku*, difficult. Not Egyptian, of course. Perhaps discovered when someone knocked a shovelful of manure into the fire. Could we stop for the *raku* pots, do you think?"

I remind him about the coffin lid, and he says, "Of course. I have a good feeling about this. It's time. To see my hieroglyphs again."

"Well, I don't exactly (have a good feeling)," I say, pitching the last part of my sentence into Rob's ear only.

It's curious; Rob and I aren't acting very apprehensive, either one of us, but we're expecting trouble. Egon said something peculiar when I called. "Several phone calls in for tickets already. Not some of our usual patrons. Of course, if they're true devotees of Egypt, they're very welcome. But I suspect perhaps they aren't."

"Yeah, I betcha they aren't," Rob agrees.

It's not very far from Conestoga to Homeland. Twenty miles, a snap of the fingers on a good road. This isn't a good road, so it takes longer. Robbie is a determined driver. "I want to get there and get it over with," Rob says when I comment on damage to the spine.

"Like riding a camel," says my father.

I'm trying to watch the road behind us, which is hard to do. First, because of the big cloud of tan dust raised by Rob's driving. And second, because of the loops and wiggles in the road. There's no particular reason for this road not to be straight, no eccentric hills or gullies, but it wanders like a sidewinder's trail; it must follow some ancient cattle track. A couple of times I see a car behind us and then tell myself not to be paranoid, why shouldn't there be a car behind us? And then I tell myself yes, I should be paranoid.

"There's somebody back there," I mutter in Rob's ear.

He grunts, "Yep."

We pass a gentle old California relic, a barn melted into the ground, its walls flattened, its roof the height of a chicken coop. "I could paint that," my father claims.

"You know, Ed," Rob tells him, "you do seem better lately. Your memory. Know what I mean?"

My father sounds pleased. "Oh, very much."

After a minute he adds, "It was the pills. The blue ones, I think. I believe they were blue."

There's an immediate tense silence in the car: Rob in the front seat, me, in the back. Rob finally says, "Pills, Ed? *What* pills?"

"The blue ones. The blue ones were the ones that did it."

"*Who* gave you the blue pills?" I snap at him.

"Oh?" He's caught the tension in my voice. "Well, pills, you know . . . on the cart. You know, the cart . . . with the pills . . . in the evening."

"Somebody's been . . ." Rob says to me.

I say, "Uh-huh."

A minute later I add, "I'm an idiot. He gave enough warning."

"Kittredge?"

"Uh-huh." I'm holding on to the fake leather armrest. I think I'm feeling murderous. "He wanted to jack up his memory. So he could find out what he knew. He could have hurt him. He could maybe have killed him. Nobody knows the side effects."

Rob is silent, from his profile he looks very angry. Finally he says, "It's probably all right. There are several kinds of stuff in Europe, and they *do* test there. I'll check. It's *probably* all right."

"For God's sake, Rob, just drive.

"There's somebody behind us," I add.

Rob agrees, "Yep."

A minute later I say, "Sorry."

"Just like a camel," my father says. "The wobble of the car. Exactly the same."

We go through a few more bends and road-curves in silence and finally, at the end of a handsome eucalyptus alley, I point, "That's it, to the left. Egypt Regained. It's pretty weird."

Rob says, "Jee-sus."

Plunked down in a little grassy field, at the end of an off-shoot of this rutted road, there it is, Egypt indeed. Some of it is pink and has arches; some of it is tan and has latticed windows, as in "Meet me in the Casbah." There is a water-fall down one side of the building, and there are narrow walled passages that meander around the outside. The building material appears to be pink or gray adobe. I've been here before, but that was three years ago; I've forgotten some of the festive details. There is a wide pond and a large parking lot, presided over by a gentleman wearing a turban and a loincloth.

If there was a car behind us it has disappeared, but it's hard to be sure. The road has plenty of ambulation.

The bad news is that there are six cars already in the parking lot. And the good news is that none of them is Dr. Kittredge's Miata.

Ever since the blue-pill discussion I have been thinking about Dr. Kittredge, very bad, evil, frightening thoughts.

We pull up to the edge of the parking lot, and the person in the turban and loincloth sticks his head in our open window and says, "Hi."

My father is thrilled. "They have a native attendant."

Native Attendant has a happy-smiles label on his turban that announces his name is Haroun. He's blond and pleasantly suntanned, with good teeth and nice surfer's pectorals.

Right now, Haroun needs to emote because the mention of Daddy's name requires a big rise. "Oh, wow. Has he *ever* been waiting for you!" Haroun parks us in the best parking space and leads us to a monstrous gold metal front door, where an Egyptian god leans out to bless, palms raised.

"Why, I remember this!" my father exclaims, sounding pleased. "I suppose it's impressive. He—what's his name?"

"The god?" I ask.

He's irritated. "The man. Who lives here. I met him."

When I tell him Egon Rothskellar, he says, "Ah, yes. Well, he knows. That figure is modern. Not real. Not even a copy! I told him, and he knows."

We're interrupted by the arrival of Egon himself, who appears, like an Arabian Nights djinn, half bent over and unrolling something as he approaches. Yes, indeed, behind him, a long red runner. He gets the last little bit of rug smacked down and arranged and then stands upright, dusts off the knees of his impeccable khakis, and holds his hand out to my father. "See? I told you! The red carpet. The only suitable greeting for our foremost scholar. Welcome, oh noble visitor, welcome." And he touches his hand to his forehead, his mouth, and his belt buckle, probably hoping this comes out as an Arab salute.

It almost does. My father is pleased. "It is good to be needed," he says.

And so we proceed through the door and into a cold carved-stone hallway, too dark for me to appraise the carvings, and finally through a second door and out into a long high-arched room with shelves and statues and upright glass cases and horizontal glass cases and stands holding pots, figures, clay models. The usual Egyptian mixture.

On either side of this room is another room with what looks like more of the same. And down at the end there's a small fenced-off sort of alcove with a sign above it.

"Now," I think, and I bend over and wonder if I can get my shoe untied unobtrusively. Because that's where the token is now, in my shoe. Not glued under the sole, the way my father did, but just resting under my sock. And surely we'll be needing it soon. I'm expecting a sudden dash or at least a purposeful march led by scholar Edward Day down to the cubicle containing his coffin lid where Verse Four will be identified and translated. I'm waiting for that. Daddy is supposed to say "My coffin lid, yes, I think it is in that space there." Or something like that. "I need to see my lid now," he's supposed to say.

So. And, no, he doesn't. He seems to remember that the lid is back there, at the end, in a special space all to itself, a place of honor, with a sign above it: EDWARD DAY EXHIBIT. "We will work our way gradually," my father announces. "There are things in this room. Some of them, surely are original?"

Egon blinks and smoothes a hand over his hair. He is thin and elegant-looking, hawk-nosed, something like one of his Egyptian kings, except that he has well-coiffed, collar-length white hair. "Such an honor," he says. "So wonderful to have Dr. Day here. How I have looked forward to it."

I am starting to feel desperate. Please, there are things we need to do, and dangers if we don't do them, and probably more dangers when we have done them, and here we are poised on the edge of disaster.

There must be a way of pushing my father. But pushing him is not a great idea; he could just fold completely.

"Daddy," I say, "your coffin lid." I gesture. "I've been wanting so much . . ." I make circles in the air to show him how much.

He smiles, his extra-sweet smile, "I wonder . . . perhaps . . . work our way around the room. Starting with this goddess . . ." He frowns. "I do know her name. It is right there, almost at the front. Carla?"

"That's Sekhmet." Sekhmet is the goddess of the brilliant midsummer sun; also she's good for getting even with your enemies. She has a lion's head and a woman's body and is both interesting-looking and scary; the Egyptians liked her. My father circles her carefully.

Should I tell him Sekhmet would like him to move on down to the coffin lid enclosure? I should not. I can imagine the debate. Did she speak? Did I hear her in my head?

He probably would tell me that hearing things in your head is bad.

There's another female figure in the room, a cartonnage, a figure made of gesso-coated linen wrapped around a mummy. My father is giving Sekhmet the appropriate attention, a little muttering and some bowing, but he's inclining his body toward the cartonnage; I'm afraid he'll be moving on to her next.

Oh, hell. Again, it's almost as if he were teasing us.

The cartonnage is a charming, cheerful, plumpish lady. A figure like this has the features of the departed painted on it. In this case the departed was black-haired and pop-eyed with a knowing, welcoming expression and lots of handsome turquoise beads.

Daddy moves on to her. He needs to flirt. "Why, hello."

I am making eye contact with Rob. My eye contact says, "Help." Rob's asks, "Help *how*?"

"I didn't know they had you here." That's my father, breathing sweet nothings to the cartonnage. "That is good. Almost as good as my coffin lid."

Rob is watching the room to the right. It's smaller than this one but also has plenty of glass cases and statues. "People," he asides to me. "Dodging around."

I agree with him. The scene is getting too active.

"At least get that thing out," he means the token.

Yes, get the token and then go down to the coffin lid, just Rob and me to start, and try hard to understand. Neither of us is very sure about our hieroglyphs. We need Edward Day. Who may not be that sure, either. But will probably join us after he sees us there. And if he's full of blue pills, maybe he has his memory of hieroglyphs back.

I try to rehearse again what I think happened between my father and Aunt Crystal.

She was on her way down to the beach.

She met my father.

She wanted to tell him where she had hidden the incriminating whatsit. Text, probably. Aunt Crystal liked pieces of paper.

So she wrote him a note in a form that she thought he'd maybe understand. Or, maybe show to me.

"Is it sometimes cold in here?" my father is asking the cartonnage lady. Solicitously worried about her welfare in the afterlife. "Is the Eye of Horus triumphant?"

I tell Rob I'll be back in a minute and snake my way out to the dark corridor and through to the ladies' room, which of course has been Egyptianed up with murals of pharaohs and pyramids and with liquid soap containers that look like canopic jars. I sit down on the marble floor and take off my sneaker and then, after I've extracted the Walgreen's receipt, have to decide where to put the damn thing. Down my bra? No. I'm not that well stacked; it's likely to drop out the bottom. My backpack is the only logical place; I put the token in the outside pocket.

And emerge from the restroom into a hectic scene.

A busload of kids, fifth grade ones maybe, children about four feet high, has just been unloaded in front of the door.

A teacher has them lined up. Brighter lights have been turned on in the hall. Egon Rothskellar is jeeping around at the head of the line. The teacher is issuing ultimatums: No touching. No running. No getting under things. No chewing gum. Yes, there is a mummy in a glass case, but anybody who runs or touches has to go sit in the bus and doesn't get to see the mummy. Now I know you're going to make me proud of you. Mr. Rothskellar has done a wonderful, wonderful thing, having a real Egyptian museum here.

The teacher assesses her line, which looks ready to explode, and signals to Egon to open the inner doors. There are about twenty kids, but it seems like more.

I remember that I am a grown-up and dodge around the head of the line and out into the main room where Daddy is still whispering remarks to the cartonnage lady and Rob is backed against the wall. Behind me the line of kids gallops in like the wolf on the fold, but trying hard to muffle their normal instincts. "Hey, wheresa mummy? In there, I betcha. Or there, or there?" they ask, pointing in various directions.

"Jeez, Rob," I take his hand, and lead him ahead of the mob down to the Edward Day Exhibit.

My phone rings. I consider just letting it ring, but after it does that once, twice, three times, and I see the teacher looking at me censoriously and a female guard plodding forward on her prison-issue shoes, after all that I answer and am greeted by the chirpy voice of Mrs. Cohen. "Carla, my dear, good morning, good morning. How are you? Where are you? Such terrible things are happening here . . . we are so interested, so worried. What about Ed? Is he there? Is he better?" The fifth grade kids, who like cell phones, have collected to watch, the guard is saying things like, "Just let me keep the instrument for you until you have seen the exhibits, please," so I tell Mrs. Cohen that yes, Daddy is okay. We're at Egypt Regained where we're going to Daddy's special room to see his exhibit. Thank you for calling; love to everybody, I have to stop now. And I hand the phone over to the guard, who goes away to check it and put a label on it.

I was glad to tell Mrs. Cohen where we were. It seems a good idea to spread the word around.

The kids are in a circle of about six, staring at me transfixed. Perhaps the charm is that the guard made me surrender the phone. Or maybe they see me acting nervous and find this interesting. Many little, round staring eyes are appraising me.

Back in the main room my father is still flirting with his gesso girlfriend.

"Father," I call, and, "Edward," and, finally, "Dr. Day."

"Dr. Day" gets a little action. He turns in our direction.

"They have made a mistake here," I say.

"What, darling?"

"Your translation is missing." And it is. There used to be a word-for-word rendering of the text pasted onto the front of the case.

A section of the fifth grade thinks this may be important and tries to crowd into the Edward Day Exhibit.

Rob bends over, to become closer to their height. "I'll

tell you a secret," he says. "The rest of your class doesn't know this yet. The mummies are upstairs. The first kids upstairs will get to stand right next to the case and see the mummy close up, see how many teeth it has left and whether its eyeholes are open or shut and whether it still has eyeballs in there; you'll see really clearly."

Rob has said the magic words. The kids near the enclosure entrance start out on the run, and then remember about running and its penalties, so they key down and are off, stiff-legged, but as fast as they can manage.

And the commotion has another result; it also lures my father down here. He says good-bye to his gesso-wrapped friend and actually hurries toward us.

Rob is an old meanie. There are no mummies upstairs, only small, mostly mud-colored ceramics. But I guess it will take the kids a while to find that out.

Meanwhile, I have ascertained that there is an actual door to the Edward Day Exhibit. It's folded back against the wall. I scoop Edward Day and Rob inside and close the door, which is tall and made of some sort of reddish wood and has a bronze clasp on it.

"Now, Daddy," I say. I unfold the token.

There it is, all our token iconology, the little figure with its arms in the air, some straight lines.

Aunt Crystal wasn't an Egyptologist at all; she was mildly critical of archaeology in general because she didn't like my mother. But she was proud of Edward Day and had learned a few things about his work. I'm almost certain her drawings will be translatable.

If there are hieroglyphs on the lid that look like these, we've got a starting point even without the text that used to be part of the exhibit. Maybe I, or Rob, can free-associate some. And if Daddy is feeling anything like his old self, he'll be translating clearly, right away.

I turn up the lights on the enclosure and twist a handle on the bronze door. I don't want to be interrupted while we're doing this. I've locked us in.

🐧 Chapter 23

We've been in a huddle inside the Edward Day exhibit for twenty minutes now, and it's beginning to feel like being barricaded in a besieged castle. Outside our door, the fifth grade has returned, and the conversation and scuffling has gotten oceanic; inside the temperature is rising.

My father seems, at last, to be delighted at his reunion with his lid. He stands, hands in pockets, beaming down into the case, murmuring little snatches of phrases. "Victorious. . . . In the underworld." I've asked him to look at the token, which I'm clutching in my hand, but he waves me away.

Rob and I are bent double near the south end of the case, trying to match Aunt Crystal's kneeling figure and the straight lines with the incisions on the lid.

This is harder than you might expect.

Incisions don't stand out sharply on old, very battered, very scuffed wood.

I've tried from every angle. The north end of the case.
The south end. With the lights turned higher, which they
aren't supposed to be, because that damages ancient artifacts. "Daddy, help me," I say. "You know what's on there.
You know it from way back." I circle the case again.

My father says something about opening the storehouses.
He's quietly cheerful.

I'm wasting energy being angry about the lack of a
printed translation. Certainly there used to be one; the big
importance of the coffin lid was that it changed hiero-
glyphic readings. But Egyptologists are always fighting
about what something means, maybe in one of those dis-
putes the text got rewritten. And yes, I see it now; there's a
notice on the wall. WE ARE UPDATING THE COMMENTARY
ON THIS EXHIBIT.

Hell and hell.

I'm glad Daddy hasn't noticed that sign, evidence of people interfering in his history. I move around the case again,
trying to get a better angle on those scratchy markings.

I kick off one shoe, the one that had the token in it. It's
come untied, and I've been tripping on the lace.

Suddenly, either light or association or the slant of the
sun from outside—something works, and I can see a whole
set of indentations. I can see them; I can follow them, and I
know what they mean. "Hey," I say. "Rob. I *get* it."

Rob says, "My God, my God," and pushes up beside me.

"See there," I say. "And there? And then the straight
lines. That's our text. Don't you think so? Yes, sure."

"Okay," Rob says. "Yep, you're right. Two lines, one
heavy, one light and serrated. Yes. So. What does the rest of
it say?"

"I can't read that part, but I can read the stuff before. I

recognize it. Sort of a preamble. It's a formulaic statement, something they ask over and over, always the same way. A ritual question. It looks like bird, pen, kneeling figure, bird, plus some other stuff. It means 'What then is it?' "

I'm so pleased at recognizing this that I don't stop to evaluate what my find adds up to for us. How does it help us right now? For the moment I don't care.

But Rob cares, big-time.

"What then *is* it?" He bleats. He says this twice, once as a simple question and a second time, loud and cross, as an angry exclamation. He follows that up with, "Jesus triumphant, you mean to say we've come so far and done so many stupid things to be asked 'What then is it?' "

My bird-pen speech has also awakened my father. "Bird, pen?" he asks. "Oh, daughter. I cannot believe it. Not *bird, pen.* A hieroglyph has a name. There is a proper noun for each hieroglyph. When I was younger I knew. I cannot believe that you would call it 'bird, pen.' "

My failure upsets him a lot. "Simplifying. Bad, very bad . . . your shorthand . . . for the hieroglyphs, my dear."

Well, at least I have his attention. I start out, "Listen, Father . . ."

Outside, the fifth grade has gotten into a fight. Feet slide, voices screech, someone calls someone an asshole, a grown-up voice says, "All right, you kids, cut it out, cut it out and get away from here. Get away from that door. Come on now . . . Nobody, nobody at all is going to see even one mummy if you don't . . . Now come on, get in line."

The outside gradually dies down into silence, and my father is still looking at me as if he's interested. I seize the day. I grab one of his hands. "Listen, Daddy, after 'What then is it,' what comes next?"

He looks puzzled. "Many things, I think."

I point down at the coffin lid. "It's too scarred, I can't read it. But you did. You read it when you wrote your book. What was the next thing it said?"

"Why, my dear." He puts his other hand to his forehead in a protective, shielding gesture. "Various things. Good things."

"No," I announce fiercely. "You *know*. Just there, on your coffin lid. It is *yours*, you know."

"Why, of course, my dear. Certainly it is."

"What came after 'What then is it?'"

"Why . . ." He waits for a minute, tilts his head. "Why, darling, a song of some kind? Maybe 'Wake up, wake up, darling Corey'?"

"*No*," I tell him, "absolutely not. Daddy, *think*."

My father surveys me and begins to get a pleased crinkle at the corner of his eyes, "Why, darling, I know, yes, of course I know. It was about the millions of years. The Dark Lake." Chin up, he shows me his sunny smile. He moves a hand rhythmically. " 'Dark Lake is the name of the other,' " he intones, the singsong voice telling me it's a quote.

"Dark Lake?" I say. "What's Dark Lake?"

"Dark Lake. A deep lake. Sacred. There are two of them. Heracleopolis. I think that's right."

I look at Rob. "Oh, my God, there it is."

"What?" ask Rob. "How? Where what is?"

I'm remembering Belle's statement about Daddy being interested in the well. The one in the hills behind the Manor. The one Rob and I walked up to. "And he calls it Dark Lake," Belle had told me. "Of course it isn't a lake, but that's what he calls it."

"Listen," I say. "Rob." My voice is high; I can hear myself

upping the volume. "It's the well, Rob, the one up in the forest, the one we sat beside and you chucked a rock into; that well. I guess she knew about it, and she knew he'd understand. That's where we have to look."

"Rob," I grab him by his jacket collar because he's staring at me as if I'm speaking a newly invented language, "listen. I get it, I get it; that's where Aunt Crystal left the stuff; I know where to look."

Rob and I are still staring at each other, bemusedly, so to speak, when there is the *skritch* and *click* of a key being turned in a lock. I remember that I have locked us in, and someone with a key is entering.

The person with the key gets the door half-open and stands in the doorway. Outside, the exhibit hall is strangely quiet and looks empty. The person comes into our enclosure.

The person is Dr. Kittredge.

He enters sideways in a strange kind of half-shuffle. He has a gun, which he aims in our general direction. He gets the door shut with his foot and leans against it.

For two days now I've been expecting Kittredge, so I am not exactly surprised, just startled, scared, heart pounding, telling myself, "Oh, Jesus." I've even been expecting a Kittredge with a gun. But still I'm not ready. My heart skips, my throat is dry; I half-open my mouth to yell and then decide that that's not a good idea.

Something is different about Kittredge, who looks at me weirdly, almost sideways, making the gun veer from me to Rob to Daddy. His face is swollen and flushed; his forehead bulges. In a minute I understand. He's drunk. I've seen him drunk before, but not this drunk, which I think is very drunk indeed. The drunkenness makes the gun behave erratically; it wavers, tries to aim at Daddy, finally settles on me.

"Thank you *very* much," Kittredge says.

He pauses, gestures with the gun, a small, dark blue, shiny type. "That's just . . . just what I hoped you'd do," he says.

He waits some more. "I heard it all. I was in the office with the sound system turned up; you enunciated great. Just . . . exactly . . . *exackly* what we needed. And now . . ."

Here he wavers enough that it skips across the back of my mind how maybe I could grab at him, or Rob could, but then he straightens up, the unsteadiness passes. Kittredge is a big man, and he can be plenty drunk before it really stops him. "Too bad," he says. "In a way. Because normally . . . Miss Carla . . . I'd just send you on your way. But *howinhell* can I do that?" He looks down at the gun and makes a noise with it that I think is taking the safety off.

Rob calls out, "Patrick. *Hey*. Don't be dumb."

Kittredge's gun heat-seeks Rob. "Dumb?" he asks. "I was *smart*. Real smart to think of that sound system."

"Oh, you were, you were," I say quickly. Inside of me the adrenaline has begun to kick in and is revving up my responses and telling me what to do. "Delay," it says. "Engage him. Talk to him. He loves to talk. Get him going. If he's talking he can't think about shooting you. Get him started."

"Hello," my father says. He sounds pleased. "Quite a few of us are here now. I think it is time to go home. Don't you think so, too?"

He asks this question of Kittredge, who ignores him and wavers his gun in Rob's direction. Rob has been making minor gestures with his arms, which I can see flexing under his jacket sleeves, and with his hands, which he's compressing into fists. He's getting set for a kung fu leap. When we were in junior high, Rob took kung fu lessons. There was a big vogue in Berkeley for that kind of thing.

I start to yell, "Rob, don't," because I think Kittredge will shoot him before he gets the leap finished, and then I decide not to yell but to take action of my own, verbal action, like my adrenaline has been advising. "There are two ways," the adrenaline whispers into my mental ear, "insult him and get him talking. Or praise him and get him talking." I start out with insults.

"I don't think you were smart," I say. "If you're so smart how come we're here? We came because you were dumb. You let us know. You were obvious. All along, you were obvious. Right at the beginning, I said to Rob, you know, I bet all this stuff, all these accidents, is Kittredge."

Rob tries his own brand of diversion. "Patrick, for God's sake, use some sense. Come on, you're a doctor, you've got a good job, you've got a future, you're going to have a name in Aging. Or in Retirement Management. People are recognizing you . . . and what you're doing. You're writing a paper; you'll get it published . . ." Rob falters here. I remember that he once told me Kittredge had never published anything and that he was at the Manor because a place like that was the only hidey-hole for a fourth-rate doctor. "At the hospital," Rob says. "Everyone respects you; everybody knows you."

Kittredge doesn't pay any attention to Rob; he spits on the finger of his left hand and polishes the barrel of the gun while keeping it pointed at me.

"You know," my father tells him, "I think I know who

you are; you're the man who brings the *New York Times* on Sunday. Am I right? I really appreciate that *New York Times*."

The gun swivels. "You . . . silly . . . little man. You're *pretending*. Don't come at me with that adorable aged Alzheimer's crap. Con man. I know an old con man when I see one."

Rob is clenching his fists at his sides some more.

"Listen," I tell Kittredge as forcefully as I can, "Doctor, I don't know anything. My father doesn't and I don't. My father is a crazy old man that you've been feeding pills to. None of us understands a goddamn thing. Something about accidents and you searching our rooms. Nobody here knows any of it, and if you sober up and let us out of here, we'll go away and not talk about it and never ask you another question."

Kittredge does some uncoordinated artillery gestures and says, "Ha, Ha." The stagy kind, meaning, *how dumb do you think I am*.

Rob is being obvious again with his flexing and unflexing.

I return to my calculated insults.

"We thought it was weird, Rob and I did. The first time we ever talked about the accidents, I said, 'Hey, I bet it's the doctor. There's just something about him, too damn unctuous. He lays it on too thick, carries on about how he loves the Manor.' "

I'm all set to continue with a description of Kittredge as a would-be lover; details about fat stomachs and panting middle-aged Don Juans, I could do that for five or ten minutes. "And the worst thing," I start out, as preamble, then I take another look at him. His face is a darker and brighter red; the gun is shaking. This isn't such a good idea.

He's trying to aim the gun right at me, at my heart or my lung or my gut.

Can I be reassured by the fact that his aim is probably terrible?

I didn't think Dr. K. would get this far this fast.

I've been halfway counting on the fact that I know him. But maybe I don't. The Kittredge I thought I knew would have to—slowly—work his way up to . . . shooting somebody.

"Okay," I say. "Okay." I stop here and swallow convulsively. That adrenaline hormone has begun to fade. Now we'll try praise.

"Hey, wait, I have to hand it to you, Doctor. You did some things right, a lot of things; everybody at the Manor thought so. I did, too. I looked at you and went, 'Hey, that doctor atmosphere. *Good*. He's got that great manner, makes everybody calm down, the ladies all notice it. Every single one of those ladies . . . '" Here I steal a side glance at Kittredge. Am I going too fast? Is even one bit of this guff connecting? Yes, the gun is hanging lower and his color has calmed down. "The ladies all had crushes on you; you knew that, I guess. You had a big lineup for your evening office hours. And then there was the *trust*. Everybody trusted you. Yes, real, heavy-duty trust. 'Our doctor,' they said. Everybody said it. Smooth. Whatever you were doing, you thought about it and you did it right. It was easy for you. You've got that smooth manner. That bedside thing. People go for it; everybody at the Manor went for it."

Holy God, I think, this is too much. But of course it really isn't.

Rob is still planning something ridiculous. But Kittredge is a lot more relaxed. I try to babble extra-interestingly so he'll watch me instead of Rob.

"And believe it or not," I say. "Yeah, I thought you were connected with the accidents somehow, but we've gotten this far, a whole month into the history of this thing, and I simply don't know what was really happening. Something about buying the Manor, first the accidents and then buying the Manor, is that right? But why? You were smooth; you covered your motives, and I never could really figure it out. Buying the Manor, that was it, right? Why on earth buy the Manor?"

I don't want him to know that I understand about Aunt Crystal. How she died, that scene on the beach.

So far, that hasn't come up. Without it he doesn't have any real reason to butcher me and Rob and Daddy.

Does he?

Rob, to the side of Kittredge, flexes into a half-crouch, arms loose at his sides, hands clenched.

But Kittredge is more aware than I'd realized. He turns and with a sideswipe of his gun clunks Rob on the forehead and knocks him down. Rob tumbles dramatically and lies perfectly still, but after a panic-stricken moment I decide he's not really hurt. On his way down he turned his face in my direction and winked. That fall was pretty theatrical.

"Ha!" Kittredge says, just like the villain in a Japanese movie.

"Pretty good, that, huh?" I guess he's addressing me while staring down at a prostrate Rob. And I guess I have to send a thank-you up to the Goddess of Combat that Kittredge felt like showing off his martial arts skill instead of his gun readiness.

"Ah, baby," he says, turning back to me, "you're askin'

why buy the Manor? Baby, you don't know a thing, not a thing. You don't know what the Manor is worth."

Kittredge has his mouth open, ready to give me his lecture on the value of the Manor, when there's a small commotion with some diffuse unidentifiable noises at the door and then the squeak of the handle being turned. Apparently Kittredge didn't lock it.

I think, *Oh, thank God, thank God; here's some Marines to the rescue. Rothskellar got free, the kids called the local cops, whatever, I don't care who it is, come in, whoever you are.*

Kittredge raises his gun.

Who comes in is Mrs. Dexter. Mrs. Dexter from the Manor, my old friend, Daddy's old friend, complete in her purple suit and Red Queen face, but not looking exactly the same, because she doesn't have her walker.

I do all this recognition in the first couple of seconds, while my mouth is open and I'm starting to yell, "Mrs. Dexter, get back, get out of here. He's dangerous, he's got a gun. Go call the . . ."

The lady cuts me off. "Oh, shut up." It's her usual crisp no-nonsense voice, maybe a little higher than usual.

"You don't understand," I blither. "He's got this gun; he's going to shoot us, and he'll shoot you . . ." This I reappraise, trying to force the scene into focus. My voice winds down.

This setup is all wrong.

Kittredge has lowered his gun.

Mrs. Dexter is standing just fine without her walker.

A little lopsided, maybe, higher on one side than on the other, but okay.

Her purple suit sits only slightly crooked over one hip.

Maybe the suit sits crooked because that side of Mrs.

Dexter is weighted down by her own gun. Bigger than Kittredge's piece, a capable, blackish-silver firearm, held firmly in her right hand.

The gun isn't pointed at Dr. Kittredge; it's aimed at me. And at Rob, stretched out on the floor, and at my father, meek beside his coffin lid.

Mrs. Dexter points her gun mostly into the middle of my shirt and says, "I hate squawking women."

My mind is racing with scraps of phrases like, "But I thought . . . ," "I don't understand," "What has happened to you," but I don't say any of this, because I am beginning to get it.

Mrs. Dexter leans up against the door. She scowls and compresses her Red Queen face and does me over with what might be scorn, except that the Red Queen face always looks scornful.

Then she turns to Kittredge. "Patrick," she says, "you always were an idiotic oaf. Stand up straight. Quit looking as if the world is imploding."

I struggle with getting my brain around some new concepts.

Mrs. Dexter knows perfectly well what's going on.

Correction: she knows perfectly well, and furthermore she's in charge of things. In charge of Kittredge. She's acquainted with him in a way I never imagined. She orders him around.

"What in *hell*," she is inquiring of him now, "did you think you'd gain by slaughtering these people in a public place? A place that afterward will be full of blood and DNA and fingerprints? And you're drunk. *Drunk*." She makes it sound like fornicating with goats.

Her gun has moved to cover the whole room, which includes Kittredge as well as us. She seems good at that: getting the whole room in her sights.

"Lou, old *girl*." Kittredge more or less hangs his head. I suppose he looks sheepish. His own gun hangs down at his side.

"You knew perfectly well," she says, obviously just warming up into her tirade, "you were supposed to get them together. Quietly, unostentatiously. Get them out of here. Quietly. Out the back door. Not making a scene. *God*, you are an *idiot*."

She must have been practicing invective in her private moments when the other old ladies weren't around. She's pretty good at it.

"Nobody knew," Kittredge tells her. He pauses and attempts to think about this. "Well, hardly anybody."

My father smiles happily. He's pleased. "Nearly everyone is here now. We sound a bit cross, but that's because we're hungry . . . I have seen my coffin lid," he confides to Mrs. Dexter.

She always appeared fond of him, and even in her new role as the Demented Witch of the West I expect her to say something like, "Yes, Edward." But all she does is look at him speculatively and say to Kittredge, "I suppose we'd better take him separately. If we have the old man with us and they know that, then they won't do anything stupid."

Kittredge asks, "Huh?"

"Patrick, you moron. We take him and hide him and tell them that if they want him to live at all, even ten minutes . . ."

Kittredge says, "Oh." Then he adds, sounding pleased, "I could give him a shot. Knock him out."

"Yes, Patrick, you could. That's one of the things you're still good for. And give *yourself* a shot while you're at it."

The new evil Mrs. Dexter is going to be harder to talk to than the evil Kittredge was. "You don't need to take him," I begin, sounding humble and plaintive. "We'll be good."

"No, you won't. *He'll* be good. When we have him, he'll be very, very good."

My stomach ties itself in a tight, gnarly knot, my throat starts to close up. I'm horrified by this prospect, but I still manage to try a new tack. One of the talking ones. "Listen, the doctor has made a major mess of this. Fifteen seconds after you leave here the entire police and fire departments of Del Oro County will come screaming up . . ."

Mrs. Dexter smiles. I used to think she had a nice smile, enlivening her crumpled, baby's face, but now she looks extremely mean. "No, they won't. Patrick is dumb, but not that dumb. He sent everybody home with a toxic-leak warning. Even the director; he's out back looking for the leak. And the phones aren't working. So let's get ourselves out of here. Come on, get your act together." She looks at me and glances in surprise at my feet. "You don't have any shoes on."

Well, it's just one shoe that I'm missing. I took it off when I kept tripping over the lace. I sit down obediently to reshoe myself. Anything to delay action.

(Mrs. Dexter is still an old lady, even though a demented one. As an old lady, she thinks I should be wearing shoes.)

"Just tell me why you're doing this," I say, conversationally, using the calm tone of voice you might try with a rabid animal, "I've not been smart enough to figure it out. *Why* would you want to buy the Manor?"

"Oh, indeed," For a moment she seems like an imitation of her Manor self. She sounds ironic. She wants to tell me about it. "Think. You're smart enough. What makes land valuable in California? Not scenery, not location, not retirement homes for the love of God, not gold. No. None of the above. *Oil*. That's it. Oil! *Black* gold." She begins now to sound a little Messianic.

"And there's oil under the Manor?"

"Oh, you betcha." She's quoting somebody with that *You betcha*. "Under it. Outside of it. Up into the hills."

I've gotten to the shoelace-tying part of my dressing project. "How do you know?"

She relaxes slightly against the door. Apparently this is sufficiently important to her that she wants to explain it fully, even to me. "I was raised next door to this ranch. I am a *niece*. I should have inherited, and the old bastard just wrote me out. Wrote me out as if I had done something, and all I ever did was hang around and tell him how wonderful he was. But he never guessed that I knew about the oil. I was just a child, you know, but I overheard it all.

"I was a child, and Patrick here was a much younger child. A little Mexican child. Weren't you, *chollo*?"

Kittredge glares at her. He is slumped against the wall, now looking very drunk indeed, with his gun dangling uselessly from a flaccid hand.

"Patrick wasn't a relative. His real name is Patrick Guerrero. His father was our fence man. He kept the barbed wire mended. Didn't he, Patrick?

"But his mama was Irish. Wasn't she, *chollo*? That's how he got to be Patrick. And now he's going to be rich. A rich, stupid Mexican Patrick."

I've reached the end of my shoe-tying now, but I quickly

maneuver the knot loose and start over. "And that's what Aunt Crystal found? The assay records?"

"Stupid, nosy, old bitch. I hate nosy old women. If people would just mind their own business. The assay place was the one you and your little boyfriend went to up in the woods. The hole was an oil-testing shaft, not a water well.

"That crazy old man," for a minute I think she's talking now about Daddy, but she adds, "my uncle. The rich are all crazy, did you know that? He decided he hated oil. Wouldn't talk about it. Kept saying, 'No oil here. Negative.' He did something to the county records—bribed or blackmailed—to get that drilling record erased. The only proof was some letters to his wife about how much he loved her and how much he hated oil and how he'd erased it from memory. So *that's* what your nosy old bitch of an aunt found."

"But," I say, "but . . ." This is partly a delaying tactic and partly because I really want to know. Also, out of the corner of my eye I can see Rob beginning to stir. "What difference can some old letters make? The oil is there, in the ground. Any geologist can prove that."

"But the Manor sale is next *week*," Mrs. Dexter says, sounding triumphant about this fact. "Nobody knows about that oil, and they won't know before the sale, they'll think the only value of the Manor is in the buildings and in the retirement home name. But what good is a retirement home with half the residents suing the board? We'll bid, and we'll bid low, and we'll get the Manor.

"But we had to keep the fact of the oil out of it. And your nosy old aunt was determined. She was going to tell the Board. She caught on right away about the sale and the difference the oil would make. She was going to tell the Board and tell the library and the historical society and the *San Francisco Chronicle*. She got really excited; such a historical find.

"And if she did . . . well, you can figure it out. You're smart enough. That was one of the things I hated about you. That you thought you were so smart. Poking your little nose into everything. Miss Smarty-pants."

People aren't reasonable, and I suffer a surge of anger that Mrs. Demented Dexter hates me. "You were okay about me saving your life," I tell her.

"Saving my life? Did you really believe that?" She now gets specific, recounting the tale of how she practiced for that accident, about the glass and her bloody lip and how the whole thing was staged. "And I had to do it several times, chomping on glass and spitting it out . . . ugh. And all that time your dotty father . . . Nobody believed him about his opera on the beach, but just suppose he had those oil papers and was going to give them to somebody. Give them to Sisal or take them to the newspapers. You couldn't tell with him. A loose cannon. I kept saying that. We had to get those papers out of him."

"Don't move." This command is for me. She'd do better to snap it at Rob, who is pushing himself halfway up and flexing his kung fu muscles.

"Listen," I say. I tell myself, *Keep talking. Deflect her attention.* My adrenaline is on command; it takes over. "The person in Mona's cloak. That was you?"

Mrs. Dexter swivels her gun into salute position. She giggles, an unlikely, scary sound.

"Why?" I ask.

"And you don't have your walker," I add. "Why not?"

She giggles some more. "Why? That's what everybody is

saying. *Why*, she asked, *oh why?* Sisal, the ice queen, the ice queen who found out too much, pleading with us, *why, oh why?*"

This lady is absolutely, seriously nuts.

There's an indeterminate scuffle behind us. Some shoe-scrape, some panting breaths, and a stifled grunt.

By the time I turn around Rob is in midair with legs spread, in a kung fu leap aimed at Dr. Kittredge's gun.

And Mrs. Dexter is reacting. And pretty damn quickly. She turns, not losing her balance, and fires from chest height, two-handed, hard and sharp. I hardly even sense her arms coming up into position. There's a muffled noise and a burned-leather smell.

She shoots Rob.

Her aim is perfect. She gets him right in the middle of his blue denim shirt. He stops in midair and puts his hand over the shirt, which starts immediately to leak a great deal of blood.

In sections, legs, hips, chest, head, he settles himself on the floor.

"You stay where you are," she says, pointing the gun at me.

This, if the Fates had unreeled their ball of yarn right, would have been the end of this story.

Because I'm not about to stop, no matter what Mrs. Dexter is set to do next. I'm going over there and look at Rob, and find out whether he's alive or dead.

Not that I'm particularly brave. Simply that I'm set to go and examine Rob, and I won't be able to stop.

Fortunately at this point the Fates apparently make a decision not to clip my life-thread.

The door into the Edward Day exhibit opens once more, and this time it admits Sheriff Hawthorne.

Sheriff Hawthorne looks just the same as usual. Rumpled, dandruffy, inefficient. But he, also, has hardware. He's handling a big dull-steel gun as if he's used to it.

"Don't," he says to Mrs. Dexter. He delivers that one syllable, *don't*, also as if he's used to saying it and has said it that way often.

Mrs. Dexter takes a second too long to think about it. She seems to be assessing the powers of the sheriff's large dull gun as opposed to her shiny one. She looks transfixed, as if someone has aimed a bright light into her eyes. Then she raises her arms and fires, but a hairsbreadth too late; Sheriff Hawthorne has fired first. Her reaction is all with the arm and the wrist. She drops her gun and clutches her arm and her side and finally falls down onto the floor, not exactly moaning but breathing in that strangled way that's almost moaning.

Maybe I was waiting for her to hold the gun dramatically to her forehead, close her eyes and *whammo*, but you can't really do that with a shattered wrist.

Sheriff Hawthorne now points his gun at Kittredge and scowls at him, and Kittredge, slowly at first and then quickly, drops his piece and sits on the floor. He doesn't breathe hard, like Mrs. Dexter. He says, "Son uvva bitch." Then he adds to it. "Goddamn son uvva bitch."

The sheriff ambles over, collects the guns, and stares down at Rob. He says, "Bleedin' pretty good. I better not touch him."

Which doesn't stop me. I'm beside Rob now with one hand on either side of his face—I know enough, thank you, Sheriff Hawthorne, not to move him or adjust him in any way; I just have my hands lightly by his head—and I'm saying, "Okay, Rob, you can do it, hang in there, Rob, it's over now. They're on their way, the medics are coming; we're getting help." And a whole lot of other stuff that I forget as soon as it's out.

Rob looks up at me, the standard Rob *I'm okay* look, and attempts to smile. I say, "Oh, shit." I'm crying.

It's a couple of minutes before the firemen and cops and trauma teams arrive.

"Lotta stupid stuff going on around here," Sheriff Hawthorne is chewing gum when he remarks this to me.

♟ Chapter 24

Rob is in the hospital for three weeks.

It is, of course, his own hospital, where he is very popular, so after he has had his first surgery and is out of danger his room is constantly full of me and Susie, plus interns, doctors, nurses, cleaning people, orderlies, switchboard operators. I sit by his bed reading *Sophie's World* and losing my place in it. I try to read aloud to him, which is mostly a bust. Susie burns herb smudges, which is strictly forbidden, and she has to throw them out the window if someone comes by, as they always do. She invokes the Goddess and puts a fat little statue of her under Rob's pillow. Rob has to have three operations, two for damage to muscles and blood supply and one for the repair of his shoulder. He will have a metal plate in his shoulder.

He says the metal plate will be better than his original shoulder was, although he will have a terrible time in airports. He had used that first shoulder too much for digging in Egypt.

I try to read to him from *Sophie's World* about Nietzsche and the strong man being the only admirable kind, which Rob correctly says is a repellent theory, and Susie objects to on the grounds that love is the only quality that counts; the only emotion that lasts, the one that moves mountains. " 'If your sorrow be high as the hill of Hebron,' " Susie says, eyes shiny and obviously quoting something or other, " 'if your sorrow be wide as the river on the plain, love still will transcend it, love will ascend, love will bridge.' "

This sounds sappy when I write it down now, but hearing Susie say it and seeing how much it means to her, I don't think it's sappy. Also, I'm feeling sentimental. I stayed up three nights in a row when Rob's case was really serious. I'm still recovering from that and am still scared by it. After Susie leaves the room in search of a bottle of Crystal Geyser without bubbles, I put my hand on his where it's positioned on the white coverlet, and say, "Listen, Rob, dear—hey, bro, how about it, let's get married when you get out of here." I try to make my proposal friendly and loving and buddy-sounding, because I think Rob will be turned off by undue sentiment.

Something comes and sits on his face, a little flinch like you'd get from a cold washcloth. He puts his free hand on top of mine, where it's resting on his other hand, and says, "Carly, I don't think that's a good idea."

I remove my hand from our hand-sandwich.

"We go round and round about this," he says. "Let's give it some air."

I wait a while longer, and he continues, "You're emotional because I'm in the hospital."

Well, no argument there. "Okay," I say, "yes, of course, well, natch. And so what? How'm I supposed to react? Jesus, Rob, do you have to be so fucking practical?" And I go out the door of Rob's room and leave the field to Susie, who will come in later that day.

Which is not okay with Susie, who comes see me that night and asks what's the matter. I tell her, "Nothing at all, Sue, you're imagining it," and the next day I'm back at Rob's bedside with a new book, *Hey, Waitress,* which is interviews with waitresses, and he and I are perfectly cheerful with each other and even do some giggling and have a friendly argument about the preferred amount for a server's tip.

Rob reaches over in the middle of a waitress-monologue and tells me that he loves me. Go figure.

He'll be out of the hospital the day after tomorrow.

Guess who has gotten to be my new best friend?

Mrs. La Salle. We got together first by discussing Mrs. Dexter.

"I'm still not used to it," I tell Mrs. La Salle. We're in her apartment with the great Japanese prints and a new beige-and-gold *shoji* screen and some new copper-colored African lamps. Mrs. La Salle herself wears a hand-woven something with leaping fish on it. "I always liked your clothes," I tell her.

She shrugs. "But not me."

I don't say, "I liked you fine. I just thought you wanted to marry my father for his money. And maybe were a murderess." Instead, I say, "I suspected everybody."

"But not Louise—Mrs. Dexter."

"It was the walker," I decide. "It made her seem vulnerable, and plucky. And innocent, some way."

"Well, *I knew* about the walker."

"You knew she didn't need it?"

"I thought she only needed it part of the time. Turns out it was none of the time. She told me she used it for a while right after the accident and figured out then that it made a good cover, got her seats on buses. Then she decided that she'd use it whenever she needed a seat on a bus or some other perk that life wasn't going to give her. That accident made her pretty negative about things.

"I also knew about her background in Del Oro County and how much she hated her uncle.

"Mrs. Dexter had been a resident of the Manor for only four years," Mrs. La Salle says. "I don't think she moved in with those ideas about the oil and buying the place. I think that plan crept up on her. But, then, she always kept it a secret about knowing Dr. Kittredge. So maybe she *was* planning something from the beginning."

"Or was ashamed of knowing him." I'm remembering the look on her face when she said Patrick had been a little Mexican child on their ranch.

Before she came in to the Manor, Mrs. Dexter lived with her ninety-year-old mother in a California town named Modesto. Mrs. Dexter was a tax accountant with an office in the Modesto mall. I tell Mrs. La Salle that, yes, I can picture all this. Modesto is one of those hot, dry, dusty places where you understand that someone could quietly lose track of their personality.

"What about Kittredge?" I ask.

"Well, what about him?"

"I always suspected him of something, but just the same I was surprised it was this bad. After all, he's a doctor. He had a life."

"He's an *unsuccessful* doctor. And a fraud. He wasn't who he pretended to be: Patrick Kittredge, the Irish man-about-town. He had to play a role all the time. He was angry, and Louise would know how to work on that. She probably promised him the earth. A clinic in Switzerland."

I sigh.

"Don't brood about it," Mrs. La Salle says. "There's nothing you or anybody else could have done.

"Here, we've got another half-martini for each of us."

Something I really like about Mrs. La Salle is that she gives you martinis instead of tea.

Another new interest of mine is the new chef. The guy who caught Mrs. Goliard when she went out the window.

He isn't a new chef any longer but that is still what everyone calls him. His name is Wayne Lee, and he turns out to be Chinese, that is, a Californian of Chinese ancestry, and six-foot-four and quite handsome, with sturdy athletic shoulders, which helped him in catching Mrs. Goliard. He was a student at Santa Cruz, in Human Relations, like me. But we don't talk about that at first. What we talk about is my aunt Crystal, whom he knew, "Well, hey, a little bit. She came around and talked to me a couple of times and left me some books. She's your dad's sister, right?

"Great old lady," he says. "Awesome. Lots of spirit. Ordered everybody around. I like that in an old person, makes them seem younger, y'know?" He shifts when he says this and moves a shoulder forward; he was on the basketball team at Santa Cruz, and he has that basketball player's gracefulness.

Aunt Crystal must have been really bored here before she began her fatal research into oil. What she wanted with Wayne was some shreds and memories of California Chinese history, which Wayne, although he's California Chinese, didn't know anything about. But he offered to write to his great-grandfather, a patriarch who still lives in Locke, a crumbling Chinese town in the California Delta.

"I loved it that she got so excited about that stuff," Wayne says. "Made me feel guilty for losing track of it. But she had that buzz, y'know? That real aliveness? You got a bit of it, too. Must run in the family."

Wayne asks me to come bodysurfing with him. "I'll coach you," he promises. "And maybe borrow a wet suit some place. Terrific exercise. And it's real easy."

So I go bodysurfing, and it isn't that easy, but Wayne is a good companion. It turns out to be one of those exercises where it feels very good when you stop. He gets me into running, too.

Mrs. La Salle, Susie, my dad, and I are climbing, bush by bush, through the woods in back of the Manor.

"This will ruin your shoes," I tell Mrs. La Salle. "It'll wreck your stockings."

"My shoes were ruined ten minutes ago. I had to do this."

We're on our way up to examine the assay hole that Rob and I thought was a well.

Mrs. La Salle has been actively curious about all aspects of our murder story, and especially about Daddy's and my involvement in it. I remember that she used to write a gossip column for a San Francisco magazine and suspect her now of planning a book-length true-crime exposé of our Manor murders. The *San Francisco Chronicle* features the Manor murders on the front page at least three times a week: "How Death Stalked the Retirement Colony."

I hope she won't get too curious about my father and his account of the woman on the beach. So far, the *Chronicle* hasn't caught on to that at all. The Manor Murders are just two murders, as far as the *Chronicle* is concerned.

"Your shoes are handsome," Susie tells Mrs. La Salle. "And a restorative shade of green. But perhaps not perfect for hiking."

"God, no," says Mrs. La Salle. To my surprise she and Susie like each other. Susie thinks Mrs. La Salle is beautiful and smart and fashionable; she tells her so. "Did you have Botox injections?" she asks.

Mrs. La Salle says, "No, but I plan to. Will you?"

Susie agrees, well, maybe. "There's an Indian tribe somewhere—I read about them. Botox resembles a naturally occurring substance, you know."

Susie isn't a fast uphill climber because she keeps getting distracted by nature. "Look at the shape of this," she says with each interesting clump of something brown, speckled, or striped. So she admires the manzanita shapes and pulls off pieces of bark and says they would make a lovely red dye, as she puffs lackadaisically along behind, catching her hair and letting the blackberry thorns pull at her long print skirt.

"Robbie is a *great* deal better," she announces forcefully into the air. "He is fighting his way through to wellness. And it is *all* owing to Carla."

"Surgery helped some," Mrs. La Salle says mildly. She

suspects about Wayne and me and understands the subtext of Susie's pronouncement. *Robbie and Carly are the ideal couple. They are made for each other. No one should get between them.*

Behind us is my father. He's behind only because he finds so many interesting things to step into and investigate. He's still perfectly spry and shows no bad symptoms from our active two months here. Of our visit to Conestoga, Homeland, and environs, he seems to remember only that he slept in the grass. "Which was frightening," he admits. "Now, why would that be frightening? But Carla found me. She always does."

"I believe," he says now, "we are on our way to Dark Lake."

I wonder why he decided the assay hole was Dark Lake. Maybe it reminds him of some place he knew early in his relationship with my mother, when they were in love. Well, they must have been in love once, mustn't they? People don't marry each other without being in love, do they? I think about this sometimes.

"I have found," he says, holding up a tiny, architecturally defined mouse skull, "an archaeological specimen."

"A skull is an ultimate," Mrs. La Salle says. "I have an artist friend who made an exhibit of ultimates."

Mrs. La Salle and I have talked about her friendship with my father. "I could see it in your face," she says. "You thought I had weird designs. Predatory woman fastens on senile old millionaire. Well, it's hard to talk about, but I knew perfectly well he wasn't a millionaire. Fact is, I'm doing reparation of sorts; my brother died with Alzheimer's, and I wasn't good about it. Not at all. He was so young, I took it personally. So now I work it out, paying up a little, with your dad. Susie would understand."

I tell her I understand, too. I don't add that I thought of an explanation like that and then dismissed it because I couldn't picture her in the penitent role. And I still don't, exactly. But I believe her.

"Your father is a very sweet man," she tells me.

I reach for her hand and call her, "Daphne." You see how far this experience has moved me along life's treadmill; I'm calling Mrs. La Salle by her first name sometimes.

Another reason why I've gotten closer to her is that she's all that remains of the trio. Mrs. Cohen has left the Manor. "I truly found every minute of it interesting," she says. "And now I am managing my emphysema much, much better and am able to return to the world. Oh, how I will miss all of you."

Kittredge and Mrs. Dexter are being prosecuted for Mona's murder, for which the sheriff must have good evidence. He just looks bored and satisfied when I ask him about it, and when I ask about Mrs. Sisal's murder, he chews gum. Maybe I wiped off too many fingerprints around her office.

I tell Sheriff Hawthorne maybe I never thanked him for saving my life. "Well, I'm doing it now. I'll think of you when I'm eighty. And that was pretty deft of you, arriving in the so-called ultimate nick of time. How'd you manage it?"

We're in a hall of the Manor. The sheriff leans against a wall and does more gum-chewing. "How did I get there so ex-pe-ditiously? Well, it was partly your friend Mrs. Cohen, who is nowhere near as dumb as she looks. She was worried about you; you talked on the phone, remember? But mostly, I'd been stickin' close to both you and Mrs. Dexter ever since you had your bunny rabbit incident."

"Bunny rabbit?" I have a moment of confusion and then realize he's talking about the hare, the poor little skinned *Lepus townsendii*. This man has a weird sense of humor.

"Yep. Because your boss, Belle, found this dried stinkin' rabbit skin in Mrs. Dexter's apartment. Seemed a bit off to me. I kept an eye on her after that."

"So you followed us, were behind us the whole time."

"Summa the time." He gives me the *And that's all you're going to get* stare.

But before he goes I try to pump him about Mona. "I mean, she came to me for help."

He regards me slit-eyed. "Help? Sweetpea, you couldn't have helped that little lady. She had the victim's personality package: devious, deceitful, dumb, a druggie. Scares easy. The sort that changes sides. And telegraphs when she's gonna do it. The other conspirators tend to catch on, right?"

I try to read his face. Does he mean Mona came to him with information? I can't read anything; all that Juicy Fruit action interferes.

Nobody mentions Aunt Crystal. The evidence about her being the net-woman is all in Daddy's head, and I think the sheriff suspects that Aunt Crystal is truly disappeared and that her going was arranged by Kittredge and La Salle, with Mona involved some way, but the one time I talk about it with him, he just shrugs and looks at me and says, "You think you can prove that? Wanna put your dad on the stand?"

And Belle has started proceedings to buy the Manor. Belle is another of those people who acts bored when you ask them questions. "Well, you're right, I didn't use to have any money," she says. "But now I do. You remember Mr. Rice?"

Of course I remember Mr. Rice, who locked his door with four different locks and told me I had really tried to help him.

"Well, him and me got married.

"It's a marriage of convenience," she says, probably in answer to what she sees in my face. "The convenience for me is money and for him is care. Real professional care. It's a bargain on both sides. We'll both keep it, and now I'm rich.

"An' I always thought I could run this place a lot better than most of the lamebrains that were trying."

Belle is going to completely revise the Permanent Care Policy. Clients will be able to buy out any time they want.

"It is only five minutes farther to the assay hole," I tell Mrs. La Salle. "It's shady there, and we can all can sit down." I take some leaves out of her hair. "You look like that Botticelli painting."

"Such a ridiculous idea," Susie says. "Oil . . . in these beautiful woods. They should leave things alone. Oil never helped anyone." She is panting hard.

That was pretty much Belle's attitude when she first learned the story. At first, she seemed to blame me and to think I had caused all these complications. And then she did a complete about-face and decided I was the heroine of the hour who had saved everyone's life. This was all happening when Rob was at his sickest, so it got very peculiar and tense.

"Come on, hup, two, three, four," I say ridiculously at Susie. "*Avant*. Forward. Chin up. We're almost there."

* * *

When we arrive at the oil shaft we establish ourselves on the platform around it. Say what you will, the place still looks like a well, a well out of a Thomas Kinkade painting, one of those village wells with a hat-shaped structure over it. What's missing is the village and the romantic smoke from the pollution-making green twig fires.

Daddy finally comes bouncing up with a newly discovered artifact: a computer ink cartridge. I don't know why people have to abandon their junk among the redwood leaves.

Mrs. La Salle lies on her stomach and tries to peer into the assay hole. "So, there is oil down there?"

"There was some. And deep down. It's not really a gusher."

Susie pulls one of her scarves up around her. She has surprised me by getting self-conscious about her fat neck. "The goddess is with us and around us and will not like more digging."

"What's going to happen?" Mrs. La Salle asks.

Belle has been keeping me briefed on this. "They're fighting. The Board is divided, and the ecology people have gotten into it. Mrs. Dexter wouldn't have had an easy time."

"She would have kept it quiet until later. She would have bought the Manor and waited and handed out some bribes. She was basically smart, but her craziness was growing and growing."

Mrs. La Salle says she saw the craziness only once. She had knocked on Mrs. Dexter's door and thought she heard someone tell her to come in. "Anyway, I just opened the door—it was hard for her to get to it with the walker. So I came in, and it took me a minute to understand. I just stood there."

I tell her, "Yes?"

"She was all dressed up. In costume. I thought of that roadhouse in *The Sopranos.*"

"The go-go bar?"

"Except she was more—well, teenage beauty contest. A low-cut velvet top with spangles. Pleated gold miniskirt.

"No walker. And the miniskirt short enough to show her ass." She delivers the word *ass* clearly, without undue emphasis. "Louise is an old lady. Older than me. She was bare under the mini, and half bent over with her flesh hanging down in folds.

"She'd been cutting something up. She had a big pair of scissors, and the floor was littered with scraps of paper.

"She turned around and looked at me, and then she went right back to what she was doing . . . cutting something up. Photographs, it looked like. And scattering the pieces. After a couple of minutes I just left.

"And, do you know, the next day when she saw me in the dining room, she didn't seem embarrassed at all. She smiled and said, 'So, you walked in on my ritual. Rituals are necessary, don't you agree?'

"She was just like normal, leaning on her walker."

I take a minute to think about this story, which I can see very clearly and still not see. I tell Mrs. La Salle that I'm still not used to the idea of the evil Mrs. Dexter.

"A lot of readjustment," she agrees. "Roads going off over the horizon. What will you and Edward do now? Sooner or later I'll move on. But maybe you should stay. Remain at the Manor."

Mrs. La Salle means not just that my father should stay on, but that I should do so, also. Belle has offered me a job, an actual job, with actual pay, as her assistant.

One of the many things I hate about that idea is I would feel like I was here waiting for Aunt Crystal. Going by that beach and checking to see if she has surfaced, all wrapped up in her gold net.

Actually, I hope she never floats back to us, but remains out in the tide, free and uncatalogued, grinding herself into the ocean floor, one with coral, barnacles, lighted jellyfish.

"It would be *so* wonderful to have Carly working here," Susie announces to the redwood trees. "Carly can be here, and Rob will work in his hospital, and Rob will be the resource doctor here, and Carly and Rob will get married—because I do think that young people should get married. Marriage is a true commitment and the most romantic condition of all, and it will all be the fulfillment of everybody's dreams."

Thank God Susie runs out of steam at this point in order to peer down into the assay hole and say, "Now who would think that was oil? That evil substance. It all looks so sweet."

I haven't told Susie and Mrs. La Salle of the latest development about Wayne Lee being a figure in my life lately, although Mrs. La S. has kind of guessed. Maybe Wayne will be an important figure, but I'm not sure.

I don't want a sensible, feminist lecture from somebody the age of my grandmother, if I still had a grandmother, about thinking through my own needs and evaluating a man as calmly as I would evaluate a new car—it's Mrs. La Salle who would talk that way. Nor speeches from Susie, sad regretful monologues about the goddess and Robbie's love for me and Susie's love for me and oh, Carly, I hate to criticize but how could you even think of somebody else after all you and Rob have meant to each other . . . When you and Rob could be set up so charmingly here . . .

I don't want to tell Susie that the charmingness of that arrangement is part of what I find depressing.

Wayne is funny and sensible and very athletic. Maybe too athletic; he knocks on my door every morning at six for me to go on a three-mile run. That is, I run, and he runs ahead, saying, "Come on, Carl, you can do it, you know you can. Just pick up your feet, one after the other, forget about the pain. Look at me, this way."

He has a very good smile and a lot of healthy Susie-type interests except that he likes a caffeine-enhanced fruit drink in the A.M., right after he gets up. He runs again in the evening and does exercises at night. He isn't the slightest bit dependent on me.

The Habitat man was totally dependent and needy, and that's what got me into trouble. Because part of me wants to be needed.

Rob needs me some, but he also likes to be the caretaker and to manage things. And Wayne, as far as I can tell . . . well, I haven't entirely decided. I think maybe Wayne needs admiration, but I'm not sure.

I am still figuring him out. The healthy running is great, like an offshore breeze across your life. Especially when your life has been burdened with stagnant miasmas, to quote some poet or other. But when I confided to Belle about Wayne, she said, "The boy scout stuff is okay for about a week. Then it starts to drag."

Belle has been around, and a person feels like listening to her.

* * *

My most recent opinion is that nothing lasts very long except for my affection for my father. And no jobs or boyfriends or murders or world events will get in the way of that.

But I'm also smart enough to know that my dad won't last forever.

Lately, he's taken to staring out his window and quoting scraps of Egyptian poetry at the scenery, or maybe to the mermaid, whom he can see beyond the bushes in the oval. "Don't feel sadness," he says. And, "Please love your life and live it now."

Those seem like pretty good mottoes, and I think I'm adopting them.